# Blood and Ballet

## MELISSA MITCHELL

Dear Mike and Wendy Mitchell,

Merry Christmas and
enjoy!

♡ Melissa Mitchell

ISBN - 978-1-7259-0773-7

*For my husband Matthew, whose support has been instrumental in my success, and for Jeanine, my bardic sister, who has undertaken this journey alongside me.*

Dance for me a minute, and I'll tell you who you are.

— MIKHAIL BARYSHNIKOV

The goddess Hecate watched from the shadows, from the darkness of the trees, eyeing the Thracian soldier with pride. He stood before his beloved Aurelia, who sobbed, falling into his arms. "Must you go?" she wept. "Must you leave me like this—alone after such misfortune?"

They stood before a small cottage. This was to be Aurelia's new home, just outside the city of Rome, while her husband served his debt. Here, she would be safe.

"You must be strong, my love. This is our only chance at freedom." As he spoke, the Thracian pulled from his pocket a jewel of protection, placing it about Aurelia's neck. Hecate felt her magic pulse as the amulet settled against Aurelia's skin. "You must wear this, Aurelia. It will protect you from those who would do you harm." Aurelia was not permitted to know any more than that—except that she would be safe. Aurelia eyed the amulet but briefly; she cared little for trinkets when her husband spoke such words of heartbreak.

"Promise that you will never take it off."

"But, why?"

"Aurelia, you must promise me. I cannot lose you," he whispered. "Not now—not when we have come so close to freedom."

"Then it will never leave my neck, this I promise." Her eyes were pools of despair. "How long must you be away? Why must you use a name other than your own?"

The Thracian answered each of her questions patiently, as a lover and husband ought. He petted her, consoled her, kissed her as if each would be the last. Finally, he was forced to leave her.

Aurelia was sent away into the cottage, out of sight. Hecate could not risk being seen by any other. Only then did she emerge to present her hand. "We must be away before your absence is noticed," she said. The Thracian nodded, his face grim. He took her hand obediently. His obedience, his love for Aurelia, were the qualities she needed. He was her best choice—her best hope—and now he owed her a debt.

Their new surroundings materialized around them—the gladiator school in Capua. She released the Thracian's hand. He turned to her with questioning eyes. "You may retire," she said. We are done for the night.

He nodded, going to lay down upon his cot. She watched him from the darkness, studying his physique. His strong build settled into a restless sleep. His silver eyes darted beneath hooded lids. His heavy brow held lines of worry. Humanity was such a fragile thing. Soon, he would be fragile no longer. She had mighty plans for him—for the war to come. This

Thracian was destined to make an impact upon the world, and she, goddess of the moon, would see it done. His achievements would echo into eternity. What a perfect creation she would make of him—the world's first *vampire*.

# CHAPTER 1

To be a ballerina is to be immortal, or so we tell ourselves. We must live for the here and now. We cannot afford to think about death. We cower away from consideration of our future. We hide signs of aging behind face paint and costumes. After all, blemishes are a show of imperfection. Such symptoms are for mortals.

If immortality is the heart of ballet, then perfection is certainly its god. It took me a long time to figure this out. Ballet changed my life. Had you asked me when I was younger, I would have told you that ballet was simply dancing. *Now* I will tell you differently.

Ballet is darkness—beautiful obsessive darkness. It rips you apart from the inside. Sometimes it's fragile as glass, one small chip and it shatters into a thousand glittering fragments. Other times it's raw, unforgiving, powerful, and yet, graceful.

People only see the sparkles and tutus. They see the smiling women on grand stages painted like dolls, and the gallant princes who rescue them. They don't see the pain beneath those bright faces; they don't see the suffering.

And the ballerinas themselves? They all dream of becoming principle soloists, *prima* ballerinas, lured in by the delusional fantasy that if they put in all the hard work, all the sweat, the tears, the man hours, they will be chosen. They will be special. *The one*. Who doesn't like the sound of that? How many of them actually make it?

I did…once.

The official diagnosis was a tear in my labrum and a spiral fracture to my left femur. When I asked the doctor if I would dance again she said, *"Perhaps."* What does that mean?

After that, I went nearly a year without putting on a single pair of pointe shoes. I could hardly bear to look at them. I simply tucked them away, even the ones I'd gotten signed by famous ballerinas, deep in my closet. I didn't need the reminder of my misfortune.

I never danced the same after my injury; my body could no longer handle the rigor of it. The National Ballet agreed to take me back of course. I had a track record with them. That wasn't the real reason. My rich grandfather was a huge donor to the company. It pays to have connections. Naturally I was demoted to corps. As you can imagine, everything went downhill from there.

My friends in the company were no longer my friends: they whispered behind my back same as the rest of them. Funny how people dissociate with you when you no longer have something to offer them, when you're no longer *somebody*. I couldn't walk into a room without turning heads and spurring whispers.

"Why did Cece come back?" I once heard someone say.

"She should give up and accept her fate. Let the rest of us have a turn." That one hurt the most.

Maybe they didn't think I heard their nasty little remarks. That's what I'd tell myself setting up at the barre. In hindsight, they wanted to be overheard; they wanted to tear me down; they wanted to remind me that my dreams were naive. They were right, because *my* dreams shattered the moment I hit the hard wooden floor.

Ballet is to blame for the turn my life took. Perhaps I could have chosen a normal path like a teacher or a doctor. Something reasonable. How differently things would have turned out had I done so. Now I could clearly see my life stretched out behind me. My past decisions culminated into a single sharp and painful moment. In that single moment, everything changed.

It was late at night in the city of Vienna when I was attacked and forcefully dragged into the back of a black van. Everything moved so quickly that I couldn't question what was happening. I soon found myself caged within in a tiny room, but otherwise unharmed. Only then did I criticize my choices as my helpless gaze circled this new enclosure, surroundings bare of all but the necessities. The mind can be a strange thing during impossible situations.

I had a long time to think about my captivity, enough for my fear to ebb into a small trickle where once a river had been. I sat cross-legged on a tiny bed watching the locked door, waiting for inevitable danger to burst through; I should have been more afraid. The fighter in me should have devised a million desperate ways to break free. Instead, I was too shocked by the events that brought me here. I'd seen something I shouldn't have, and it was either going to kill me, or set me free. The only problem was, deep inside, I was already dead.

I waited until at last I heard the jingle of keys. Then a latch clicked, and the door opened. My regard fell upon a man. He looked like all the rest of them, tall and powerfully built. His brown hair was short, curling this way and that, and his heavy brow creased as his eyebrows drew together. His accusing gaze left me uneasy, but there was something more pressing behind those brown eyes. He looked at me like he was hungry for something—they all did.

I'd already convinced myself that my captors belonged to some sadistic cult that enjoyed killing people and kidnapping little girls. I was merely waiting for my theory to prove true.

"You have been summoned." The man had a strange accent, not Austrian like so many others. "I am to take you before Caius."

I swallowed, my throat suddenly dry. "What's going to happen to me?"

"Do not keep him waiting." My escort motioned with his head and stepped out into the hallway, immediately shrouded by darkness.

I rose to my feet—and perhaps to my doom—which was now heavy and unmoving. Suddenly, my little room didn't seem so bad. In the hallway, the man's hand wrapped around my upper arm as if to say, *don't even think about escape*. His grip was painful. It would leave a nice set of bruises to go with the others.

My guide led me through a fifteenth century Austrian castle like those I visited on tour, except this one was extremely modernized. I saw plenty of signs of electricity—televisions, computers in a little alcove, and wall-mounted touch screens. The technology was a facade that failed to hide the castle's age.

Our destination was a large study with richly carved shelves and nooks. My eyes circulated the vast chamber as I inhaled the scent of varnished wood. Unlike the other rooms, this one was not technology heavy. My scrutiny paused at the shelves laden with hundreds of books. Many of them would have fetched thousands with their gold-embossed pages and pristine bindings.

I became preoccupied with the dominating feature: a highly-polished desk in the middle of the room. Behind it sat a dark-haired man wearing an impassive expression. He watched me, his body motionless. Only his silver eyes followed my movements, glittering with judgement; those inhuman eyes were enough to make anyone balk.

"This is the girl you spoke of?" His voice was rich and pleasant; I found myself surprised. My guide nodded.

I assumed the man behind the desk was Caius. His importance echoed in his commanding voice. If respect was given for looks alone, then his position was evident, with his angular cheekbones and pointed chin, his fine appearance, and erect posture. Caius was simultaneously fearsome and striking. If such a thing were possible, he made it so.

There were a number of other occupants in the room, men and women. They were finely dressed in silks and lace. They stood still as statues except for their eyes. It was creepy the way they followed me like prey, and the hairs of my arms stood on end. The very air around me was thick with their pride and superiority. I was suddenly reminded of the way I used to feel during ballet class after my injury, as if every inch of me was up on the chopping block.

I kept my eyes forward and tried not to appear fearful. For me, acting has always been second nature. After all, all ballerinas are actors. We are trained from a young age to display grace and beauty, not our true feelings, and never our pain. So I did exactly that.

Caius didn't bother with introductions. Why should he? "Tell me about the man you were found with, *girl*. How well did you know him?"

I wasn't a child, and his use of *girl*—the way he said it—rubbed me wrong. I wanted to say something scathing, but my fear was too cold. Instead I said, "I hardly knew him." It was difficult to find my voice, harder still to control it from squeaking. "I only met him a few days ago."

The man I saw them kill was little more than an acquaintance. Now I was here because of him, because of what I'd seen. Was this to be my death sentence? "What's going to happen to—"

"Silence," Caius hissed, sharply cutting me off. His manner turned frigid. "It is *I* who ask the questions, not you."

"Well, that's not very fair, is it?!" I regretted this immediately, clenching my jaw closed before I said anything else rash.

The grip on my arm jerked painfully. "Do you wish to die?" The hiss in my ear reminded me of a snake's.

"Do not get smart with me, *girl*." Caius's piercing eyes left me trembling as the prospect of death unearthed its hoary fangs.

"I—I already told you, I hardly knew him. We met four days ago at a café. His name is Thrax."

"Yes, yes. I already know his name." As he spoke, I saw his fingers twitch. They drummed against the desk's glossy surface, but only for a moment. It was the first and *only* emotion I'd seen beyond what lurked in his eyes. I clung to that display, assuring myself that he was merely human. *Surely he was human?* Caius spoke again, "When my men found you with Thrax, you were in the alley outside of Fluxx. Why?"

An image of the alley resurrected itself in my mind. It's tall multi-story walls loomed above me ominously, casting darkness upon my soul. I shuddered. "Thrax took me to Fluxx," I whispered. He took me for what was supposed to be a date. Now I could only summarize it as the date from hell, for I had surely found myself within the fiery tongues of the underworld after what I'd seen.

"Go on," Caius drawled.

My hands balled up into fists as I spoke, "Not long after we arrived at Fluxx, Thrax wanted…he wanted to leave. He seemed…" I struggled to verbalize his strange behavior. "I think he was agitated." I recalled the way his eyes flashed, the hunger displayed within them, the same hunger I saw reflected in each pair of eyes I now met.

"So let me get this straight. You decided it was a good idea to go into the alleyway with Thrax, a man you'd just met?"

My face burned. "No! Of course not!" Did Caius think I was a desperate floozy eager for a creeptastic bang beside a bunch of trash cans with a psychopath? I was appalled. "Once we were outside, I tried to leave. He scared me. I insisted—I insisted on going home." The angry curl of Thrax's lips when I told him I was no longer interested, swam into my mind's eye. That look left me panicking.

"If you insisted on going home, why didn't you?"

"I tried," I whispered. "Just as I was walking away, he dragged me into the alley." My voice was barely audible as I relived the shock, and my eyes having a mind of their own, widened. In reality, my story wasn't perfect. Thrax never *dragged* me. As soon as I took two steps from him, I felt a whoosh, some kind of forceful contact knocking the wind out of me, then I was barricaded against the wall in the alley. None of it made any sense—not then. Now, I had my theories.

"I see, and after that? After he dragged you into the alley?"

My heart began to race. I didn't want to think about anything after that part. "Thrax got aggressive." My throat tightened. I swallowed, trying to fight my emotion. "I tried to get away from him. I tried to fight him, to call for help...I just...he was too..." I helplessly looked around the room, desperate to end the discussion. Why did they need to hear anything beyond the horror I already revealed?

My audience hadn't moved, but a voice that didn't belong to Caius proved that they weren't merely made of wax. "Would you say Thrax *pinned* you against your will?" It came from a man standing at Caius's shoulder. Caius glanced up at him before looking back at me.

Wasn't the answer to that question obvious enough? I couldn't speak anymore so I nodded.

"Then it is as I suspected, Caius." The man and Caius exchanged a look. Something was settled. The man stepped back, and that was that.

"Very well then." Caius looked at my guide. "You may return her to her room." The grip on my arm returned. My guide began dragging me away, but I wasn't done yet.

"Wait!" I pulled. "What did you do to Thrax?" I couldn't hide my frustration as I tried to look over my shoulder at Caius. I needed to know. Not because I cared about Thrax. The son of a bitch could rot in hell for all I was concerned. I asked because there was nothing normal about the way his body withered up into ash when they'd stabbed him.

Caius held up a hand, halting our retreat. "Tell me, does it *anger* you that we took his life?"

Of course not. I shook my head.

"I see. And what do you think he was about to do before we found you?"

"I…" I very quickly regretted my original question.

"Answer me, *girl*!"

"He—he was going to rape me, I think…" My voice was hardly a whisper.

Caius afforded me a look of condescension. "Rape? How very naive of you. No. What he intended was far more sinister. It was your blood he sought, and ultimately, your death. A sore death it would have been. The life of a night-walker is a grievous end indeed."

# CHAPTER 2

*N*ot all things lost can be found. There are some things that no matter how hard you try, elude you, and if you push too far, you break. When it was clear that I would never dance as I once did, there were no words to describe the overwhelming depression that took me. My determination had nearly broken me.

While recovering from my injury, there was hope. I hoped once I was permitted to dance again, I could get my body back to where it once was. When my injury healed, that hope evaporated like water on hot asphalt. I realized there would be no going back. That realization left me lost in the dark without so much as a candle.

Most who cared about me encouraged my delusions—perhaps they didn't want to be the bearer of bad news. "Just keep trying," they would say to me. "It won't happen in a day."

It was my father who spoke reason; he was the one who pulled me from my pit of despair. He saw my depression for what it was. He knew what I knew, that there would be no going back. So, he offered me an escape.

In reality, I think he was tired of watching me suffer. One day he came to me with a big manila envelope stuffed full of train tickets, tickets to various destinations across Europe. Ballet was developed in Europe, and selfishly, I still couldn't release that part of my life.

"Cece," he'd said in his somber voice. "It is time for you to find happiness. You will get none here."

He was right; I would never find true happiness beating a dead horse. So, I begrudgingly agreed to his offer. Not long after, as I traveled through Europe, I began wondering if I would *ever* find what I sought. Happiness was always out of reach, like chasing a mirage in a hot desert. I was left asking: was it possible? All the dreams I had would no longer come true. The only way to fix that was to pick *new* dreams.

That's what Vienna was supposed to be, a place to make a fresh start. Now, all I could think was, *look how great it turned out for me*. I say that with the largest amount of sarcasm I can muster. I was hardly two weeks into my new life before some guy posing as my date tried to eat me alive. Was I to be grateful towards my captors for rescuing me? They took me from one alarming situation simply to throw me into another. After five days of being stuck in a tiny room playing prisoner, I was beginning to believe there might be no place left for me in the world.

On a separate note, I finally learned the name of the man who so forcefully took me to see Caius. For the first couple of days I called him *Jailor*, which earned me a hard look every time. His name was Felix, and he was my only visitor after arriving.

I saw him three times a day—breakfast, lunch, and dinner. He delivered my food, took me upstairs to use the restroom, and said hardly anything at all. If it weren't for my ventures upstairs, I wouldn't have known the time of day. Those short trips were the only instances where I was exposed to windows, and I couldn't help but look upon them longingly.

On the bright side, Felix stopped treating me poorly after the first night. I think he realized my innocence after first believing me in league with Thrax. Still, I didn't know why I remained a prisoner.

My persistence in questioning Felix regarding the reason for my imprisonment annoyed him. He showed this by clenching his jaw and avoiding my gaze. In fact, he frequently avoided my gaze during our brief visits. When I did catch his eye, there was always the same hunger lurking beneath his stare. Even still, I think I was slowly growing on him.

When I woke up on day six, things began to change. Felix was absent in delivering my breakfast. I had no way of keeping time, but I could tell because my stomach wouldn't stop growling. If someone didn't come for me soon, I was worried I'd pee myself.

My anxiety increased as time passed. Perhaps they'd given up on me. For the millionth time, I tried the door. Felix never forgot to lock it, but I pulled on the knob anyway, letting out a long string of profanities when it expectedly didn't open.

Not long after, I heard the familiar jingle that marked his approach. Going without social interaction for a week made me look forward to seeing him. I was supposed to loathe him for keeping me here.

When the door opened, I squealed with fright and stumbled

backwards onto my bed. It was not Felix who stood in my doorway, but Caius. His tall frame filled the entry, and he stood gazing down as if my behavior was ridiculous. "Expecting someone else?"

"Where's Felix?" I demanded.

Caius dramatically looked over his shoulder before turning back towards me. Then he shrugged. "He's not here —obviously."

My gaze narrowed; his sarcasm was not amusing.

"All right. Fine. I released him of his duties." He let himself into my room and went directly to the shadowy corner where he took a seat to watch me.

I refused to say a word and simply glared at him, though I quailed inwardly under his sharp gaze. Perhaps he'd simply come to gawk at me.

At last he did speak. "How are you finding your stay?"

Was he trying to be funny? What a pompous bastard! "I'm finding my stay quite well, actually." I mustered up some fake sarcasm of my own. "I'm enjoying it *so much*, as a matter of fact, I was going to ask if I might stay indefinitely." Two could play this game.

"I thought you might ask. We can certainly arrange something."

"Wonderful. You are too gracious, Caius. I cannot thank you enough."

"Think nothing of it. It is the least I can do."

Ugh! I wanted to scream, I was so infuriated. He appeared to enjoy my temper. How fantastic that I could offer him amusement.

"Cece, is it?"

"Celine," I muttered. Felix must have told him my nickname.

"Ah. I see. How *fitting*. Cece for people you like, and Celine for those you don't."

"No." I felt an angry blush creep onto my cheeks. "Cece for friends and family. Celine for strangers and people I don't trust."

"Oh, terrific. Cece, then, since I am no stranger. You told me moments ago that you wish to stay in Anghor Manor indefinitely. We are hardly strangers if we are living together."

"I do not *wish* to stay in this manor forever!" I finally cut the bullshit. "I want to leave. Immediately! Why are you keeping me here against my will?"

"Ah-ha. We get to the crux of the matter." He rested his elbows on the chair's armrests and steepled his fingers, gazing back at me with calm collection. I was neither calm nor collected. "You see, Cece, you cannot leave, otherwise, I would have released you days ago. We vampires do not take kindly to sharing our secrets with the outside world. You have seen too much."

"Vampires?"

"Of course, my dear Cece. *Vampires*. Why so shocked? Surely you've had enough time to work it out for yourself."

I most certainly had not, and I told him so.

"Be that as it may, I am afraid you are stuck here forever." His silver eyes gleamed wickedly. I felt my soul wither. I was never getting out of here. It was hopeless to fight him. Fighting Caius was exactly what Caius wanted. He enjoyed toying with me. "Yes. Difficult realization is it not?" He paused, feigning consideration. He must have thought himself the world's greatest actor. "Although, I suppose there *is* a way," he lured. "But you seem so cross! Perhaps this discussion is best left for another time."

A tiny glimmer of hope sprang up within me. It was nothing more than a candle flickering in a dark room. "There's a way?" I regretted my question almost instantly. He was still baiting me, and the moment I realized it, I burned hot with frustration.

"Why of course, my dear Cece. I should have said sooner. Let me explain. Seeing as you are an outsider, you pose a threat to us. Loose cannon and all that." His face was calm as he spoke, void of emotion. "We cannot risk anyone running around aware of our existence. However, if you choose to become one of *us*," he paused, "let's just say your circumstances will be quite different."

"Become a vampire?" This was another joke. He was still playing with my head. "I thought—wasn't that what your people *rescued* me from? Becoming a night-walker?"

He threw his head back and laughed. It wasn't the feel-good kind of laugh that's contagious. It was the kind of laugh that says, *you're doomed*. "My dear Cece, your ignorance amuses me. Night-walkers and vampires are so very different. Perhaps the only similarity is that we both require blood to stay alive. No matter, you will learn in time."

"I don't want to learn. I don't want to become a vampire." My anger had all but dissipated. All that was left was the desperation of being trapped.

"No? Why ever not? Do you think we are monsters? I assure you that we are nothing like those night-walkers your friend Thrax intended you to become."

"No. I just—I don't want to. I want to go home."

"This is your home now."

"No, it's not! I don't want to become a vampire. I've got to get out of here. Is there no other way?"

"Well of course there is! Of course, my dear Cece." His grin was malicious. If a beautiful man could be fatal, my heart might have frozen in my chest.

It took great courage to speak. "I'll do anything. What is it. I'll do it."

"You can die."

"What?" The warmth drained from my body.

"You heard me. There are only two ways to leave Anghor Manor. You have two choices. You may choose to become one of us, or you may choose death. It's your decision."

"But, what if I don't want either of those choices?"

"Then, my dear Cece, I am afraid you are stuck with me forever."

# CHAPTER 3

*T*he day I decided to give up dancing was one of the longest and hardest in my life. I pondered it for weeks. With each passing moment of consideration, a little more of me died.

Some decisions are strengthening, like when you make positive steps towards becoming more responsible or take the higher road in a tough situation. Doing what is right will always make you a stronger person, even if it hurts. Other choices can destroy you. I'm talking about the ones that make you feel *so* guilty inside, it appears you might wither and die.

It took time and many long train rides through the European countryside, but after a while I realized that giving up ballet was the right choice. After getting kidnapped, I was faced with a *different* choice, and this one made the previous look like cake. Just like the last, I felt a small part of me wither.

After Caius left me with an ultimatum, he relocated me to a new room. Anghor Manor, he called his abode. Although he

MELISSA MITCHELL

got the definition of manor wrong, because it was very nearly a castle.

When he showed me to my bedroom suite, he told me in his rich accent, "These are to be your accommodations for all of eternity. Unless you decide to die before eternity comes to pass." He said this with a sadistic grin like he was Dracula, and my life merely a game.

I didn't find anything funny about his rude joke. Just before leaving me on my own, he told me that I was permitted free range of the manor. "Do not try to leave; you will find the doors secured."

The first day I was too frightened to venture beyond my new haven, but eventually hunger drove me out. I was never told where I would find the kitchen, so I began an exploration of Anghor Manor that lasted many days. I found the kitchen of course, but I also stumbled across much more.

Caius was correct: every single door and window to the outside world was hardwired into the high-tech alarm system. Each had its own keypad, and without the code, wouldn't open. After trying to guess the code several times, triggering the alarm, I admitted defeat.

Not long after I set off the alarms, I tried to escape through other means. There were computers around the manor, but every single laptop computer was locked with a password. There were no phones since these vamps all used cell phones of their own. The security seemed a bit extreme. I couldn't understand why they'd gone to such great lengths against me, that is, until I realized I wasn't the only prisoner here.

I didn't see them at first—the other girls. Once I discovered them, I figured out where all my clothes had come from. It was quite a shock the day I stumbled across Adel. Eventually, she became my first true friend in what I began to consider a gilded cage.

"You don't look like a vampire. Did they take you too?" I asked when I discovered her in the hallway outside my room. She didn't speak great English, but yes, they'd taken her too. After a long conversation, mostly whispered, I learned that she and the other girls were *never* given the option I was, to become a vampire or die. Why was that?

When she heard my fate, the choice I'd been given, her eyes grew wide before she turned and left me standing in the shadowy hall. It wasn't exactly the reassurance I was looking for. All I could think was, becoming a vampire was a horrible act to be avoided, so I had every intention of doing so.

Felix still visited me daily. I told you I was growing on him. In time, I began to see him as less of an enemy. I also came to understand why his gaze was so hungry: he was a vampire and I, a human.

I read in some stories that Vampires were seductively good looking. I found that to be true. Every male and female vamp I'd seen was jaw dropping good looking. So much for creepy Dracula and red eyes.

As the days passed, I began to wonder about Adel. One day I mustered up enough courage to ask Felix. "I met another woman recently. Fancy that. Why are there other women here?"

"There are other women here? Humans?" He wasn't the greatest actor.

"Don't play dumb! Come on. What's the deal? Why are they here?" What I really wanted to know was, why were the other women treated differently? I wasn't sure how far I should push my luck.

Felix was quiet for a minute before answering. "To understand that, Cece, there is much you must learn about our culture."

I waited, finally lifting my brows and telling him to enlighten me.

"Vampires do not believe in draining our snacks dry. Well, let me restate that, vampires who follow the true vampire code, do not believe in draining a human dry. There are plenty of rogues who love nothing more—your friend Thrax for example. They get a certain high from it."

"Thrax was not my friend!"

Felix ignored my protests. "When you drain a human dry, they die, but they are not truly dead. They turn, and when they next open their eyes, if they are in the sunlight, *then* they truly die. If they aren't, then they get very hungry. Can you guess what they crave?"

Was this a trick question? "Um. Blood?"

"Yes. If they get it, their turning becomes permanent. You've already heard the term *night-walker*."

"What's so different between a vampire and a night-walker?"

He sat back against the sofa, relaxed, as if he gave this lecture regularly. "Vampires are day walkers. Anytime walkers. More importantly we have self-control, unlike night-walkers, whose thirst for blood is never quenched. Vampires do not have this problem. Furthermore, we don't feel the need to bite every living thing with a heartbeat."

"Is that why you haven't bitten me? Because you have self-control?"

"Partially. Mainly because Caius commanded us not to."

Well, that was news. "So why are they here then? The girls?" I had a hunch, but I wanted to hear him say it.

"Can you not guess?" He studied me for a moment. "Very well. The girls serve two purposes, blood, obviously, and they work at Caius's club."

It took me a moment to register all that he'd said. Those poor girls! Some of them were still in their late teens. A few of them looked to be in their early twenties. "How many are there?"

"Twenty? Twenty-five? Give or take a few." He winked.

I shook my head. It was sick! Completely sick. But was I really surprised? They were vampires, and their whole world was fucked-up. Most likely it was a world they hadn't chosen, but I had a choice.

A new thought crossed my mind. "When you say they work at the club, do you mean Fluxx?"

Felix nodded.

"What exactly do you mean by *work*?" I was afraid to know.

"They dance."

My mouth opened, and then closed. It wasn't the answer I was expecting. "You mean, Caius isn't—he isn't selling them off as sex slaves or anything?"

He grunted, as if the thought disgusted him as much as it did me. He also looked at me like I was crazy. "They serve us with their blood—that is enough."

"Oh." Thank heavens!

Our conversation didn't go much further than that. As I've said before, Felix wasn't one for giving many answers. I was surprised I got as much out of him as I did. But, I still had one burning question: why was I given a choice when the other girls weren't?

If I chose to become a vampire, Caius had promised me freedom. Or at least, he said I could come and go as much as the others did. I'm sure he'd give me the passwords to the doors and I'd be allowed to do what I wanted. There would be no going back to my old life. Then again, I had no old life to return to.

After my conversation with Felix, I spent a lot of time with Adel. I wanted more information about Anghor Manor, about her job at Fluxx, about the outside world, since she got further out of the manor than I ever did.

"I work three days—Thursday through Saturday. It is only time I truly happy." She smiled as she told me; she didn't smile often.

"Because you get fresh air? Because you can get out of here for a little while?"

She shook her head. "No, because I dance."

Her words shocked me for a number of reasons. I was left wondering what her old life had been like. Why did she love dancing so much? Would I be allowed to dance at Fluxx for a chance to get out of Anghor Manor? Could I find a way of escaping Fluxx easier than I could my current cage? Was Fluxx my key to being free? So many questions were flashing through my mind.

"When I dance," Adel explained in her broken English, "I am free. The music wash over me, and I dance."

"Is it a stripper kind of dancing?" I tried to remember if I'd seen the dancers when Thrax had taken me to Fluxx. Yes, there had been dancers. I recalled barred cages set on pedestals all over the huge dance club. There had been girls in those cages, scantily clad girls, but they hadn't stripped.

"No, Cece. No. Never take clothes off. But the people—they like watching us. Some of us girls truly good."

"What about you?"

She smiled shyly. "Me? I not too good. But I try maybe."

I was sure she was better than she gave herself credit for. "Do you think I would be allowed to do it? To dance I mean?" No! I tried to tell myself. No dancing. No! No! No! Even if it wasn't ballet, I'd left that life behind. I couldn't resurrect it. I feared that dancing of any kind would be like pouring salt on an open wound.

"I—I don't know." Adel was hesitant. "Maybe?"

A new hope sprang up inside of me, and so did a plan.

# CHAPTER 4

*I*'ve never considered myself pretty. Most girls say that, I know. I have always been a bit of a *plain Jane*. Luckily, I was blessed with a ballet body. I'm told that women would kill for that kind of physique.

Me? I'd kill for a nice rack. Ballet dancers—most of them anyway—don't have big chests. So naturally, I've always wanted one.

It's silly how we want what we can't have, like going outside. After arriving at Anghor Manor, I constantly dreamt about going outside. I couldn't help but gaze longingly through the windows. Sometimes I'd drag a chair to one simply to watch nothing in particular—the birds, the trees, anything really.

You're probably thinking, what's so bad about living in a high-class manor? It's got the latest and greatest technology. It's got stunning fifteenth century charm. Why leave? Well, like I've said, knowing I couldn't leave made me want it more. Why did Eve try the forbidden fruit when she was already living in paradise?

Escaping Anghor Manor was never going to happen. I knew that. It was a fortress. Still, I had hope. There was the possibility that Fluxx was less guarded—the possibility that I might sneak away through the crowd. To find out, I needed to get to Fluxx, and for that, I needed permission to accompany the other girls. The only person to grant it was Caius.

It took me days to find Caius's study. I knew it lived behind one of the many locked doors, so you can imagine my surprise when I stumbled across it unlocked. I half expected to find Caius at his desk. Pleasantly enough, I found myself alone. So, I began to explore.

The ceilings were vaulted; I couldn't keep myself from gazing up into the rafters with wonder. There were alcoves and smaller nooks, loaded with shelves of books. Elegant, fine looking books they were—the kind you'd see in the house of a collector.

The central study was filled with Caius's grand desk. To the side sat an impressive couch arrangement with rich, coffee colored leather sofas and ottomans. The arrangement faced a massive fireplace. I gazed at it, awed by the handsomely carved marble.

The back wall impressed me the most. It hosted a vast display of books three stories high. Two narrow walkways spanned the length of it, one on the second level, and one on the third. Two wrought iron spiral staircases with gold railings led up to these.

Eagerly, I went from one alcove to another, thumbing through books, delicately sliding my fingers across their bindings. I was too nervous to pull them out at random, so I contented myself with gentle caresses. Most of them were not in English. Quite a few were in Latin, and many more were in languages I didn't recognize.

I squealed gleefully when I discovered a section of titles that I could read. Then I found the holy grail of all books: a section containing English literature. My heart skipped a beat, and I eagerly swept through them. I was looking for several books in particular—books that I'd read a hundred times over.

I sighed when I found them. My hand settled on *Jane Eyre* first. I pulled it out. Immediately thereafter I saw more of my favorites. I removed another, and another. When I had a nice stack, I retreated to the nearest plush couch and took a seat, setting my spoils upon the end table.

*Pride and Prejudice* was on the top, so I took it up. It was a first edition—no surprise there. Still, I was amazed to be holding it. Eagerly but delicately, I began flipping through the pages to my favorite part, the part when Mr. Darcy proposes and Elizabeth cuttingly turns him down. I'd read the story so many times, but that didn't matter. It was the most familiar thing I experienced since arriving at the manor.

I cannot say how much time passed like this, going through my favorite parts from each book. I lost myself, and for the first time, I felt comfortable.

"How did you get in here?" Caius's voice startled me. I gave a little yelp. *Northanger Abbey* tumbled out of my hands onto the floor. I quickly picked it up and turned to see Caius standing with his arms crossed. His eyes were stormy.

"How do you think I got in here, Caius? Through the door of course." If I was going to be stuck here, I needed to stand up to him.

His jaw flexed. I could tell he was clenching his teeth, hopefully infuriated by my smart-aleck response. What was the big deal? It's not like I hadn't seen the place before.

"This is my private study. I do not appreciate asking twice. How did you get in?"

His anger cut through my courage. "I'm sorry. I didn't know."

"Didn't know?"

"The door was unlocked. I was looking for you. I thought..." What did it matter? He didn't deserve my explanation. "It won't happen again." I set the book on the table with a thump and stormed away to make a quick exit.

I was steps from the door when I felt a whoosh of air. Caius stood before me, blocking my exit. The anger was gone from his face, replaced by impassivity. Taken aback, I stopped dead in my tracks.

"Do I scare you that easily?" he asked. My blank look forced him to elaborate. "You flee before finishing your errand."

I fidgeted. My growing dislike for him left me befuddled. I struggled to remember my errand.

"Well? I doubt you came here simply for the sake of *seeing* me."

He was right by that account. Seeing him was the *last* thing I wanted. "I wanted to ask you a question."

"Obviously." He arched a perfectly shaped eyebrow.

"I wanted to ask..." I faltered. My lack of courage was embarrassing. "I want to work at Fluxx with the other girls. I want to dance."

"You're joking, right?"

"I'm not," I said, immediately defending my wounded pride. His surprise left me miffed.

"I don't want you at the club."

"Why can't I go?"

"Because you are a liability."

I frowned. Moreover, I was offended. "Why?"

"Don't you know the meaning of *liability*?"

"I know what it means." I did not appreciate his condescension. "Why am I a liability?"

"Because your blood isn't like theirs." He was referring to the other women. "Why do you think Thrax attacked you?"

On cue, my heart began to pound as memories of Thrax resurfaced. Caius noticed. A hungry look lurked in his sliver eyes. Why was my blood different?

"Try not to look so confused, Cece. It happens. It's rare, but it happens."

"I—I don't understand."

"Then let me make something clear." Caius moved so fast he knocked the air from my lungs. I found myself pinned against the wall, his exposed fangs inches from my skin. I was too terrified to make a sound.

"When we vampires smell *blood*, something inside our brain takes over. Instinct kicks in. Unlike our filthy cousins, we can control ourselves, most of the time."

I gazed at him in horror. Was he going to bite me? My heart was racing so fast I could hear the blood pounding in my ears.

"Some blood, Cece, like your blood, is different." He moved his mouth close to my ear and lowered his voice to a whisper. "Some blood *smells* better, *tastes* better."

His breath tickled my skin. I wanted to fight him, but I was too terrified.

"When we smell blood like yours, our self-control begins to falter." He slowly moved his head so that the points of his teeth were resting on my neck. I didn't dare move. "It is safest for everyone if we steer clear of the temptation." He pulled away to look at me. "One little taste, Cece, that is all it takes."

In that moment, I finally saw him for what he was. "All it takes for what?"

"For a vampire to lose complete control." His teeth shrank back to normal. "Oh stop it, Cece. Not all of us are monsters."

I continued to look at him like he was one.

"You should know that strong bloods make the best vampires, and we haven't changed a strong blood in a long time. That is why I gave you the option. The other girls won't survive the change."

I was stunned. I could only gaze at him dumbfounded. At last, many of my questions were answered, creating more.

"Never mind that now. You don't appear inclined to become one of us."

If I was a liability, how could he be so sure his vampires wouldn't bite me? No wonder they all looked at me hungrily. I was the most expensive bottle of wine in the house, and they were dying for a taste.

Caius seemed to read my mind. "Never fear, my dear Cece.

You are off limits to all vampires. Those of my coven have exquisite self-control. The young ones, not so much, which is why they do not live in Anghor Manor. I cannot risk the girls' lives. But those of us living here in the manor are seasoned."

"Is that another word for old?"

I wasn't expecting it, but he threw his head back and let out a booming laugh. It was different from his usual, menacing laugh.

"Yes, *old*, if you must put it so bluntly. You see"—suddenly his fangs returned—"if I so desired, I could break into your vein this very moment." His mouth went back to my neck. His lips brushed my skin. I expected prickles of fear like before. Instead, my abdomen clenched with desire.

"What's the matter, Cece?"

Afraid of the way I felt, I tried to get free of him.

He chuckled, tightening his grip. "Don't you want to be like the other girls? That is why you came into my study with your request." His breath moved across my neck, taunting me. My body begged me to relax, so I ceased my struggle, going limp as a rag doll.

"I could do it, you know." His whispers were gentle caresses. "I could have a taste. My control is absolute. I would never *drain* you. But you would like it—yes. You might not think so now, but you would enjoy it."

Yes, I would enjoy it. I wanted him to. I would beg him if that's what it took to feel his teeth on my neck.

"Do you still hate me Cece? Tell me you don't."

"I don't hate you," I mumbled. How could I hate him? He

was so…

Something in my mind snapped like shattering glass. I did hate him! Fury erupted in my brain. "I do hate you!" I hissed. I pushed with all my might against his chest. He let me free. Scrambling away, I distanced myself from him. "I do hate you, Caius. And don't do that to me again!"

He eyed me warily. It was an improvement over his usual looks of hunger.

"What was that you just did? Were you—were you *bewitching* me?" I was appalled.

An amused smile spread across his features. "I was bewitching you—yes. Trying to anyway. Your mind is terribly strong. Did you like it?" He cocked his head to the side like I was some interesting creature placed in the world to stimulate his curiosities.

"I most certainly didn't like it!"

"Oh, very well then." His face returned to its emotionless facade. "You're no fun, Cece. None at all."

My jaw dropped in disgust. Before I had the chance to say something insulting he said, "So, you really want to work at Fluxx?"

I shut my mouth and nodded.

He was silent a moment as he regarded me. "Very well. Have Adel help you get something to wear. You start Friday. Now go." He side-stepped, clearing the way to the door. I marched out without bothering to thank him. It was the least he could do after that kind of behavior.

I didn't go back to my room immediately. Instead, I found Adel and told her. She and Felix helped me order some ridiculous outfits online. Felix wouldn't let us see the computer password when I tried to spy it.

"Nice try, Cece," he said over his shoulder, perceiving my intentions immediately.

"Do I really have to wear that?" I asked when Adel helped me pick out my things.

"It not so bad, Cece. We all wear this—less than what you have chose anyway." I made sure to select the *least* revealing lingerie outfits from the sites we surfed.

Felix stood by, amused by our arguing. We bickered over colors, styles, and everything else girls nitpick when deciding on clothes. A sudden thought struck me, "Felix, what about normal clothes? I need normal clothes too. If I'm going to be here forever"—I paled at the thought—"then I can't borrow Adel's stuff all the time."

"Girls," he muttered, before reaching into his pocket for his wallet. An Amex black card clanked down onto the keyboard in front of me, like it was no big deal.

"Well, aren't you hot stuff," I muttered. Adel laughed.

When I finally returned to my master suite, the first thing I wanted was a shower. I needed to wash off Caius's fang cooties from my neck. I also made sure to check in the mirror, thankful that there wasn't so much as a red mark. A hot shower heals many woes, and it certainly helped me with mine.

I didn't notice them at first, but before I crawled into bed that night, I discovered a neat little stack of books on my bedside table. They came from Caius's private collection. He had included all the ones I picked out, and a few extras. Turns out, he had a heart after all.

## CHAPTER 5

*I* was nine the first time I danced on stage. It was for a local ballet school where I took lessons. I worked hard to prove I was a perfect fit for Clara in the *Nutcracker*.

When I was selected, I ran straight home to tell my mom. It was all I talked about. I carried my *Nutcracker* doll everywhere, and practiced my solo with him no matter when. I wanted to be perfect.

As the performance loomed near, a nervous tension built inside of me. I began questioning my abilities. What if I tripped? What if forgot part of my solo?

When the day came, I was a wreck. Kids aren't supposed to stress the way I did. My mom must have hated my mood swings, because she said something to my grandmother, who was visiting for Christmas.

*Grand-mère* came to my bedroom while I was sitting at my vanity. "Cece," she said. "I have a way to melt away your nerves." I will always fondly remember her French accent and the way she smiled at me.

Leaning over me, she pinned a beautiful pearl pin onto my costume. "This is a good luck charm. You must wear it. I wore it *always* when I danced. It got me through." She'd been a ballerina in France when she was younger. "The pin is magic. You will dance like an angel."

I believed her of course, proudly displaying it on the front of Clara's nightgown for all to see. And she was right, I did dance better than ever.

That pin became my constant companion. I wore it for every ballet performance I ever danced. Of course, when you get to the professional level, you can't simply put whatever decorations you want onto your costumes. In fact, most times you cannot wear jewelry of any kind.

You'd be surprised by the good-luck charms ballerinas manage to hide under their tutus. I once knew a girl that wore the same hair scrunchy for all her performances. When she wasn't permitted to wear the ghastly thing in her hair, she'd hide it under her leotard some way or another. We all have these weird rituals and habits that get us through performances. That pearl pin was mine.

So when Friday approached, I began to get very nervous. Sure, Fluxx was just a night club. I wouldn't be dancing ballet, but that's what scared me. I only ever danced ballet. This kind of dancing, sexy dancing, was not my forte. I simply couldn't do it without my good-luck charm. I *needed* that pin.

Thursday afternoon, I went for it. I had to bang on Caius's study door for nearly a minute before he opened it. "Caius, I want my purse."

"What purse?" His eyes narrowed.

"My purse. The purse I had when you kidnapped me."

"You must be mistaken, my dear Cece. I never kidnapped you."

I wanted to yell at him. I *always* wanted to yell at him; he had that effect on me. "Whatever, your little *gang* of vampires kidnapped me. Where is it?" I tried to keep my voice calm.

At last he gave up. "I suppose you are hoping to use your cell phone to escape?"

"I'm not that stupid. Like you would let me have it. Keep the phone. I want my purse and the other belongings in it."

"Why?"

"That's none of your business."

"Then I suppose you won't be getting your purse." He tried to shut the door in my face.

I slammed my palm against it to keep it from closing. "That purse is mine. Everything in it is mine. Give it back."

Caius's lips twitched. "Tell me why you want it, and I will give it to you."

"Because there is something in it that I need. In fact, you can have the damned purse and everything in it. I just need one thing. Please." I gazed back at him, unyielding.

"Very well," he sighed. He stepped aside and let me pass. "Have a seat." He went to rummage around in a cabinet. When he removed my purse, I breathed a sigh of relief.

"There'd better not be anything missing." I wouldn't feel

better until I had that pin in my hands. I reached for the purse, but he did not give it to me.

Instead, he took a seat across from me and unclasped it. My jaw dropped. His audacity astounded me. What kind of guy goes through a lady's purse? But I said nothing, schooling my features.

He began removing objects, studying them intently, talking to himself. "Hm. What could Cece want *so* badly that she's willing to brave *my* presence?" He took out several items of makeup, and of course, my cellphone. Then came the keys to my new apartment, the apartment that I'd never get to live in now. Out came a couple of feminine products; I felt my cheeks go red when he removed them, but he didn't look up at me, thank goodness. He kept going, and whenever it was something of interest, he made eye contact with me to analyze my behavior. Receipts from cafes and take-out, my wallet, a tiny case of band aids, the list grew. What can I say? I carried a big purse.

I tried my hardest to keep my face straight when he removed my pearl pin. I could feel my heart flutter in relief. It was still there, exactly where I'd put it. Maybe if I wore it that night at Fluxx, my luck would have been different.

Caius must have sensed my heart beat, because he considered the pendent much longer than he did most of my things. At last, he set it on the pile and continued until my purse was entirely empty. Then he leaned back and watched me. "Well? You said *one* item."

I looked from him to the pile, glancing at the one item.

"Let's play a little game, shall we? I guess what you want, and if I guess correctly, *I* get to keep it."

"Are you kidding me? That's the stupidest thing I have ever heard!" Trying my luck, I reached for my pin. I'd forgotten how fast vampires were. His hand wrapped around my wrist before it got anywhere near my prize.

He clicked his tongue, scolding me. "Now, now. Let's see." He released my wrist and I sat back on the sofa with a huff. He reached out and picked up the pin. I silently cursed. "Obviously this is what you want. I am trying to understand why. Is it a gift from your lover?"

Like I had a boyfriend! Pfft. I wasn't that lucky.

"No? Hmm…" He turned it over in his hand. "Genevieve DuPont." He fell silent for several breaths while I eyed my pin with desperation. "I know this name."

My eyes widened. Goose bumps prickled my skin. Maybe he was bluffing.

"How did you come by this pin?" He waited for me to speak. To be honest, it was none of his damn business. "Do you want it or not?"

I nodded eagerly. "It—it belonged to my grandmother."

"Your grandmother was Genevieve?" He cocked an eyebrow as if my answer didn't quite make sense.

"No. My *great* grandmother was Genevieve."

His face was impossible to read. "Genevieve was a famous ballerina at the Paris Opera House, was she not?"

How could he possibly know this? I nodded, taken aback. He was correct: Genevieve DuPont was famous in her day. She danced until she was in her mid-forties; most ballerinas didn't make it past thirty. I'd seen pictures of her, so I knew that she was beautiful, but my grandmother never said much about her.

Ballet ran in my family. It was a huge part of our family's history on my mom's side. That's why my grandfather was a big donor to the National Ballet Company. My great grandmother, Genevieve, started the tradition. She passed the pin down to my grandmother, who also danced in France before coming to America. My mother didn't, but I did. So the pin passed to me.

Caius regarded me for a moment. "You have her auburn hair, Genevieve's hair, did you know?"

My heart skipped a beat. I didn't know. The photos I'd seen were black and white. He looked over my pin once more, as if it held new meaning. It certainly held plenty of meaning for me, and I wanted it back. "It's all I have left of her. Please. Give it to me. You can have everything else there. I just—I just need the pin."

He shrugged then handed it over. His eyes were full of curiosity. "I watched your great grandmother dance ballet many times in Paris. She was a particular favorite of mine." The way he said it made me uneasy. I looked at him with disgust, unsure of what he meant by favorite. He laughed. "Relax, Cece. It is not what you think. I spent some time in Paris during the twenties, that is all."

I had very mixed feelings at this point. Knowing he'd seen my great grandmother dance was a little alarming. I wanted to ask about her, but I was also eager to get away from him. Fortunately for both of us, I didn't have to struggle with my indecisiveness. He put an end to our conversation. "You may take the rest of your belongings and go. I have no use for them." He snatched my cell phone and left everything else for me to grab.

Friday evening came extremely quickly. I clung to Adel more and more as it approached, and was grateful for her help in preparing for my debut at Fluxx. The packages I ordered came the day before my performance. Adel went through them with me, helping me to choose the perfect outfit for the big occasion.

I settled on a black lace mini dress. By mini I mean, barely covering my behind. Since it was lace, it was quite revealing. Underneath it, I wore a black bra and panties, and a garter belt with straps to hold up a sleek pair of pantyhose.

"It complement your hair, Cece!" Adel fawned over me in front of the mirror. The other girls were likewise excited for me to join them. Marie and Sophie were in Adel's room hogging her second mirror. Their happy chatting decreased my nervous jitters. They mostly spoke German, but sometimes I heard bits and pieces of English. I gathered that they too enjoyed dancing at Fluxx.

When it was time to go, each girl had a vampire escort who led them down the grand staircase in the entrance hall of the manor. Felix was mine. "Are you nervous?" he asked. I lied and shook my head no. "Beautiful pin, by the way."

I wasn't sure if Caius had informed him of our interaction, but I thanked him anyway.

"Ready to go?" He took my hand, holding it firmly. I knew what the gesture really meant. He was prepared should I try to dart off. When I stepped through the large front door into the fresh evening air, I hesitated on the vast front landing. Several deep breaths were necessary before I could continue on.

The outside world! I'd finally made it. It wasn't freedom, but it was a step in the right direction.

# CHAPTER 6

When a ballerina dances, she becomes an actor. It's a different kind of acting, in a way more difficult. A ballerina must tell a story using only the music and the movements of her body. There are no words, no vocals, only what she can portray through her face and through the motions she makes. I always loved this about ballet. You become a different person. You are no longer yourself. You can escape your mind—escape the world you live in. It's like trading one life for another.

The night I danced at Fluxx, I became someone entirely different. I didn't need to do this, no one was forcing me. I could have danced as Cece, but where's the fun in that? Cece's life wasn't exactly going well, so I didn't want to be myself.

I suppose you're wondering what happened after I stepped outside of Anghor Manor? I'd never seen the front of it, but I quickly discovered that the manor had a humongous circular drive. There were twenty-two of us that Friday night. Our escorts turned out to be our drivers. Lined up along the circular drive were an equal number of exotic cars. My eyeballs nearly fell out when I saw them. I'd never ridden in anything so glamorous. "Which one are we taking?" I breathed with excitement.

Felix grinned. He held up a set of keys and pointed. "The red Maserati GranTurismo, there."

I squealed. Suddenly I was more excited than nervous. "Can we drive fast?"

"Maybe on the way back," he chuckled.

I soon learned the reason for the use of such opulent cars. After all, they could have piled us into vans. To understand this, we need to backtrack for a moment.

Fluxx was the *only* vampire club in Vienna, and it was owned by Caius. I'm sure vamps went to other bars and clubs, but this one was considered the *crème de la crème*. Cover charge wasn't cheap; it wasn't a place for cheapskates. And the dancers who danced at Fluxx? They were considered celebrities amongst the clientele there. Sure, they were *only* human, but there is something fascinating about humans where vampires are concerned.

When we arrived at fifteen minutes to eight, there was already a giant entry line stretched all the way down the block. Each of the cars pulled up, and we were escorted in. The crowd was cheering, going wild with excitement. I saw bright flashes as our onlookers snapped photos of us for their Instagram accounts. I clung to Felix's hand. "Are they always this excited to see the dancers?"

"Of course. You ladies are the unobtainable. That makes you both mysterious and sought after."

"But not unobtainable for you guys," I corrected. I watched

him smirk. "Does Caius ever come out?" I wasn't sure why I asked. I guess part of me was hoping he didn't. I already felt vulnerable enough around him. Now I was wearing hardly anything under my sleek black trench coat.

"Of course he does. This is his club. He doesn't *always* come out, but tonight is a special night. Tonight is your opening night, so he will be here."

"My opening night?"

"Yes. Why else do you think there are so many people lined up waiting to get in?"

My jaw dropped. "They are here for me? But I don't get it."

"Word travels fast, Cece. There's a new girl in town, a new girl in Fluxx, I should say. Everyone is eager to see who it is. Oh, and I should mention something else. The rules." I had wondered if there would be rules. "Under no circumstances are you permitted to speak to anyone, no matter how badly they wish to talk to you, no matter how much they call you or try to get your attention."

We were walking down a dark inner corridor that spanned the inside of the club. The walls were illuminated by lights that stained them blood-red. I took note of my surroundings, looking for exits, and anything that might be used as a future escape route. "If, in the event that someone tries to reach through the bars of your cage, you must expect the worst— that they are trying to bite you. Move away from them. Patrons know the rules, and Caius is not tolerant, but we get many newcomers. Anyone who tries to climb up on your cage will be removed immediately. But, just in case..."

Was it too late to get cold feet? The cages were used to keep people out, not to keep dancers in. The iron bars would be our only protection from the vampires. The way Felix talked…let's just say I was wary. I nervously fidgeted with my pearl pin.

Felix led me to a dressing room where the rest of the girls were. "Five minutes, ladies," someone announced. The air was electric; it reminded me of being backstage before a performance. We were each given our own vanity area to apply our final touches: lipstick, hair pins, and whatever else we might have forgotten. It wasn't necessary though; we were already ready.

Adel moved over to me and held my hand. It was a welcome gesture. "Remember, look sexy, Cece. They love you." I gave her a brief smile, ignoring my fluttering heart.

After a few minutes, I could hear music playing loudly. Doors opened at eight. "It's almost time, Cece," Adel whispered in my ear. I gave her a brief nod. Our escorts collected each of us. We were led downstairs into a basement.

I grew apprehensive. "Aren't we going into the club?"

"You are," Felix answered. "We don't walk you through the crowd. That would be too dangerous." Suddenly it was clear to me: our escorts were more like bodyguards. To be honest, the way Felix made it sound, I was *glad* to have him there with me.

It didn't take long to figure out how the dancers got into their cages. There were lifts all around the large basement, which mirrored the club above. They were the same type of lifts used on a stage to bring a person directly up into plain sight.

"Each lift brings the dancer into her cage," Felix explained. "We keep guards down here at all times. No one is permitted below. You will be safe." I nodded, hardly listening as my gaze circled the room. Guards at all times eliminated any hope I had of escaping through the basement. "You are over here—the middle cage." Felix led me onto a large platform that would soon become my dance floor.

"It's larger than I thought it would be." And it was, *much* larger. I could have cartwheeled twice in the space I had.

"You are the debut dancer, so you will have the center cage." The other platforms were only half the size of mine, and located randomly all over the vast basement. The placement would allow the crowd to gather around in between the cages. "All eyes will be on you, Cece."

"But…" That was not how I expected things to go down. "I said I wanted to dance. I didn't mean I wanted to be the center of attention!"

Felix shrugged. "Caius's rules, not mine." Of course it was always Caius's fault. I rolled my eyes.

"Take your places, ladies," someone called. My heart thumped. I heard the music above us stop. Everything fell silent. For a moment, you could have heard a pin drop. "You'll do great," Felix whispered into my ear, giving my hand a final squeeze before moving away.

I heard a loud voice above me. I strained my hearing, listening to what it said. The DJ was announcing me. I tried to understand everything he said, but he was speaking German. It sounded like he was telling a story of some kind. All I understood were the final words in English, which were ringing in my ears as the floor began to lift. At that moment, he switched to English. "Ladies and gentlemen, give a warm welcome to the fiery redhead known as *Ginger*!!"

My heart began racing. The crowd was screaming, going absolutely wild. Slowly, I was lifted upwards towards the club floor. Music was already playing. I recognized the song: *Paris*, by The Chainsmokers. How fitting. Did Caius pick this one out?

"Shit!" My mutter was drowned out by the music. With the kind of attention I was getting, everyone would be watching me, eager to see who this *Ginger* was. What had I gotten myself into?

At first I only saw shoes, designer men's and women's dress shoes. Were those a pair of Giuseppe Zanotti's?! Then I saw more: ankles, calves, entire legs. Was I supposed to start dancing now? I decided I had better get moving. The last thing I wanted was to look like a scared little girl.

My body was reluctant at first—hesitant—but I let myself sway to the music, getting a feel for the beat, letting it wash over me, sink into me. I was a different person tonight, I reminded myself; I was Ginger. I didn't need to be *scared Cece* anymore. I only needed to be Ginger, who was apparently a fiery redhead.

At last, my stage clicked into position. The crowd cheered, so I flashed them an alluring smile and flicked my red hair with as much sass as I could muster. They responded with a roar of delight. Just like that, Cece was snuffed out.

I danced my heart out, shaking my hips back and forth to the beat of the music, strutting around my cage in circles so that everyone could get a good look at me. Every so often, I made sure to flick my hair one way or another. Sometimes I used the bars, letting my body slide down them. My audience ate it up. Silently, I was thanking God for the hip-hop classes I'd been required to take. "A good ballerina is a well-rounded ballerina," my teachers always said.

By the time *Paris* ended, I was actually disappointed. I'd forgotten how much I loved the attention; moreover, I'd never had such an adoring, lively crowd.

As the next song came on, the DJ got back onto the mike. "Isn't she lovely?!" The audience screamed. "Now, let's give it up for the rest of our ladies!" Still more shouts and cheers followed. One by one as the next song played, each of the other girls were lifted into their cages. Adel was one of the most popular. The crowd loved her. She was beautiful with her poufy blonde hair and her teal bralette with matching panties. I could see why they loved her.

We danced the entire time. I was too enamored by the bright lights and loud music to pay much attention to the patrons gathered about our cages, drinking and dancing. Fortunately, no one threw themselves at my cage, but they did call my name and stick their hands in, to try and touch me.

I couldn't help but wonder, who were the vampires and who were their human dates? Furthermore, did their human dates know what they were? How did that work, anyway? There were so many questions, still unanswered, that I couldn't seem to get out of my head.

I was grateful for my endurance. Nearly eight months had passed since I'd given up ballet, but I still had it in me to dance without stopping for the six hours I worked. I was equally impressed with the other girls. They didn't need breaks either, though, I did notice that they developed a routine for slowing down and speeding up. It gave them time to catch their breath.

In case you're wondering, I did not allow myself to move in

any way that was seemingly similar to ballet. That part of my life belonged to Cece. Ginger was *not* a ballerina. I wanted to keep that aspect of Cece's life under lock and key. It was the only thing Caius couldn't take from me, or use against me. He already taunted me enough.

As the night came to a close, there were so many emotions flowing through me. I was thrilled to have survived my first Fluxx shift. My audience was *crazy* for me; nothing leaves a performer feeling more fulfilled. I was reluctant to return to Anghor Manor. I liked my new cage much better. However, I was also relieved to be done, exhausted both emotionally and physically, and my ears were ringing.

As our DJ dismissed us one at a time, the remaining crowd gave long, loud cheers for us. I was the last one to be lowered. The moment my platform clicked into place in the basement, Adel threw her arms around my neck, hugging me warmly. "You did it!" she squealed. "You did it, Cece!"

Other girls gathered around me too, congratulating me. They were all so nice, nothing like the cut-throat ballerinas I was used to competing with. I was so overwhelmed by their support, that for the first time since getting kidnapped, I thought I might burst into tears. That was saying something because I *never* cried. And I mean *never*.

"Well done, Cece. Well done." Felix was standing off to the side of my platform. He was smiling wide. I smiled back. The other escorts stood around too, but they did not rush us along, or break up our fun. In fact, I heard a bottle pop, and then another. All of a sudden, champagne glasses were passed around, and I found myself sipping Krug Vintage Brut.

We were all celebrating in the basement, relishing in a

successful night. It was the happiest I'd been in nearly three weeks. Adel stayed by my side, paying me one complement after another. I returned the favor, telling her how much the crowd adored her.

"Do you think?" she asked apprehensively.

"Adel, you should have seen how they cheered for you when your platform came up!" I gushed.

"But not like they did for you," she whispered into my ear. "And did you see Caius?"

I choked on my expensive champagne, not expecting to hear Caius's name. "No, I didn't." In fact, I'd forgotten he was even going to be there.

"Well I did, Cece. I saw him. He couldn't take his eyes off you."

CHAPTER 7

*I*'ve never been a people person. It's not that I'm socially awkward, I simply don't enjoy being around people for longer than what is necessary. I like my personal space, my alone time.

Perhaps it's because alone time has always been a rare commodity, especially when I joined the ballet company. If I wasn't in class, training, or taking private lessons for my solos, I was stuck at home with my family. If I wanted to go out, there were always hundreds people doing the same thing.

Unlike some ballerinas living on their own in New York City, my family followed me when I relocated to join the company. I guess that kind of unyielding support is hard to come by, and I appreciated it at first, but all I had was my bedroom, which was my only sanctuary of solitude.

Anghor Manor was much of the same: the only quiet place was my own bedroom suite. Aside from the twenty-one human girls that resided within, a number of male and female vampires also lived in the manor, not to mention all the visitors. Anghor Manor was definitely a headquarters of some kind. Vamps were coming and going frequently. There was never a moment of peace, unless you were tucked away somewhere. Since Caius made clear that his little library-study was off limits, I kept to my room, mostly out of shyness.

It didn't take long to learn that the girls were quite the opposite. They were social butterflies, making use of the television room, the game rooms, and various other living spaces in the manor. I suppose now is a good time to familiarize you with some of the daily tasks of manor life.

The first couple of nights I ate alone in the kitchen at odd hours. Not long after discovering the other girls, I learned that they cooked dinner together each night. If you're curious about the kind of dinner to be had when twenty-one women are available to prepare it, well, mealtimes were nothing short of a feast. Strangely enough, I enjoyed cooking with them.

I found this intriguing because ballerinas have a love-hate relationship with food. It isn't easy maintaining a ballet body. You must be careful of what you eat. But I wasn't a ballerina anymore, so I no longer held back.

I was pleasantly surprised to find that vampires ate human food. "You don't live on blood alone?" I asked Felix when I discovered this.

He laughed at me. "You humans have such odd preconceived notions of how we vampires behave."

Despite my inclination to remain in my room during the day, reading mostly, I came to enjoy dinner time. I always helped the other girls in the kitchen. Adel and I had endless things to discuss while we sliced and diced, mostly pertaining to her life. I tried to steer the conversation away from my life as much as possible. She knew I was from New York, that was all.

Once I began dancing at the club, we had even more to talk about. It was during this time that I discovered how she and the other girls came to be at Anghor Manor. I found out how the vampires managed to drink from humans without giving up their secrets.

Each girl's story was similar. Adel in particular had been at Fluxx the night she was taken, just like me. She was on the dance floor with her date when a big fight broke out. Things got pretty nasty. "There was blood everywhere," she explained while we cut carrots. "Vampires stab vampires. Bodies fly across dance floor faster than I blink. I so scared. I screamed and screamed." She was only sixteen at the time. "I had fake ID. And you know vampires, anything for blood."

"So they took you because you saw too much?" I was very curious. That had been *my* case. I'd been taken because I'd seen the vampires stab and kill Thrax.

Adel shrugged. "Other girls saw same. They allowed to go home. Their mind weak. But not me."

"What do you mean?" I loved Adel's patience. She never made me feel silly for asking questions.

"Vampires are *persuasive*," she said. "They have ability to bewitch mind. Most humans, vampires tell them anything. The human believe them. That how they clean up."

By the end of the bloodbath at Fluxx, the vampires had managed to reprogram the memories of their human witnesses. "Except for me," Adel said. "My mind too strong. I not forget." She looked around the kitchen before adding, "That is what happen to all girls to come here. We are ones who fail. We have strong minds."

"But, what about the males? Where do *they* go?"

She gave me a blank look, as if the question never crossed her mind. "Don't know. But vampires do not kill. Good vampires do not kill. Caius vampires good. Only rogues do that. Rogues will suck humans dry."

So the question remained, what happened to the male humans who were strong-minded? I knew one thing though, a strong mind did not mean strong blood. Caius made it clear that these girls were not strong blooded enough to survive the change of becoming a vampire.

As my time with them stretched on, I began to make more sense of things. I also noticed something else. I became more extroverted. Perhaps it was my homesickness. Or maybe I was changing. I was becoming more like *Ginger*. I began spending more and more time outside of my bedroom.

It started with dinner. Dinnertime in Anghor Manor reminded me of the family dinners my mother required me to attend when I wasn't working. I disliked those because I had no choice. In Anghor Manor, there was always a choice, or rather, the illusion of choice.

I was never required to attend dinner if I didn't choose to. Aside from forcing me to remain here, I had a choice in all else, including whether I became a vampire, lived as a human, or opted for death. Mind you, I had a very strong will to live, so the third option was out of the question.

The dining room at Anghor Manor was breathtaking. Its stone walls were covered with woven tapestries depicting

Roman battles and gladiators in the Colosseum. The table itself was a magnificent monstrosity. It seated fifty-two people, and it was *always* full. The best part was, there were no assigned seats; we sat wherever we wanted.

There were always more vampires present for dinner than lived in the manor. If a vampire was visiting on business, he or she stayed for the evening meal. I think Caius liked playing host, and the girls *loved* cooking for them.

So far, Julia was my favorite of all the vampires, aside from Felix of course. She didn't live in the manor, but she visited often. Whenever she did, I sat by her.

"Tell me about your debut at Fluxx," she asked Sunday night. "I hear you were a big hit. Has dancing always come naturally for you?"

"It has," I admitted, washing down my steak with several sips of wine from a Baccarat crystal glass. Another thing I liked about the manor—wine was always served at dinner.

The wine cellar in Anghor Manor was beyond imagining. It was a giant undercroft filled wall to ceiling with casks and dark bottles. I was honored to choose the selection for this meal: a vintage Penfolds Grange Shiraz that went down so smoothly, it should have been criminal.

"*Well…*" Julia shifted to better look at me. "I've already heard so much about your performances. I'm determined to go to Fluxx next weekend to see what all the fuss is about."

"You should come." I smiled. "I enjoy it more than I imagined." And that was the truth. I was still riding the high.

"Good! It's like I always told Caius, letting you girls dance is the best thing he's done for the strong-minded."

I nearly choked. "You're the one who talked him into letting us dance?"

"Of course. Before that, there was nothing for you ladies to do. You poor things—just sitting around the manor all day. I couldn't live with myself if that was to be your end."

"But, what about boys?" I asked. "What happens to strong-minded men?"

"Oh, honey." She afforded me a patient look. "Strong-minded males? There aren't any."

My jaw dropped. Julia laughed. "Men are fickle creatures, dear. They can have the strongest blood, certainly. But when it comes to the mind? They are as pliable as clay."

At this, I burst into a fit of giggles. She had me laughing so hard, that the entire table went silent. Everyone looked over at me, including Caius, who happened to be sitting three seats down on the opposite side. My eyes met his and I immediately felt my cheeks burn. I quickly looked away and went back to my food.

"What are you telling her over there, Julia?" His rich voice rang out into the silence. "Not our *secrets*, I hope?"

Julia turned to me and winked before addressing him. "Quit toying with my little pet, Caius."

There were a good number of reasons why I liked Julia; her sticking up for me was one of them. Caius simply shrugged, "Perhaps if she wasn't so easy to tease..." With that, he returned to his conversation.

*Easy to tease?* I wanted to take his plate and shove it into his face. Before deciding otherwise, I loaded up a spoonful of mashed potatoes and flung it at him. My aim was true. It splattered all over his cheek. He froze.

At that moment, I second-guessed my behavior. Making a fool of Caius probably wasn't the best idea. In fact, it was a terrible idea.

Suddenly, faster than my human eyes could follow, I was smacked in the face with a handful of mashed potatoes. The warm gooey mess splattered all over me. It got into my eyes, and dripped down my shirt.

Immediately, the table erupted into chaos. If you've never seen a vampire food fight, well, it's quite a show. Although, not so much for the humans involved; all I could see was a blur of flying food.

It lasted a minute at most, and when it finished, the entire table erupted into laughter. Every plate was empty, except mine and the others who could never hope to move as fast. When I managed to wipe my face clean, I noticed that Caius was watching me. For a brief moment, I saw something in his eyes, but it wasn't the usual impassivity. Was he impressed that I had some gall after all?

*"You're no fun,"* he'd said to me earlier that week. Well, I showed him! That marked the start of many changes between Caius and I.

$\mathcal{T}$he average pain tolerance of a ballet dancer is three times higher than normal. I've heard the statistic and never questioned it. Why would I? I lived it. Have you ever seen a ballerina's feet from dancing pointe? They're disgusting, with accentuated knuckles, scabs, blisters, and missing toenails. It's a good thing they're covered with pretty, pink-ribbon shoes.

I never questioned my own pain tolerance—it has always been high. When I suffered my life-changing injury, I finished the entire practice gritting my teeth before seeing the company specialist. I could have quit directly after falling. Sticking it out was probably the worst thing I did. Although, it wouldn't have changed the outcome.

I think most ballerinas are like that. A ballerina will do anything to prove that she's tough enough, especially the ones who haven't landed solos and prima positions. But you know what's really sick? Ballerinas like pain. They wouldn't be dancers if they didn't. It takes a special kind of person to become a ballerina. Having a high pain tolerance is an absolute must.

Why do we enjoy it? Because it makes us feel alive. In the stressed-out world ballerinas live in, it's easy to feel dead. Only two things fix this terrible lifelessness: pain, and the exhilaration of performing live.

When I quit dancing, I was deprived of the constant battering my body was subjected to. Perhaps that was good. Like many aspects of dancing, I missed the pain.

One blessed day, I discovered a room in the basement of Anghor Manor that offered me the pain I was robbed of. I was exploring the manor like I often did, when I worked up the courage to venture into the basement. I heard shouts coming from down the hallway and was immediately curious.

At the door, I listened for several minutes, trying to understand the variety of sounds coming from within. The thud of wood, the clang of metal, the shouts of triumph, the cries of pain, they were all intriguing. So, I pushed the door open.

I found myself in a large training room. It had mirrored walls and tall ceilings. There was a large sparring ring, soft mats for fighting, punching bags, numerous weapons, you name it. I was immediately enticed by what it potentially offered me.

"You shouldn't be here," a voice sounded beside me.

"Hi Titus," I said, turning to greet one of the many vampires I'd come to know. He brushed aside a few stray locks of shaggy blonde hair as he regarded me with sparkling green eyes—eyes that weren't so different from my own. "What is this place?"

"It is our training room."

I studied the scene before me. There were pairs of vampires everywhere. I recognized many of them, and some I'd never seen before. "What are you training for?" Weren't vampires already powerful enough? Their human counterparts didn't stand a chance, so what was the point?

"I am not at liberty to say."

"Oh come on, Titus. Who am I going to tell?" My argument left him thoughtful. I scanned the room. Felix was off in a corner wrestling with an unfamiliar female. He knocked her to the ground before offering her a brilliant, dimpled smile. Then he gave her a hand, bringing her to her feet. My gaze narrowed suspiciously. "How come no one is moving in blurs? Don't you guys have like, super human speed?"

He smiled. "Rules of the room. No use of special powers beyond our own strength."

This sounded particularly appealing to me. I'd never done fighting of any kind. Seeing this, I was driven to desire.

"Do you think—" I hesitated. "Can I try?" I expected him to laugh. More so, I expected a no.

Titus shrugged and led me to a punching bag. After I had a pair of boxing gloves, he showed me how to hit it properly, back and forth. "Move your body with your punch," he instructed, demonstrating in slow motion. I followed his movements. When he was satisfied, he left me to myself. I cannot stress how fulfilling it is to punch something repeatedly.

After about ten minutes, I went back to Titus. "Why do I have to wear gloves?" They were bulky and made my hands all sweaty. I wanted to feel the thing I was hitting. The gloves weren't a requirement, he simply didn't want me to damage my hands. Like I cared! I welcomed the pain. So, I ditched the gloves and went back, starting anew.

The first hit was a shock. I slammed my fist into the bag and felt the pain reverberate through my knuckles, up into my wrist and arm. I clenched my teeth and struck the bag with the other fist. Again, the same feeling. Over and over I began punching. It was like a drug. The burn on my skin increased. I thrived on this kind of hurt.

Excited, I began throwing myself into my punches, letting my entire body carry the momentum of each fist forward before slamming them into the bag. Faster and faster I moved. With each hit I felt better, *happier*, more like my old self.

It took several minutes for me to become aware of the still- ness in the room. I abruptly stopped, looking around in confusion. Every face was turned towards me. Each wore the same expression of savage hunger.

My heart rate spiked. I looked at my fists. The skin had broken and was bleeding freely. My eyes widened.

Titus rushed over to me. "That's enough for one day." He ushered me out of the room before anything escalated.

"But…" I wasn't ready to stop.

"I've never seen a human so enthusiastic about self-inflic- tion. I'm not sure what point you're trying to prove, Cece, but Caius would have my head if anything happened to you."

"Is it really that bad? My blood?"

"The instant your skin broke, every single one of us wanted *one* thing."

My eyes grew large. Caught up in the moment, I'd neglected my conversation with Caius the day his fangs grazed my neck. "I didn't mean to be so…"

"Careless?"

"Yes."

Titus didn't scold me. Nor did he send me away. Rather, he offered me something I needed. "The training room is empty in the morning. Meet me here at seven if you still want to *purposefully* injure yourself."

"Really? You mean it?"

He crossed his arms, eyeing me curiously. He was trying to figure me out. I'm sure he'd never met a human in my position, eager to hurt themselves for fun. "Yes. Really. As long as there isn't a sick reason why you want to do this to yourself. It will be painful, you know."

"How do you mean?"

"Well, learning to fight, if that's what you're after, will require you to subject yourself to a number of beatings. The only trainers here are vampires. I assure you, most of us won't go easy on you."

"Not even at first?"

He flashed me a brief smile. "Well, maybe at first, but not for long."

"Good. Then I'm in." What the hell was I getting myself into? Crazy enough, the thrill was a welcome one.

"Very well. Just remember—this was *your* choice."

*My* choice. There. He'd said it. Everything in their world was based on choice. If only I could make the one important choice still waiting on me.

It took two days for Caius to find out about my new hobby. I came to dinner sporting a black eye, which immediately betrayed my secret. "What the fuck happened to your face, Cece?" Caius's voice cut through the room as he got to his feet. Everyone fell silent.

"Nothing," I squeaked, sinking down deeply in my chair. Under his penetrating gaze, time seemed to stop.

"Come with me." It was not a request.

I was too afraid to argue, so I followed him out of the room. He said nothing as he strode through the manor. I had to jog to keep up with his unfair pace. As soon as we entered his study, he slammed the door and rounded on me.

"What the *hell* is going on? Did you fight with the other girls? I will not allow conflicts in my house."

I backed up towards the door. I'd never seen him like this. Not even the first night when I was brought before him. This emotion was a direct contrast to the stony contempt he'd offered me then.

I shook my head violently. "I would never fight with the girls, Caius. It's nothing."

"Who did this to you?"

"No one. No one did it to me. I did it to myself."

"You did it to yourself," he repeated. "I do not tolerate lying, Cece."

"I'm not lying! I swear. I like the pain. I was in the training room. I asked Titus to train me. It's my fault. He warned me."

"You like the pain…" His tone was even. "Cece, that's the most fucked-up thing I've ever heard."

"Why? Because I don't fit your perfect little *stereotype* of how a lady should behave?" I clenched my fists and held them tightly against my body. "Don't you *dare* tell me who I am, Caius."

My tirade caught him off guard. He opened his mouth, closed it, crossed his arms, uncrossed his arms. More importantly, he didn't know how to respond.

"Are we done now?" I didn't need his judgement.

"No, Cece. We are not done."

"What more do you want, Caius? To lecture me? To harass me? Taunt me? Tease me? Go ahead." I was done playing his stupid games.

His jaw tensed. "I am not going to lecture you, Cece. What I was going to say is, you're scheduled to dance at Fluxx tomorrow. Do you expect to go on stage with bruises covering your body? What kind of message does that send?"

Oops. I hadn't thought about that. I felt a surge of adrenaline as I considered the implication of my actions. Caius was right, I couldn't dance looking like this.

He didn't say anything else, he didn't need to. Instead, he walked over to his wine cabinet. I watched him pensively as he reached for a glass and filled it with wine. He set the bottle down with a louder than necessary thud. I'd definitely ticked him off.

He walked back with a glass of dark red wine—the color of

blood. My eyebrows knitted together as I watched him. Then my stomach dropped. Right in front of me, he elongated his fangs and bit into his wrist. I flinched as his skin broke. He held his dripping wrist over the glass. Blood streamed into the wine.

My eyes were wide with horror. I took several steps backwards until my back was flush with the door. My hand reached for the knob.

"Oh no." He glanced up at me before returning to his task. "You aren't going anywhere." Satisfied, he licked his wrist and the blood stopped. Then his fangs receded and disappeared.

"Drink this." He held the wine out to me. I remained frozen in place. His eyes narrowed. "Vampires do not shed their blood lightly, Cece. Nor do they shed it for just anyone. Take it."

Like a puppet, I walked forward and took the glass, but I did not drink. "I don't want to become a vampire," I whispered. Was this my punishment? What about my choice?

"Jesus Christ, Cece, drinking my blood isn't enough to turn you into a vampire. Drink the fucking glass. All of it."

I shook my head, fearful of his intentions. He was tricking me. That's how he liked to play; he loved games.

"No?" He arched an eyebrow at me. "You won't drink?"

I pursed my lips tightly together and shook my head.

"Let me make things *very* clear then, my dear Cece. You are not permitted to dance with a bruised body. You either drink that, or you can stay home tomorrow and every day after.

Furthermore, you can kiss the training room goodby—that and your fucked-up desire to inflict pain on yourself."

His threat brought panic. He would take away everything that made Anghor Manor tolerable. There was a choice: his blood for the lifestyle I wanted to maintain. I looked from him to the glass, utterly uncertain.

"Blood for dancing, Cece. Blood for pain. Your choice."

And so, I drank.

# CHAPTER 9

*E*arning pointe shoes is a ballerina's coming of age. It's a turning point in her career. For males, it's different. Males often dance on pointe to begin with, to improve their technique and strength. In fact, it can be disheartening to demote a male to pointe when he falls short. During a performance however, you rarely see male ballet dancers on pointe.

For females, it's the opposite. When a ballerina's feet are strong enough and her technique developed, she's ready. If she's lucky to have a good teacher like mine, she will be presented with a pair of satin pink pointe shoes. It's symbolic. It says, *you're ready for the next stage of your career*. It took me nearly five years to earn my pointe shoes. When I did, it was one of the most fulfilling days of my life.

Of course, it took less than twenty-four hours to completely change my mind. By the end of my first practice I was dying to take them off, but that's not the moral of my story. The fact is, I worked hard for years to get to the next level—I *earned* it.

Dancing at Fluxx was entirely different. I never got demoted from my front-center cage. I thought I would have it for a week, two at most, being the new girl and all. But every week I was led to the same exact place in the basement.

"When do the other girls get a turn?" I whispered to Felix.

He shrugged. "I do as I'm told." He didn't see anything wrong with the arrangement.

Maybe I was simply overthinking it. Still, it didn't seem fair. All the girls had been working at Fluxx far longer than me. I hadn't put in the time. Without question, every one of them earned the position more than I had. Why was I being handed stardom so freely? It was a cheat. I never liked cheaters—I certainly didn't want to be one.

I know; it shouldn't have been a big deal. A cage is a cage. Mine was simply twice as large, slightly more elevated than the others, and in the center of the room. It was the first thing guests spotted when they walked in. It was a statement: look at her, she's the best of them all.

My biggest fear wasn't fairness; I was worried I might be ostracized from the group. These girls were my only support, and they had become akin to sisters. I couldn't lose them.

In the ballet world, it's all about *sew* and *reap*. Your peers rarely question the solos you are given, or why you receive a promotion. You dance with the same people daily. They see your struggles and you see theirs. You know that when something good comes their way, they've earned it.

There's nothing a ballerina hates more than a cheater—more than seeing someone in the company get something they didn't work for. And believe me, it happens.

When it does, that person is shunned, albeit not publicly. It's a silent affair. Everyone pretends to treat you the same. They act as though they think no differently of you. They play the denial card, but secretly, they begin to hate you. And after the seeds grow, you reap an empty harvest.

I thought that would happen with the girls of Anghor Manor. I was used to it happening. After all, I didn't deserve a position with the company after my injury. I should have gone through a fresh tryout like all the newbies. But nope, my grandfather gave the company plenty of money. Without knowing whether or not I'd be capable of dancing adequately, the company handed me a corps position. Corps is base level, but plenty of people reach for the position without ever receiving it.

As the weeks in Anghor Manor slipped by, I became more and more shocked. The girls treated me the same. If anything, better. Adel and I grew closer. She never once brought up the fact that I didn't deserve the star cage.

"It doesn't seem fair," I told her. "You should have a turn. You are prettier than me, and you've been here longer."

"Oh Cece. You best dancer! The crowd loves you. Caius would be stupid to put me in."

"Have you ever danced center before?" I asked out of curiosity. I wasn't really sure how the rotations worked, or who decided where each of the girls were placed.

She paused. "Yes—first time. I hated it."

"You're kidding?" I was shocked, but still, I pushed a little harder. "I could tell Caius to give you a turn, Adel. I'm sure he would listen." Pleading with Caius was worth a try. "You deserve to be noticed."

"No," she insisted repeatedly. "It must be *you*, Cece."

I finally gave up. Sometimes I questioned her constant loyalty to me. Was she simply being fake? Did she secretly hate me for getting handed something I never earned? It certainly happened like that when I was in the company. Girls did it to me all the time. That's how I learned to keep my guard up. And that's why it was difficult to accept that Adel wasn't that way.

When I failed with Adel, I asked the other girls too, and soon found their feelings were much like hers. I went to each with similar proposals. They all assured me that I was good, that I deserved the position. And so, I remained the main attraction at Fluxx.

I'm sure you are wondering what became of Caius's initial reaction to my debut, when he apparently couldn't keep his eyes off me. I thought perhaps Adel had made it up. Why on earth would Caius be interested in watching me?

I was told he didn't visit the club often. Since my debut, he never missed a night. I paid careful attention to him, conspicuously, as I didn't want him to know that I noticed his attentive eyes.

Watching him became instinctive. After Caius gave me his blood, he was easier to locate. I later came to understand the reason why. His blood in my body created a connection. At the time, I simply believed I was getting better at my *Caius awareness*, some kind of sixth sense I was developing.

The blood might have dissipated and our connection faded, but I continued my training with Titus. Each time we practiced, I came away with bruises. Caius hated it. I once overheard him attempt to dissuade Titus. They were in the training room, but they didn't know I was listening just outside the door.

"You enjoy using her as a punching bag, Titus? Is that it?"

"She asks for it, Caius. I've never seen a human this eager to fight, not since our days in the ring."

"She reminds you of Flavia, doesn't she?"

"Quite a bit," Titus admitted. I could hear something in his voice. Sadness? Who was Flavia?

"Well, I don't like it."

I grew tired of hiding, and entered the training room saying, "You don't have to like it, Caius. My training isn't your choice."

"Well, it should be," he answered as I approached the mats. He returned his attention to Titus. "You know it weakens my body to shed blood for her."

"Um. I'm standing right here." My words didn't matter. They ignored me.

Titus was silent for several moments. "We could help, Caius. I wouldn't mind sharing blood. Besides, you should not put yourself in a vulnerable position. We need you to remain strong."

"No, no sharing. It is my choice for Cece to remain bruise-free. So it will be my blood she drinks."

"Still standing here." I glared at them.

I wasn't sure what they meant, arguing about weakness and vulnerability. They obviously didn't care that I was clueless. But, I couldn't help picking up on Caius's protectiveness. I think that was the first time I became aware of it. I felt it too, within me.

Each night after training days I found a goblet of blood-laced wine the color of Malbec sitting on my nightstand. It was always Caius's blood. Thus, my ability to locate him in any part of the busy nightclub, or any room in the manor, became a normal thing for me. That was both a blessing and a curse.

I could have done things differently. I could have given up the training room or dancing. But I loved them both. They were two different sides of me that were constantly in disagreement.

Plus, I'd finally reached a level of comfort in Anghor Manor that I could handle. After going through so many extreme changes during the past two years, I welcomed the settled-down feeling that formed.

It was dangerous. I knew it was. Getting comfortable meant accepting the fate of being trapped. Did I really want to die in this place? What about my family? They had to be worried sick. Thinking of their pain churned my stomach.

If I stayed here, how could I possibly have a life of my own? I tried not to think about it. It only brought sadness.

It was strange the way Ginger began mixing with Cece forming this completely new person with new dreams and new aspirations. Both personalities battled one another, each trying to establish itself inside of me. Cece was easy—I knew her. But Ginger? Ginger was different.

Ginger liked Caius's games and his frequent notice. She was flattered by it. Ginger loved the attention gained by dancing at Fluxx. She didn't care that she hadn't earned it. Frighteningly enough, she didn't want to leave Anghor Manor.

Cece, on the other hand, enjoyed tormenting herself. Cece *thrived* on pain. Cece loved berating Ginger for her boldness.

Cece hated Ginger. She hated Ginger's eagerness for captivity. Most of all, she hated the competition.

The worst part was: I couldn't escape either of these personalities. Like Anghor Manor, I was probably stuck with them for all of eternity. Was that something I could live with?

CHAPTER 10

hen I was promoted to principle dancer at the National Ballet, I made myself one promise. I vowed I would give a live performance at the Paris Opera House. Ballet has deep roots in France, so it held an appeal other places couldn't.

Once I quit dancing, I knew I would never fulfill my promise. I accepted that. But I made a point of visiting the Paris Opera House while I toured Europe. *La Valse* was playing live, and last minute tickets were insanely expensive. I purchased one anyway, blowing most of my spending money.

*La Valse* is a lovely ballet based on the end of World War One. The costumes are to die for. The choreography is so traditional, so classic.

It probably wasn't the best thing to do considering my fragile condition. Regardless, I held myself together. On the inside, unknown to everyone else, I was weeping the whole time.

Every arm motion, every *jeté*, every *pirouette*, every *fouetté*, brought back painful memories.

Once the performance ended, long after the reception was in full swing, I snuck back into the theater. I crept onto the stage and stood there in the dim light. How grand it must have been to be a dancer for the Paris Opera House. It was every ballerina's dream.

The vast theater was peacefully quiet. Sounds from the reception hall drifted in. I simply stood, absorbing everything. I imagined what it might be like to perform there. I pictured the seats full. I allowed seeds of envy to take hold within my heart.

Goodness, I was so stubborn. I could have taken my shoes off and danced whatever I wanted. I still had it in me, to some degree. I could have performed some of the same solos I'd just seen hours before. There was no one to stop me. There was no one at all. Just me. Instead, I simply stood there feeling sorry for myself.

After I left, I immediately regretted not dancing. I reminded myself that although ballet wasn't a part of my life anymore, it would always remain a piece of my past. I would never again let an opportunity like dancing at the Paris Opera House pass me by.

After nearly a month and a half dancing at Fluxx, when the battle between Cece and Ginger reached its height, and I came to believe Ginger might stay for good, Cece resurfaced. By this time, I'd explored the manor in its entirety, or so I thought. I was wrong; there was one last room.

In the entryway of the manor stood a set of double doors opposite the front door. They sat directly under the grand staircase, whose ornate stairs crept up both sides of the room and met in the middle. The double doors were always locked. As such, I developed a fascination with them, always imagining what I might find inside. A closet? Another dining room? A living area?

Every so often when walking by, I would try them, mostly out of boredom. They never opened, and I knew they wouldn't. Checking them became a habit.

One night, I was striding through the entryway after dinner. The double doors taunted me the way Caius might. I decided to try them once more. Hesitantly, I placed my hand upon a knob and turned. It clicked open. A thrill shot through me. I quickly looked over my shoulder and found myself alone, so I slipped inside.

I know it's silly, but I shut my eyes. I waited so long for this, I wanted the moment to be perfect. The door quietly closed behind me.

I stood for several moments taking deep breaths. The air was cool. Everything was silent. The lights were on because I could see bright illumination through my closed eyelids. A strange feeling came over me, similar to what I felt standing alone on the stage in Paris. It seemed so long ago. Slowly, I counted to three and opened my eyes.

The moment I saw, I gasped. My imagination had not prepared me. First, what I saw didn't make sense, because the world around me was slightly out of place. And second, its splendor was enough to take anyone's breath away, especially mine.

I walked forward until I stood in the middle of what was clearly the most extravagant ballroom I had ever seen. It was out of place because its creator designed it with the Paris Opera House in mind. The Paris Opera House was built in the nineteenth century, and didn't coincide with the circa fifteenth century manor.

The room was rounded on one side, with a painted ceiling nearly identical to the one inside the opera house. Landscapes and figures were depicted in vibrant colors representing the luminaries of opera and ballet across the ages. I gazed up at it in awe, picking out scenes from my favorite pieces.

The rest of the room was done almost identical to the giant entry hall at the forefront of the opera house. Multi-tier chandeliers hung above me. Gold pillars spanned the walls with decadent vines and leaves. The floor was glossed white marble. Looking down at it, I noticed how it reflected the world above me, twinkling from each of the hundreds of glittering lights.

The far wall was covered with vast, multi-paned windows. These were also separated by pillars. The drapes were pulled back, and since it was dark out, I only saw the reflection of the room with myself standing in the middle.

I should have found it odd that the lights were on and door unlocked, but I could hardly breathe, let alone think. I wasn't simply stunned by its beauty, I was stunned by how it made me feel. It made me want to dance—truly dance. Cece began clawing her way from the depths of my soul.

Perhaps this was a chance to fix the mistake I made in Paris. How ironic that such a room looked so similar to that masterpiece. Caius's words came back to me. He'd seen my great grandmother dancing there. He'd spent time there. Could this be his doing? Perhaps he designed it when he returned from Paris. Did that famous architectural wonder hold a secret fascination for him too?

I closed my eyes for a minute, letting my world fall away. Tchaikovsky's *Swan Lake* began playing in my mind. I still remembered every note of the second act. I once danced the Odette solo for *Swan Lake* during one of my first performances as a principle soloist. The music in my head washed over me. I was Cece once more, but, I was Cece as Odette.

I moved to the corner of the marble floor—the corner of my new stage—and set up in Odette's starting pose. The music for Act Two, *Odette's Dance*, began playing inside of me. I lifted my arms gracefully, letting them rise and fall as I tiptoed across the room to its middle. I conducted myself the way a swan-turned-human might.

This was the part of the ballet where the swan queen goes to the prince in the form of Odette, a human girl, to tell him of the curse put upon her by the evil magician, Von Rothbart. The solo has extensive fancy footwork. In the first part, it is only Odette and the prince, until the evil magician makes his appearance.

I took myself through each motion, letting my arms rise and fall, moving onto one foot and then the other. There were a number of *arabesques* to complete before the rest of the swans would emerge. Some of these *arabesques* I performed with my leg extended and slightly curved upward, and others with it straight. I arched my back to meet one of these, surprised by the flexibility I still possessed. Then I went into a final bow, low to the ground, to bid the prince farewell.

As the solo ended, I pictured the rest of the cast moving in around me—my swans. I blended in with them as I went through each of the *corps de ballet* movements. I jumped up on one foot, performed an *arabesque*, then a jump, then bounced up onto the other. Taking a moment to pause, I gazed out upon my audience before turning. Sweeping my arms up and around, I paused again. On and on I danced.

I wasn't on pointe, but that didn't change much. My feet still pitter-pattered just as quickly—*tap, tap, tap*—in my thin little house slippers.

I was pleased to discover that I had lost none of my gracefulness. I moved myself around the large floor taking up the entire stage. In fact, I was stunned by how strong I felt. All the pain from my bad leg was gone. It was as if I'd never been injured.

A profound feeling came over me. Was it wonder? Awe? I couldn't quite place it. I continued my movements, letting my swan have her moments.

Never had I danced in a place so eternally beautiful. I missed the adoring crowd, but it was almost better this way. The dark windows were like mirrors, reflecting my movements. I looked at my body in between each turn, checking to make sure that my posture was correct. Having danced *Swan Lake* an immense number of times, every motion was etched into my soul.

Unexpectedly and quite out of character, I turned and nearly slipped. A reflection flashed past me in the window—a reflection of Caius. I attempted to catch myself to avoid falling. When I looked up again, his face was gone. I turned, but no one was there. Had I imagined it? Was I so affected by him that I was seeing his face everywhere?

No, I was sure he'd been there. My heart was pounding. I calmed my nerves and extended my senses outward to feel him. He wasn't nearby, but I couldn't be certain he hadn't been. I was so wrapped up in Odette, that I never paid attention to his coming. How utterly careless!

A sinking feeling formed in the pit of my stomach. I quickly stumbled out of the room, giving it a regretful backward glance before quietly shutting the door and returning to my bedroom. Had I made a mistake? Did Caius now know the one secret I hoped to keep locked away? If he did, would he use it against me?

In case you are wondering how the story of *Swan Lake* ends, Odette and the prince vanquish the dark Von Rothbart, but only because of their undying love for each other, effectively breaking the spell on all the other swans. Yet, they still die in each other's arms as a result of the prince's refusal to marry the dark magician's daughter. The entire story is quite sad.

I couldn't help but wonder, was Caius the prince, or the dark magician? Ginger insisted that he was the prince—devilishly handsome and powerful—ready to sweep me off my feet. Cece saw him as the dark magician Von Rothbart, intent on cursing me for all eternity.

Back in my bedroom, a familiar glass of wine sat on my bedside table. I looked at it angrily. Within me, Cece was at the height of her power. I was back to my old self, fighting for freedom. I didn't yearn to drink a concoction that connected me to a man I was so intent on hating. But if I didn't drink, I would either have to give up dancing, or the training room.

My time in the training room that morning was pretty brutal. Titus never did anything too intense, but I still came away with plenty of bruises. I needed Caius's blood to heal my ailments.

Finally sighing, I picked up the glass and went to the mirror, studying my bruised shoulder and cheek bone. It was only temporary after all; it would be gone within minutes.

Without further ado, I drank the entire glass in several large gulps. As I waited, I watched my reflection with a kind of sick fascination. The developing darkness from each of the bruises receded. They turned to yellow, and then faded completely.

With Caius's blood continuously replenishing my body, I was the healthiest I'd ever been. I was whole. In that moment, I realized something astounding. Caius's blood allowed me to dance Odette better than ever before. It was his blood I needed to break the powerful spell that could free me from my curse. The only question was, with the curse removed, would I die in the prince's arms the way Odette had? There was only one way to find out.

CHAPTER 11

There's an obscure ballet named *The Red Shoes*. I danced it once when I was a soloist. Acting as understudy for that solo landed me my position in the company as a principle dancer. The ballet is based on a movie about a woman, Vikki, who gets hired to dance in a ballet based on Hans Christian Anderson's fairytale of the same name.

The gist of *The Red Shoes* is this: A woman stumbles across a pair of red shoes in a shop window bewitched by a demonic shoemaker. He entices her into taking them, showing her all the things she could be, and the lovely way she might dance in them. Convinced, for she dearly loves to dance, she puts them on and goes to the carnival. That's when strange things begin to happen. She loses complete control of her choices and can't stop dancing. Once she discovers the deceit of the shoes, she tries to free herself from them. The only problem is, she can't. The shoes are controlled by the shoemaker.

On and on she dances uncontrollably, all the way into the netherworld. Eventually she dances herself to exhaustion and near death. In the last moments of her life, she stumbles upon a church, where a priest removes the shoes. Finally at peace, she dies within his arms. The ballet ends with the demonic shoemaker who returns for his shoes, to be used by his next victim.

Pointe shoes are nearly always a light pink color. Occasionally they are black or white. There is only one instance when they are red, for *The Red Shoes*. I loved my ruby red pointe shoes. They were destroyed after a single night of rigorous performing. Still, I saved them, wrapped in tissue paper in a little box under my bed at home.

After my questionable run-in with Caius in the ballroom, questionable because I still wasn't convinced that he'd actually been there, I couldn't stop dreaming about Odette. Every night it was the same. I found myself in the ballroom. This time, instead of being me, I was a beautiful white swan, and the marble floor beneath me was liquid. Frantically I searched for the prince, desperately needing his love to remove my curse. The world around me would then grow dark, and the magician would constantly toy with me. "I am the prince," he would say. "It is me you should love." I always woke up the moment he began laughing his laugh of doom.

Because of these bad dreams, I couldn't get the ballroom out of my head. Every day thereafter I found it unlocked, but I could never bring myself to go back in. What was I so afraid of?

Day by day, Cece began to slink back into the shadows. One night nearly a week later, everything changed. I'd just finished dinner and returned to my room, when I found a small box on my bed. It wasn't wrapped, but it was a familiar shape. I stood for several minutes eyeing it from afar.

After a time, I approached it apprehensively. It wasn't a bomb, but I acted like it might be. Somehow, I knew exactly what I would find. There was a note on top, a small slip of paper with a single line of calligraphic text. *Cygnus inter anates*, is all it said. I gazed at it fruitlessly before dismissing it. I later discovered it meant, *swan among ducks*. Caius always did have an unparalleled sense of humor.

After puzzling over the note, my curiosity got the better of me. I pulled the lid away and removed the tissue paper. Nestled inside was a beautiful pair of red satin ballet pointes. *The Red Shoes!* I hadn't expected this. Pink? Yes, but not red.

How could Caius possibly know what *The Red Shoes* meant to me? They were from Caius, of that I was sure. At last I had my answer to a week's worth of wondering. He saw Odette petitioning the prince. He knew of the curse put upon the swan queen by the evil magician. He knew Odette needed to fall in love before it was too late. The prince was the only one who could save her.

There was no more hiding my secret. Ballet was supposed to be mine, a part of me that only I controlled. I felt cheated, as if Caius had stolen from me.

I gazed into the depths of the box, studying the shoes. They silently enticed me, and suddenly, I didn't feel quite so angry. Had they been pink, my feelings would have been different. See, that's what *The Red Shoes* are all about. Their color is meant to ensnare their victim's mind, bewitching the wearer into putting them on, bewitching the wearer into *dancing*.

I knew now what Caius was attempting to convey. Once the dancer puts the shoes on, she must dance until she dies. I couldn't help but see the similarity between the choice I'd been given to become a vampire, and the shoes. His gesture hit me hard in the chest.

I knew then, if I decided to become a vampire, if I took up *The Red Shoes*, I could dance for all of eternity. If I didn't—if I put them away—that part of my life, Cece, would fade away forever. Ginger would win.

I didn't *hate* Ginger. Actually, I liked her quite a bit. But I didn't want to be Ginger, nor did I want to be Cece. I wanted the two of them to be at peace with each other. Only, I had to find a way to join them in harmony. I had to create a new life for myself. It was the only way.

I sat on my bed holding the shoes, looking at them as I caressed the soft red satin. I longed to wear them, but feared the consequences. Putting them on, trying them out, it didn't mean I was agreeing to anything. Surely this was meant to be a kind gesture from Caius—surely it was a coincidence that he chose red.

I turned them over in my hands. Red—oh so red. I wanted them. I *needed* them. Making up my mind, I rushed to Adel's room.

"Cece!" She greeted me as she opened her door.

"Do you have a sewing kit?" I held out my shoes.

Her eyes widened. "Wow! Ballet shoes?"

I nodded. She let me in to her room and rummaged around, locating her sewing things. The red ribbons weren't attached yet; ballet ribbons never come attached to the shoes. The elastic needed fitting as well. Once Adel found me the proper tools, I got started. First I sewed everything into place before beating, bending, and stomping on the points of the shoes to soften them up.

"Cece, no!" Adel gasped when she saw my strange behavior. "You ruin them!" Most people are utterly shocked when seeing what it takes to prepare a set of ballet pointes. Adel was no exception.

"I must do it like this, Adel. I need to make them soft and flexible." I had none of the usual padding that I generally wore. Light as such padding is, I wasn't going to need it. I knew this because something was happening in my body as a result of Caius's blood. I was stronger, and I had a feeling that I would be able to do things other ballerinas couldn't.

The final touch, something I did with all my point shoes (every ballerina has her own ritual), was use scissors to make gashes and slices in the fabric on the pointe of the shoe. I didn't want to slip on the marble floor; this would create my much needed friction.

Adel gasped when she saw me do it, her eyes wide as I destroyed this small section of fabric. The look of disbelief she wore was absolute. "It's okay, Adel. They will work exactly as I need them to." Suddenly, I had an idea. "Do you want to come watch?"

The cat was out of the bag, so to speak. Everyone in the house would learn my secret in a matter of days. I owed it to Adel to believe she was the first to know. She was my best friend.

She nodded vigorously. "You true ballerina, Cece?" She sighed with wonder when I told her that I was. "I always knew you good dancer."

"You're good too, Adel," I assured her.

It's different for every ballerina, but the average time for me to sew and prepare a pair of pointe shoes is an hour. When I was dancing as a prima, I generally went through a pair for every performance. If I was *lucky*, I could stretch a practice pair to three, maybe four days. It all depended on how rigorous the work was. I got used to sewing them in front of the television.

As soon as my red pointes were finished, Adel followed me back to my room where I changed from my jeans into a pretty white summer dress. Now I was just like Vicky from the netherworld scene. The light dress would allow me to move freely. Plus, it looked lovely with my new shoes. Ready to go, Adel and I tiptoed through the house giggling.

I tried not to think about Caius. I was confused. He read me so well. He knew giving me a pair of pointe shoes would bring Cece back, and with very little effort, too. Would he show himself tonight? Was this his way of tempting me back into the ballroom? Was my life still a game to him, and *The Red Shoes* simply a move on the never-ending chess board? I pushed the thoughts from my mind.

"Crap!" I stopped abruptly.

"What is matter, Cece?" Adel stopped beside me.

"Do you have an iPod or something? I don't have any music." I didn't need music, but I wanted it.

Adel's eyes lit up, happy to contribute. "I do! And speakers." I knew she would, because sometimes I walked in on the girls practicing dance moves in their rooms together. "I be back." She rushed off while I waited for her outside the ballroom.

I began going over the solo in my mind. My fingers gripped the pointes tightly, unconsciously bending and flexing them back and forth while I concentrated. When Adel returned, I led her into the ballroom. Her reaction was much the same as mine. She explored the architecture while I got ready, stretching, moving my arches and toes around, and doing warm-ups that would prepare me for going on pointe. As I did this, I shuffled through her music for a song to use. There was mostly techno, but she did have some classical music.

"Here, you be my DJ. But *only* classical." I handed her the iPod.

"Of course," she breathed, happy to have a job.

I got into my pointes, wrapping the red ribbons around my ankles and tying them in little knots. Then I moved my feet in circles to make sure the elastic bands were tight enough. They were perfect.

"Beautiful, Cece!" Adel cried. "So beautiful."

I smiled in response, giving her one last look before assuming my starting pose. On cue, the music began to play and I began to dance. The moment I lifted my body onto pointe, it felt as if I'd never quit dancing. The red shoes bewitched me as they were supposed to, and I found myself dancing a lovely rendition of *The Red Shoes* solo. The violin instruments echoed about the ballroom with ethereal beauty. I melded myself to the melody as I too flowed across the floor.

As I completed a set of *fouetté* turns, Adel's gasp sounded behind me. I didn't look back at her, but instead, focused entirely on my movements. I lost myself.

At first I tested my boundaries, careful not to over-extend. As the song progressed, I discovered there was nothing stopping me. The solo began to take on a life of its own. With liberal creativity, I began free-forming the movements, telling the story *not* of *The Red Shoes*, but of my own struggle.

I poured everything into my rendition, all the time I had lost, all the suffering I experienced when my dreams were ripped from me. I took the last two years of my existence, and emptied it all into this *one* piece.

The song was much longer than the three minute solo I was used to, so I continued on, blending with the music. My confidence soared. I attempted jumps I hadn't done since my prima days, stunts no one should attempt without proper training. Caius's blood proved true.

My dancing was invincible. The moment I realized this, an extreme joy took me. I felt it burst from my very being, as if I was becoming the swan queen herself, taking flight and escaping the confines of land. Dancing like this—the true happiness I derived from it—made me feel as though nothing else in the world would *ever* matter. And in that instant, I understood that there wasn't anything I wouldn't sacrifice for it. I wanted it to last forever.

The curse of *The Red Shoes* had finally taken hold of me.

Twirling around the room, my white dress fluttering around me, I felt more beautiful than ever. I was so absorbed, so lost in the music, that I was back in my old life. I was happy once more. I had a purpose. I had goals and dreams. I was Cece as she was meant to be.

And then, slowly, the music came to a close. I too followed its melody, decreasing the speed of my dancing, until I came to a halt with the silence. I held my pose for several moments, breathing hard, but not as hard as is normal.

Adel's enthusiastic clapping rang out into the room. I dropped my arms and smiled. Her praise was immediately followed by a very slow, powerful clap. "Bravo!" I heard

Caius's rich voice behind me. "Bravo, Cece. Truly *magnificent*."

I turned. Standing beside Adel was Caius.

A million emotions came crashing down on me at once: confusion, jubilation, frustration, helplessness, accomplishment. It was the most unlikely mixture conceivable, and it surrounded me the way the music had, forcing me to confront my inner demons.

I never cried when ballet was stolen from me. People believed I was emotionally bereft because I never cried when I injured myself. I never wept when I decided to give up my dreams. I tucked the pain away, turning it into years of anger. For the first time in a long time, for the first time that I could remember, I burst into tears.

Utterly embarrassed, I cowered away from my audience, covering my face in my hands and turning my back to them as giant sobs wracked my body. I wanted to crumble to the floor.

"Some privacy, Adel," I heard Caius say.

I was horrified with myself for losing it in front of him. Of all people—*him*! Before I had a moment to regain my composure, before I had a moment to do anything at all, he was beside me. He gently pulled me against him, cradling my head to his chest. It was the most surprising, most unexpected gesture he could have offered me.

"It's okay to cry, Cece." Those few words made me weep harder. Someone was finally giving me permission to do what I had refused to do, even when I realized I would never dance again.

Most ballerinas have small bodies. Mine was no exception. I

came to the middle of his chest. He wrapped himself around me, warming me like a blanket and a cup of hot tea, making me feel safe and comforted.

I stopped thinking about how much I disliked him. I let Ginger come out; she was the one who wanted this. I tried to force Cece to be at peace with her. To my utter disbelief, while I felt most broken, Cece complied.

"It was all taken from me, Caius! It was supposed to be *me*," I said through my sobs. "My whole life…just ripped from me… my dreams…" I could hardly breathe as I tried to explain my frantic breakdown.

"I don't know if I can ever be *her* again. I want to be." I hiccuped. Caius continued to hold me. "But everything"— hiccup—"is *different* now."

"Celine, you can be anyone you want." His voice was a dark purr in my ear. "You have a choice. If you want to dance, if you want to be a ballerina, then that dream belongs to you. No one can take it from you."

"My injury…I'm not sure I can—"

"You have my blood. You are strong and whole, and you will stay that way, so long as you drink. If dancing will make you happy, I will gladly give myself."

I pulled my head from his chest in disbelief, and looked up at him, astounded by what he offered—not simply his blood, but the chance to reclaim a career that had slipped away from me. He gazed down at me, but for the life of me, I could not read him.

"You said I had to become a vampire."

He sighed. "My rules are my rules. If you do not wish to be a vampire, I cannot force you. But if you love ballet, then why not dance for eternity? Why not become a vampire? Not now, necessarily, but perhaps someday?" He looked down at my red shoes, then back at me.

"Is that why you picked these?"

The side of his mouth curved upwards. "I thought it apt."

"And if I don't want to become a vampire?" I arched away from him to get a better view of his face.

"Then you may remain a human, become a human ballerina, dance with the Royal Vienna Ballet, and live here. You'll probably need to audition, and you'll need bodyguards to escort you whenever you go into the city, but we can make it happen, if that is what you want."

"But, I can't go home?"

"I am afraid the answer is *still* no, Cece."

I saw something in his eyes—sadness. Then it hit me, it *finally* hit me. He didn't like locking me up, he didn't like locking any of us up, but these were his rules. He was simply following a code that he believed in—a code that protected the survival of his kind. It didn't make him a monster. If anything, it made him a creature of value, someone who remained true to his word no matter the torment it caused.

"Cece, in spite of all that has happened over the last few months, is leaving still what you most want?" His voice echoed defeat.

I thought about his question, taking careful consideration of my heart. He was offering me a chance to recapture the dreams I'd lost. With his blood, even if I didn't become a vampire, I would never get sick, I wouldn't succumb to injury, and I would dance better than ever before. *The Red Shoes* proved what they were meant to prove. They also illustrated that I would do anything to dance again, anything for ballet. My decision was made.

"Well?" Caius's eyes probed mine. "Do you really hate it here so much that you wish to abandon your dreams?"

"No, Caius," I whispered up at him. Suddenly Ginger and Cece were shaking hands inside my mind. "No, I don't think…" I shook my head. "I don't think I want to leave anymore."

And there looking down at me, Caius smiled the first genuine smile I had seen.

# CHAPTER 12

*O*h, how arduous decision-making can be! We make
countless choices every day without realizing it:
what to wear, what to eat, what to do with our time. Some
choices are far more tiresome than others. These can take the
longest. There is always that subtle fear you might choose
poorly, like when I was uncertain about quitting ballet.

Yet, have you ever noticed what it feels like once you've
settled on your answer? The moment you make up your
mind, a weight is lifted from your heart. You feel lighter,
peaceful. That's how I felt after I decided to remain at
Anghor Manor. As soon as I acknowledged this, I was
happier. However, there was still one thing weighing heavily
on my heart, and I wasn't sure how to fix that.

I was certain my family was sick with worry. They'd not
heard from me in months, and had likely started a manhunt
for my dead body. I couldn't bear the thought of them
believing me dead. It was eating me up inside. In order to
finally accept my new life, I needed to tie up my old one. I

needed to come up with a way to approach Caius on this matter.

Aside from this little hiccup, life in Anghor Manor vastly improved. Caius and I experienced a breakthrough in the ballroom after *The Red Shoes* incident. It was a personal transformation, but we went through it together. That completely changed the dynamic of our relationship.

Sure, he teased me more than ever, but now it didn't seem mean or underhanded. He wasn't trying to maliciously *hurt* me. He just wanted to have fun. I suppose old vampires get bored. As soon as I gave in, once I stopped fighting him, I had fun too. Moreover, I was flattered by the attention.

Sometimes, if I found myself walking alone through the hallways of Anghor Manor, I might suddenly hear my name off in the distance. "Cece…" If I turned in search of the source, naturally I would see a dimly lit corridor. But I would always hear my name whispered again. "Cece…" Still, there wouldn't be anyone. This often carried on until the scene around me became something like a haunted mansion. My name would echo from all directions, "Cece! Ceeeeeceeeee…" The calling voice loved to taunt me.

When I ignored it, it never stopped. So I always forced myself take a deep breath before demanding, "What, Caius?!"

"Want to play a round of darts with me in the billiards room?" he might say. And there he would be, standing in front of me holding a set of darts, grinning like a little boy, pleased with himself.

Occasionally at dinner, if I was ever too intent on a conversation, I might hear, "Oh my God, Cece, what's wrong with your hair?" I would immediately begin patting my head, thinking something happened.

"Nothing wrong with your hair, Cece," Adel might whisper, and I would look up to see Caius grinning at me, eyes glittering with mischief.

It never seemed to stop. The longer it continued, the more I enjoyed it. His mischievousness was a part of his personality. My being in the manor brought out a different side of him. In time, I was okay with that.

The Thursday night after *The Red Shoes* incident, I found Caius in my room before I was set to leave for Fluxx. I'd come back for my makeup bag to find him sitting in one of my arm chairs, looking amused and relaxed, as if he was in the middle of a private joke. I stood gawking at him because I'd never seen him perched comfortably in my bedroom before.

His eyes looked me up and down, appraising me. "I'm going to escort you to Fluxx tonight."

I arched an eyebrow at him. Felix usually escorted me. "Making demands are we?" My words set the side of his mouth twitching. "Since we are on the subject, Caius, I have a demand of my own."

"Oh?"

"I want to call my family. I want to tell them I'm okay."

His demeanor completely changed. Instead of smirks and glittering eyes, his face grew impassive. "I can't let you do that, Cece."

"I think you ought to. I want to accept my life here in Anghor Manor, but the thought of my family nervously worrying over me is tearing me apart. I'm losing sleep over it."

He was silent for several moments that seemed like a lifetime. "So you want to call them and tell them you've been kidnapped? That sounds like a great idea."

I shook my head. "No. It's nothing like that. They just need to hear my voice. I promise I won't reveal anything."

He sighed. I could tell he was thinking it over. His consideration meant a lot to me. I knew the girls were never given the opportunity. Maybe they'd never asked. I had no problem asking, because I needed this. "You want to escort me to Fluxx, don't you? So let me call my parents."

"Oh, I think it's going to take a lot more than that."

"Then what?" By now, I was familiar with his nature. He was going to bargain and earn something sweet out of the deal.

He was quiet for far too long. I began adjusting my silk minidress out of nervousness, while I watched his impassive face. At last he spoke, "All right, Cece. I will let you call your parents because I don't want you to fret. But in exchange, you will owe me something in return."

I waited in suspense. I didn't like the idea of owing him anything. Owing a vampire seemed ominous. When it became clear he wasn't going to tell me, I was forced to ask, "What do you want in return?"

"A dance, and afterward, I want to ask you something."

My brow furrowed. A dance? A question? My immediate thoughts were a bit raunchy. I pictured myself with him in a dark room offering him a lap dance. My cheeks immediately burned.

He must have sensed my discomfort. "Get your head out of the gutter, Cece. Tonight after Fluxx, you and I will go into the ballroom and you will give me one dance of my choosing."

I breathed a sigh of relief. He wanted me to dance for him. He loved ballet, so it made sense. "Okay, deal."

He got up from the couch and handed me his phone. "You've got thirty seconds. I don't want the call traced."

My fingers were trembling as I punched my mom's cell number in. The phone rang and I waited anxiously. "Hello?" The moment I heard her familiar voice, my chest tightened.

"Mom?" My voice wavered.

"Cece? Is that you?" There was a pause. I heard whispering in the background.

"It's me."

"Baby, what's going on?" She was panicked. "What's happening?"

"Everything's fine, Mom. Don't—don't worry."

"Honey, we've been worried sick. We thought you were..." Her worry twisted my stomach. "The Vienna police department has been searching for your body. Your father's there in Vienna working with them. You've been missing. What's..." It was exactly what I expected to hear.

"Mom, I'm fine. I promise."

"Explain yourself, Cece." Her voice changed. She wasn't angry, but she was deeply upset.

"I can't Mom. I can't tell you what's going on. I just—" I glanced up at Caius. His eyes were narrowed suspiciously. "It's going to be a while before you hear from me again. But I'm okay, I promise."

"Please, baby, just tell me where you are. I'll speak to your father. He'll get the police there to rescue you."

"I don't want to be rescued, Mom."

She was quiet for a moment. I watched Caius as he crossed his arms. He probably didn't trust me. Truthfully, I didn't trust myself. I wanted so badly to tell my mom what had happened.

"Mom, I need you to know I'm okay. Tell Dad to stop looking for me." She didn't respond. "I love you Mom, okay? I love you. Tell Dad and Austin I love them too. I promise I'll call when I can."

"Don't do this, Cece. Don't hang up."

"Goodbye, Mom." I hung up. I couldn't look at Caius after that. I returned his phone and went to collect my things. I was glad he didn't say anything. I wasn't in the mood for conversation.

I was quiet for most of the drive to Fluxx, deep in thought. I caught Caius glancing at me often. "What are you thinking about?" he dared to ask. I shrugged my shoulders. I didn't want to tell him that I was worried about my parents or obsessing over the dance I'd promised him.

Instead, I changed the subject before he pressed me further. "What did you want to ask me later?"

He kept his eyes on the road and remained silent. If he didn't want to answer my question, then I wasn't about to answer his.

The manor was nearly an hour outside of Vienna, but the time in the car passed quickly. We emerged from our respective cars in the usual fashion. Caius's Bentley Continental

GT was first in line, so I was out before the rest of the girls. The entourage always went into the club as a procession. And of course, there was the usual patron line halfway down the block. The usual cheers of excitement followed our arrival.

I plastered a fake smile onto my face and waved at everyone. Some of them called my name, snapping photos. I was good at acting.

Caius took my hand the way Felix did. Instead of holding it normally as I expected, he laced his fingers sensually through mine, caressing the back of my palm with his thumb. He continued to glance at me apprehensively. Maybe he worried about my phone call. Maybe he perceived my grief.

I didn't want to think about any of it as I danced that night. For the first time, I boldly allowed both Ginger and Cece out to play. I found sexy ways to incorporate ballet movements into my dancing. The crowed noticed and shouted gleefully each time I threw something fancy in—an *arabesque* here, a spin there.

There was an instant when I stood on one leg and pulled my other up behind me into the splits, sweeping my body towards the ground just as I noticed Caius. Our eyes met and my heart jumped. I had to look away.

At last when the night ended, Caius drove me back to the manor. My racing pulse pounded in my ears. I was sure he noticed, but he said nothing. Once we arrived, he led me to the ballroom. The other girls said their goodbyes and went off to their rooms. It was nearly three in the morning. We did not follow them. I owed Caius a dance, and it was time to make good on my promise.

# CHAPTER 13

*A pas de deux*, which is French for a dance of two people, is a type of ballet usually done between a man and a woman. *Pas de deux* dances require a lot of trust between partners, because they involve significant lifting, and a ballerina can get severely hurt if her partner doesn't know what he is doing. And then there's all the touching. Many famous *pas de deux* dances are meant to be intimate, with lots of stolen glances, swooning, and batting of eyelashes.

The only boyfriend I ever had was when I was sixteen. He was the *pas de deux* partner assigned to me when I first danced with the National Ballet. His name was Simon, and he was a bit goofy in a nerdy way, but I really liked him. I am certain that our dancing together had everything to do with our romance. We weren't like normal couples: we never went on dates because we were already together most of the day training. But we *did* kiss. I always liked kissing him.

Things didn't end very well between us. When we broke up, it created so much tension in our dancing that we were separated, and I was given a new partner. I learned early on that getting involved with a *pas de deux* partner was a bad idea. But I'm sure you can see why it happens. The intimacy that takes place when dancing *pas de deux* is stirring.

So where were we? Ah yes, the night I owed Caius a dance. At the end of the night, we stood together in the middle of the ballroom, Caius wearing his familiar smirk, and me, eager to know why. He'd been holding my hand, fingers laced through mine, just like they were at the beginning of the night. I dropped his hand, becoming suddenly self-conscience, and turned to him. "Well, *sir*," I said, smiling sweetly as I faced him. "I believe I owe you a dance."

His grin widened and his eyes brightened. "Yes, *my lady*. Indeed, you do."

"What shall I perform tonight?"

"Are you familiar with Manon?"

"Um." My brain skidded to a halt. I was confused. "Manon like the ballet *Manon*?"

"Yes, *Cece*. Exactly like the ballet."

"I do know it." I knew it well.

"Have you ever danced it?"

"Yes and no. I've performed *parts* of it." I'd performed the obscure parts just for practice during class. I kept quiet, feeling inclined to look smarter in front of him.

"Good. I wish to dance the bedroom scene with you."

My jaw dropped. I had to collect myself. "The—the bedroom scene?" I squeaked, growing entirely nervous. My eyes darted to the door. Maybe I could simply make a run for it.

"Yes, the bedroom scene."

"But, that scene is a *pas de deux*!"

"Good observation, Cece. I'm glad you know your ballet terms."

"You want to dance a *pas de deux* with me?" I was a bit stunned. Surely he was joking. Especially because *this* step of two was the most sensual I'd ever seen. He could have requested any of them, but he'd chosen *Manon*.

"Don't you trust me?"

I squared my shoulders. "I trust you. I—I'm just surprised, that's all."

"Excellent. I love when I can surprise you."

"I know you do." I moved over to the side of the vast room to dispose of my purse. Then I returned to him. "I don't have my pointe shoes."

"Neither do I," he joked, without looking up at me. He was on his iPhone scrolling through music. "I'm sure we will manage without them." When he was done, he looked at me. "I believe you start over there."

"So bossy!" I rolled my eyes and moved to the side of the room, where I took a good long look at what he was wearing. He had on dark denim jeans and a steel-gray, long sleeved button down. His attire was sexy as hell, especially against his olive skin, but definitely not dance material. My eyes lingered on him for a moment longer than they should have. "You realize you're in jeans, right?" I called from across the room.

"Am I?" He looked down at himself with feigned surprise.

Hands on my hips, I blew the bangs out of my face. How the heck did he think he could dance ballet in what he was wearing? Matter of fact, how the heck did he think he could dance ballet at all? But whatever, if he wanted to make a fool of himself, that was his problem. I'd agreed, after all, so I would do my part.

He cranked up the volume on his iPhone, and the music began a moment later. He then set it at the side of the room and moved back to the center, waiting for my start.

I knew exactly how this dance was supposed to go, and my heart was already racing nervously for what was to come. I didn't know *every* movement, but the important ones, yes. I could easily improvise the rest.

Ever so gracefully, I lifted my arms in a sleepy stretch, as if just waking up from a nap. I even gave a feigned yawn. Caius's eyes followed me the way a wolf watches its prey.

*This* scene is the part of the ballet where Manon and her new lover Des Grieux are lodging together in Paris. At the beginning of the *pas de deux*, Manon rises from her bed to go to Des, who is writing a letter at his desk. To dance this, I had to become Manon, and Caius had to become Des.

I sauntered playfully over to my Des, gracefully placing my feet along the floor, then leaned in close to get his attention. This act from me was the cue, it marked the beginning of the *pas de deux*.

Caius immediately and obnoxiously interrupted me, clicking his tongue. "Now, now, Cece. If I remember correctly, you are *supposed* to caress my cheek before doing that." Was he serious? I was hoping he'd miss my avoidance.

"Again." His eyes narrowed in warning. "This time the *correct*

way." He was right. There was no way I was going to successfully perform this piece without *touching* him. The entire act
was about touching, caressing, hugging, kissing. It was
unavoidable.

I dropped my arms where they were held frozen in place,
sighing dramatically. Then I returned to my previous
position.

He restarted the music and I began again. This time when I
reached him, I forced myself to remember that this was
simply a ballet, nothing more. I sensually caressed his cheek,
teasing him with my fingers.

Our *pas de deux* began. I tiptoed back to the middle of the
floor, where he rushed after me with a degree of grace I had
not anticipated. Taking my hand, he lifted his back leg into
an *arabesque* as he turned me on my tiptoes.

He moved with trained perfection whilst exuding masculin-
ity. The blue jeans did limit his flexibility, but I was never
turned on by the overly flexible male dancers anyway. For a
moment, I was stunned. I stopped and said, "You know
ballet?"

"I have lived a long time, Cece. I know a great many things..."

I gazed at him with a newfound respect. All this time I
thought he was simply pulling my leg—trying to play some
big joke on me. But, he was really going to dance the
bedroom scene with me the way it was meant to be danced.

"Shall we begin *one* more time? This time, no interruptions?"

I moved back to my starting position for the third time. I was
beginning to wonder if we would ever get through the dance.
Despite the late hour, I was no longer tired.

The music started again, and this time we ran through the movements perfectly. I went to him, caressing his cheek, gazing into his eyes with increased wonder, then moved back to the middle of the floor. He followed after me, pulling me in towards him as he held his *arabesque*. That was all it took for me to lose myself in the dance—in him. He wasn't perfect, I didn't expect him to be, but he knew all the right places to lift me, twirl me, hold me, touch me…

His eyes never left mine.

If you are unfamiliar with this particular piece, there are *many* intimate moments. They begin subtly, a slight caress here, a heartfelt hug there, and then the intensity heightens. There are a few times where Des tries to kiss Manon but she demurely turns away, hugging herself to him instead.

Every instance when he pushed his fingers seductively into my hair, or smiled down at me, my breathing hitched and my heart constricted with nervous excitement. I was supposed to be Manon and he Des, but Cece and Caius hadn't entirely departed. They could be seen it in the way his eyes sparked at me, or the way I couldn't abandon my racing mind.

All the while my anticipation grew. I knew what was to come. In the middle of the dance, there is a part where Manon and Des do finally kiss. It's not the typical kiss that takes place in most *pas de deux* routines, where two lovers engage in a subtle peck, which is often feigned. No, when Manon and Des kiss, they stare deeply into each other's eyes for at least ten seconds before kissing, and it's *not* a peck, but a full-on kiss, tongue and all.

Suddenly we were at that moment! Caius had one arm tightly around my waist while I balanced on his knee in a graceful pose. There he gazed into my eyes so closely, so intimately, that our noses touched and I felt an electric tingle. Then, ever so slowly, he brought his hand down to caress my back, trailing his fingertips along my skin before standing and setting me on my feet. Pulse racing, I moved my hand to his shoulder leaving it there to rest. My heart wouldn't stop fluttering.

Even on my tiptoes, the top of my head barely reached his chin, and it was tilted back, looking up at him expectantly. Our bodies were touching, mine perfectly curved against his. I did not expect it, but I was becoming aroused, keenly aware of the growing warmth in each of the places that our bodies met.

And then, as if he couldn't wait any longer, he brought his mouth down to mine. On cue, I closed my eyes, letting my other senses take over. His touch was playful at first as his lips touched mine, sucking and tugging, before releasing. My tummy clenched, and I responded without thinking, kissing him back. My arms wrapped around his neck and my fingers crept into his hair.

He took hold of me, standing fully upright, lifting me such that my feet were no longer touching the ground. I felt his tongue as it caressed my teeth, begging entry. So I opened my mouth wider, inviting him to explore. The exotic way his tongue toyed with me, leaving no place in my mouth unin-vestigated, left my muscles quivering.

The music continued, but I think we both forgot that we were supposed to be dancing. We were no longer in control, neither of us.

I'd never been kissed like this. *Never*. Caius kissed so ardently, I couldn't breathe. The intensity increased, until I became utterly lost. If he was bewitching me, I no longer cared.

At last, he set me down and reluctantly pulled away. I was reluctant too; I kept my eyes closed longer than necessary, wishing the moment might last forever. The music had already ended—we'd missed the entire second half of the dance. He realized this and a smile spread slowly across his face. It wasn't the kind I was used to seeing. It was gentle, even a bit shy.

He gave me a single chaste peck on the lips before placing his forehead against mine. He held me there, looking into my eyes. "I haven't felt this way in a long time, *Celine*..."

It took a moment for his words to sink in. He was open about his feelings, something refreshingly unexpected. Why couldn't I be like that? I was too shy. So instead I gazed back at him, saying nothing. I loved the way he said my name, too. It was rare for him to call me anything other than Cece, or *my dear*. When he called me Celine, it sent tingles of pleasure down my spine until they raced around to my abdomen.

"I suppose we should start again?" he said at last. "Since we missed the second half." His eyes danced.

I gazed back at him. "*No*, that was your *one* dance, Caius. You chose to spend half of it kissing."

The side of his mouth curved up into a half smile. "Another kiss then?"

"No," I insisted. "I need to catch my breath." Inside I was screaming *yes*. Yes, please!

He feigned a pout before nuzzling his head into my neck, laying kisses along the underside of my chin and jaw bone. I stifled a giggle. His lips were relentless as they made their way to my ear, where he grabbed my earlobe with his teeth, pulling gently. I almost cried in delight. So did my core, which shuddered.

I allowed my body to fall deeply against his. He pulled back to look at me again. His mischievous grin returned, the one I knew so well. And then before I could push him away, he took advantage of his superhuman speed and pecked my lips, planting another kiss there.

"Sneaky," I scolded. He laughed before nuzzling his nose against the side of my cheek, which he kissed before releasing me from his hold. I staggered backwards a few steps.

I almost wanted to grab his arms and put them back where they'd been. But instead, I stood there watching him with fascination. He was so full of surprises. I never expected him to be interested in me. Goodness, I certainly never expected him to know anything about dancing ballet. He'd planned this entire thing simply to kiss me.

"Why—why did you kiss me?"

His face was illuminated with amusement. "Cece, when a man desires a woman…"

"That's not what I meant!" I moved forward towards him like a moth to light.

He grabbed my wrist, pulling me back to him, wrapping his free arm about me once more. "I kissed you because I *want* you, Cece. I like you because you are fiery and spirited. I like you because you stand up to me, because you're fun, and I enjoy being with you."

"But you could have *anyone*. The women I've seen here, the vampires in your coven, they're stunning."

"You think I care about surface beauty? I've been around that for a long time, Cece. To me, you are the most graceful and beautiful of them all. And when you dance, I am undone."

I wanted to argue with him. I was *not* beautiful. He had it all wrong. Maybe when my face was covered in makeup. Perhaps when I was dancing in a lovely gown. But where looks were concerned, I was always ever plain. I couldn't understand why he didn't see that.

"It's time for you to head off to bed," he added before I could say anything more. "But, one last thing before that."

"You wanted to ask me something—your question."

He smiled. "Yes, I wanted to ask you something. Would you and the other girls be interested in throwing a vampire ball here in the ballroom? It's been so long since I've used it. Seeing your joy dancing—it has reminded me why I built this place. I think it should be used again. Perhaps a Parisian masquerade theme?"

"A ball?" Christmas had come early. I smiled so hard it hurt.

"Yes, a ball, if you will arrange it. My vampires are at your service."

"Can I be Cinderella?" It sounded far stupider than it did in my head. I half expected Caius to laugh hysterically at me. I asked because I had always wanted to dance the *Cinderella* ballet, but I never got the chance.

"Only if I might be your prince."

I swallowed my surprise. "Yes, I would like that."

"Then a ball we shall have!" He tightened his hold on me, and we shared a long goodnight kiss.

# CHAPTER 14

*A*ll ballet dancers live with fear. From the moment we discover our love of ballet, we are all afraid of losing it, of losing our identity. Our fear arises for different reasons and changes from dancer to dancer. We fear our finances may not be enough to pay for the classes needed to reach company level. We fear failure, forgetting our steps while we are on stage, or misinterpreting the choreography. We fear rejection, getting turned away at every audition until no one wants us to dance for them. We fear the unknown, worrying about contract renewals and salary once at the company level. Finally, we fear injury, that one small instant when a mistake is made, everything is taken away. We live with these fears until we become tethered to them.

The most afraid I have ever been was the night I was taken. There are certain things my mind won't block out no matter how hard I try, like the way Thrax looked when my captors stabbed him, the way his body withered into ash. I can't forget the way I froze against the wall as they pulled him off me, nor the way I trembled and fought as they dragged me into a van. And I'll never forget the terror coursing through my veins when a sack was thrown over my head. Little did I know, a few occasions would come close to the fear I felt that night.

In the days following Caius's kiss in the ballroom, our dynamic changed again. He had tricked me into the first kiss under the pretense of a dance, and though I enjoyed it, I needed him to know that I *wasn't* easy. I didn't kiss just anyone, no matter how good it felt. So I held back.

He went from teasing me, to ignoring me. I wasn't the least bit offended, because his behavior was feigned. He wasn't *truly* ignoring me. In fact, he couldn't take his eyes off me, and every time I caught him watching, he would suddenly turn away. I played along. By now, I enjoyed our little games. This one was especially easy. So I ignored him too, waiting for him to come to me.

He did, a mere three days later. I was walking to my room after dinner when I heard my name whispered behind me seductively. "Cece…" I kept walking. "Ceceeee." Again, more whispers sounded in front of me, behind me, to the side of me. Playing along, I continued down the passageway, ignoring them. The cry became more insistent, more alluring. It was always that way when he said my name. My body responded differently than when others said it, especially after our kiss, and he knew it.

"Yes, Caius," I answered, finally giving in. Just to be funny, I gave a graceful ballet curtsy to an empty hallway. I knew he was hiding somewhere. As soon as I stood, he swept up behind me.

His arms wrapped around my waist, pulling me against him.

He buried his face in my hair, inhaling deeply. "I miss you Cece," he said. "Why do you avoid me?"

"You seem busy." I lied because I was wary of my own feelings. I no longer hated or feared him, but what I *did* feel scared me.

He gently kissed the top of my ear, causing me to gasp with pleasure. I was a terrible faker when it came to how he made me feel. For all the ignoring I'd done, my true sentiments were easily uncovered.

"You haven't come to see me for *three* days."

"Me? Come see you? Caius…"

"Let us have a fresh start. Perhaps we might take a turn about the grounds?" He removed one of his arms from my waist and gently pulled my hair to the side, brushing his fingers along my neck before kissing me delicately. "What say you?"

I let my guard down because Caius was offering me something that I very badly wanted. I'd never been out on the grounds, but I knew they were extensive. The grass park alone was surprising in size. Every week I longingly watched a yard worker mow it on a big tractor.

Surrounding the perfectly manicured lawn was a dense wood. Woods have always enamored me with their hidden secrets.

"You'll let me go outside?"

"Yes, outside, Cece. Come for a walk with me."

I simply couldn't refuse. We walked along the grass lawn just beside the woods. Caius had his fingers entwined with mine. The trees loomed over us, beautiful trees of birch, eucalyptus, and pine. Above us the stars twinkled. It was a new moon, so all was dark. "I've wanted to come out here for ages," I admitted, sighing with delight.

"You should have come and asked." He glanced at me but I said nothing. "How are the preparations for the ball coming along?"

At the mention of the ball, I grinned ear to ear. "Preparations are going wonderfully. I've never seen the girls so excited."

"They are helping you, I hope?"

I nodded. The girls were helping a lot. We spent all our time drawing out plans for the event. In fact, it was all we talked about.

"And the dressmaker? Is he to your liking?"

I laughed outright. "You mean, *Fredrick*?" I said his name with a perfect, well-trained French accent. Fredrick was the most entertaining vampire I'd ever met. He seemed to be stuck in the eighteenth century. His powdered face and white wig were laughable, especially his wig, which was decorated with bright colorful bows. When I first saw him, I thought he'd come straight from a movie set, given his rich costume attire. I quickly learned he didn't consider his clothing a costume.

Fredrick had two large poodles that followed him everywhere, Bella the Fourth and Tisha the Sixth. Supposedly, he was the most talented designer in the world. And although he was overly eccentric, I loved him immediately.

Without keeping Caius waiting, I went into robust detail regarding my first impressions of Fredrick and our interactions thus far, finishing with a report of our progress to date. "He's taken all my measurements," I explained. "The only problem is, I can't decide what I want my gown to look like."

The other girls had already made their exceedingly detailed requests, some of them completely outlandish. Fortunately, Fredrick was French, so he'd put a lovely Parisian spin on everyone's vision. The ball was to be a Parisian masquerade, after all.

"I might have some ideas for *your* gown," Caius said, "if you're open to hearing them." Of course I was, so I nodded. "I was hoping your gown would be something ballerina-like, so that you might perform a dance or two."

I stopped walking. "You mean, you want me to dance for your guests? Dance a ballet?" I hadn't expected to be on display for a bunch of vampires I hardly knew. This wasn't a problem, since I danced at Fluxx as Ginger, and before that, performed for plenty of packed theaters. It was merely unexpected. The gears in my mind began turning.

"I know ballet is a part of your old life, Cece. I understand that you are hesitant. I've been bombarded with requests for you to dance. *Everyone* is eager to see you perform a solo or two."

"Caius!" I turned to him. "Why are people requesting solos from me when they don't know I'm a ballerina?"

His grin was wicked. "A little bird told them."

"Are you serious?"

"I couldn't help it, Cece. You are a beautiful dancer, one of the most graceful I have seen. And we vampires, we love ballet so very much. I've never met a distinguished vampire who doesn't."

I eyed him for a moment, not sure how best to respond.

"Say yes," he whispered. In the dark his eyes gleamed brightly.

As I stood gazing at him, I felt a sudden tingle of unease pass over me. It felt very isolated from the moment. I was certain that it had nothing to do with our conversation. "Yes," I said at last, distracted. Caius's back was to the trees, but I was facing them. "I'll perform if it will make *you* happy." As I said this, I scanned the tree-line. I felt like I was being watched. My skin began prickling uncomfortably.

I'm not sure what Caius said after that. My attention was entirely on the trees. Something watched us.

I saw a gleam of red, a little pinpoint of light, somewhere off in woods. It blinked, disappearing and reappearing. I noticed a few of these red points and stared at them, fascinated. What could they be?

"Cece?" Caius tried to regain my attention.

"Caius, I think there's something—"

Caius spun around and pushed me behind him. "Don't move, Cece." His command froze me in place. He must have known what lurked in the dark. "Titus," he quietly called. We'd walked some distance from the manor, and my human hearing barely discerned his summons. "Julia, Marcus, Nero. There's trouble."

"Caius, what is it," I whispered. Fear set my limbs quivering. My blood turned cold. I'd not felt this afraid since I was taken. Caius's disquiet didn't improve matters.

"What is it?" I whispered again. I didn't need him to tell me by this time. Leaves were crunching, and in the darkness, I could make out first two, then six, and then ten glowing red eyes. My heart raced until my blood pounded in my ears.

"Stop it, Cece," Caius whispered. "Your fear will spur them on."

"That's really going to calm me down, Caius!" I took a deep breath, trying to slow my pulse.

Caius began backing up, keeping me behind him as he carefully retreated from the tree-line. "Don't make any sudden movements. They are creatures of instinct. If they sense your retreat, they will give chase." Caius was terrifying me with his words.

Without his telling me, I knew these were night-walkers. These were what I would have become had Caius's men not saved me from Thrax. "They look like—like zombies."

"They very nearly are."

I felt a whoosh of air. Suddenly Titus, Julia, Marcus, and Nero were beside us. All were fully alert, ready for a fight. With the five of them, I was probably safe, but that didn't alleviate my panic.

"Where did they come from?" Titus asked. Caius's vampires were forming a barrier around me.

"From the trees," Caius answered. "They must have smelled her."

"Bull shit." Marcus's voice was low. "Her blood may be strong, but our guard was up, Caius. Nothing wandered past my eyes. These were planted."

"Nonetheless, praeparet bello." Caius crouched low.

"Et nos tecum sumus, Caius." Marcus gazed fiercely at Caius before looking at the enemy. They were speaking Latin, but I didn't know Latin. I held my breath as I watched them. For a moment, everything was silent.

"Autem!" Caius's voice rang out. With a speedy blur, one by one, my protectors converged on the night-walkers. It was a frenzy of fighting, which I could hardly follow. There were too many quick movements. I saw three of the night-walkers wither when they were staked in the heart, but Caius and Julia didn't have stakes. Caius grabbed the nearest one he wrestled with and twisted it's head, ripping it clean from its body. Only then did it shrivel and disappear. The night-walkers screamed as they died. It was a harrowing kind of hissing cry that stole the breath from my chest.

Caius would never let any harm come to me—I saw the frenzy in his eyes, the way he looked at me when he removed the night-walker's head, but that didn't mute my terror.

It was over in a few brief minutes. There was nothing left of the bodies. Caius turned to his vampires. "Back to your posts. Marcus, it's time to double the watch. Have Cato round up six more for tonight."

Everyone but Julia sped off into the night. She regarded me curiously. Caius looked shaken. "Cece," he said, shaking his head. "I put you in unnecessary danger."

Julia took my chin and tilted my face upwards, turning it this way and that to study me. "Are you going to be all right, my little pet?"

I nodded.

"She'll be fine, Julia. I'll see to it. You may leave us now."

Julia turned to him. I couldn't be sure, but she appeared pensive. Perhaps she hadn't expected to see us out together in the yard. Or maybe it was something more. Maybe she wondered about his protective nature towards me. Following his orders, she too darted off, leaving us alone.

My nerves began to relax, but my fear never quite dissipated. Caius watched me. "Time to return you to the house."

The night-walkers had ruined what should have been a nice evening walk. "Please don't take me back yet." I wasn't ready to go inside. I wasn't ready to give up my freedom of the outdoors.

His expression softened. "Aren't you afraid?"

"Not anymore. Not with you." This was only a half-truth. I was too used to living with fear to release it entirely. I took a step closer to him and grabbed his hand, lacing my fingers with his.

He glanced down at our hands before meeting my eyes. "Perhaps we should stay away from the tree-line, then." He led me to middle of the large grassy lawn.

I laid down to watch the stars. I felt much better laying in the cool grass. The smell of damp earth pervaded my nostrils, and I inhaled deeply. Caius took a seat beside me, keeping his eyes trained on the woods.

"Caius?"

"Hm?" He was still holding my hand, caressing my fingers, but I knew his mind was elsewhere.

"If vampires don't believe in draining humans, why are there night-walkers?"

He brought his gaze down to mine. "The vampires are at war."

My stomach sank deeply. I sat up to watch him.

His regard returned to the trees. "I never intended it to be this way, Cece." I was afraid to interrupt, so I just watched him, hoping he would say something more. He did, "Some vampires refuse to follow the code. They believe themselves above it—younger ones mostly. We call them *rogues*."

I frowned. "Was Thrax a rogue?"

Caius turned to me. "I wish I could have killed him myself."

My frown deepened. "I never really understood what I was saved from, until tonight." I shivered at the thought of becoming like what I saw stalking us from the woods.

"You would have been entirely lost to the world, Cece. You would have become a monster, a bloodthirsty monster." The horror of the thought reflected in his eyes.

"But you saved me."

"I wish I had."

I didn't know what he meant. Was he being literal? Did he wish he would have been at Fluxx to pull me from danger? Or was he being figurative? Did he regret the life I was resigned to live because of it?

"We hunted Thrax for a long time. He was part of the rogue's innermost ring. We never expected him to come out in the open. Ultimately, it was *your* struggle in the alleyway that alerted my vampires."

"Thrax wanted me because I'm a strong blood, right?"

"Yes."

My eyebrows knitted together. "Sounds like I'm vampire bait without even trying." My blood endangered me. No matter where I went, I had a target on my head. After living with so many ballet-related fears, I had a new fear to wrestle with.

"Vampire bait, indeed. But at what cost?" He lifted my hand

to his lips, keeping our fingers entwined. I watched him while trying to suppress my new fear.

"I do not want you to be afraid, Cece. You have been through enough."

That much was true. I swallowed. Perhaps Caius didn't realize I was used to it: fear and I were old friends who couldn't seem to part ways. I didn't *want* to be afraid, but, I didn't see a way not to be.

"I will keep you safe," he said. "I promise." His words were like the rope I required to climb from my tower-prison to freedom. Once more, he was a valiant hero offering me exactly what I needed. So I stuck out my hand, and clung tightly to that rope, climbing to my freedom. Fear might have kept me going for many long years, but with Caius, I no longer needed it. With Caius, I could finally be free.

CHAPTER 15

*M*y grandmother was a huge part of my life. As I got older, we went from having tea parties to getting pedicures, from talking about Disney movies to talking about boys and first kisses. Yet, ballet connected us on a deeper level than anything else could.

When she died, a piece of my identity died with her. At the funeral, they decided to have an open casket. I'd never seen a dead body before. *Grand-mère* looked so peaceful, but you could tell she was dead. Her skin was waxen, her eyes were closed, but her face was happy. Someone had dressed her in her Sunday best, a green floral blouse and the straight black skirt she liked wearing so often. It wasn't frightening to look upon her. I always thought it might be.

When you experience a loved one's death, you get a free pass on many things, like crying at a funeral. No one expects you to hold yourself together. They don't expect you to be strong, or brave, or composed. What people *do* expect, is that you'll be an emotional mess, and my mom was.

I wanted to be emotional, believe me. I envied the mourners's tears, while I kept my face impassive. Someone had to be strong for my mom. Someone had to be brave. My dad played that role well, but for some reason I did also.

I think I've always been like my dad in that respect. I wanted to be Mom's rock. Caring for her helped me put aside my own pain, avoid it even, to help her through hers. That was my coping mechanism. It healed me.

I discovered many things about my own inner strength during that phase of my life. I grew as a person. And, a time quickly came at Anghor Manor when I would need those same qualities.

The morning after the night-walker attack, I woke to screaming. It sounded like Adel. I'd been having nightmares filled with glowing red eyes, so at first, I thought the cries were part of my dreams, perhaps my own. I ripped my covers back and rushed down the hall, rounding the corner to Adel's corridor.

Light flooded the hall from an open door near the end. It was Sophie's room. I sprinted in, surprised to find Adel standing motionless in the middle. Her hands were clasped to her face. She wore a look of absolute terror. That expression would haunt me for a long time.

I followed Adel's horrified gaze. I think I screamed too. I can hardly remember. Sophie lay nearly naked in a bra and panties, stretched diagonally across her bed. The bed was still made from the day before. She'd not yet slept in it. Her arm was dangling limply off the edge. Her mouth was slightly open, and so were her eyes, as they gazed blankly at the ceiling. She'd been completely drained of blood. There were fang marks on her neck.

An instant later, Caius arrived. I turned to him in horror. "Is she dead?"

"Come away, Cece. Felix, take Adel out. Don't let them see this." He pulled me from the room.

In the hallway, I rounded on him. "Did—did you guys do this to her?" I wasn't thinking rationally. Of course they hadn't.

"My vampires do not *drain*, Cece. Remember?"

I gazed at him with wide eyes, trying to make sense of everything. He gathered me into his arms. I buried my head in his chest, trying to block out the disturbing image that I saw every time I closed my eyes.

"Nero, Felix, take all the girls to my study. Post guards. Gather whomever is off duty. We will meet in the hall. Cece, you need to go with the other girls."

I refused, tightening my arms around him. I was scared. I was shocked. I was sick to my stomach. I needed Caius's strength now more than ever. I wasn't going anywhere. He sighed compliantly, and kissed the top of my hair.

"This is a cruel blow, Caius," Marcus said. I kept my face hidden as he spoke. "How did they gain entry?"

"That is what I would like to know," said Caius.

"Has our security been breached?"

"It appears so. Have you any idea how it happened, Marcus?" His arms tightened protectively around me as he spoke. I buried my face deeper into his chest, letting his musky smell console me.

"My guess? Last night's night-walker attack was a diversion. Sophie was the true target all along."

Upon hearing this, I shuddered. I'd been with Caius on the lawn, and so had his guards. The thought of Sophie helpless in her room left me to despair. It could have happened to any of the girls. It could have happened to Adel!

"Why Sophie?" Caius asked.

"Perhaps it was random?" Felix had returned.

"Who can say." Caius rested his chin atop my head. "The rogues are sending us another message, it would seem."

"Ever since Thrax died, they have been—"

"Not in front of Cece, Felix." Caius silenced him. "She's been through enough. At any rate, I agree with your speculations. Sophie has been cold for eight hours at least."

"This is low." I'd never heard Marcus sound so angry. "The girls are not part of our fight." Marcus was fond of his human family. They all were. Marcus was especially fond of Sophie.

"It is low indeed, Marcus." Caius sighed heavily. "You and Felix know what to do."

"What are they doing?" I lifted my head as Felix and Marcus went into the room. What did they want with poor Sophie?

Caius looked down at me, his face full of sympathy. "I'm sorry, Cece. We must dispose of her body before she turns."

"Turns?" I squeaked.

"Yes, she's been drained."

"But, she's dead! She's not a night-walker."

"She will be. We must remove her head for safe measure, and burn her body."

I blanched.

Caius led me to his study a few minutes later. The girls were huddled around the giant fireplace. A roaring fire had been lit. I was grateful for the soothing orange glow.

Most of them were hysterical. Adel was sobbing in Marie's arms. They clung to each other. Only a few refrained from crying, myself included. Caius led me to a secluded alcove. "I need to meet with members of my coven."

"You're leaving us?" I was appalled.

"Cece, the girls respect you. I need you to be strong. Can I trust you with that? I won't be gone long, I promise."

I squared my shoulders. "I can do it."

"Thank you." He wrapped his arms around me briefly, kissing my hair. Then he disappeared from the room.

The days following Sophie's gruesome death were trying. None of the girls wanted to leave their rooms alone. They traveled in packs, afraid to be by themselves. I spent nearly all my time with Adel after it happened, even sharing the other side of her bed. She cried in my arms the first few nights.

During those days, I became the rock the girls needed, doing everything to keep them occupied and distracted—television, board games, crafts, you name it. It helped my own needs, too.

It was nothing like *Grand-mère's* death. When she died, it was her time. Poor Sophie had her life ripped from her when her blood was drained. The image of her lying across the bed wouldn't stop appearing when I closed my eyes.

After her murder, I discovered that I didn't need to feel

courageous to display courage. I did what I could to reassure the girls that things would get better, that Sophie was in a better place now, smiling down on us. She would never *really* leave us.

Three days after Sophie's death, we decided to have a memorial for her. We held it out on the back terrace overlooking the giant lawn. I was stunned to see so many vampires in attendance. Every one of them mourned, dressed in black. Marcus shaved his head, removing his beautiful, dark locks of hair, making his blue eyes stand out more so than ever. I always admired him for showing his grief so openly.

It was Sophie's memorial that truly opened my eyes to the relationship between humans and vampires. They never saw us as sacks of blood. Our lives mattered. We weren't simply food for their survival, we were their family.

Most of the girls gave eulogies. Even though I'd only known Sophie for several months, I felt the need to as well. I talked about her bubbly personality, and how much she meant to everyone. We would all miss her, Adel most of all.

Adel cried on my shoulder for most of the service. I held her hand tightly. It helped to know she took solace in my friendship. It was all I could offer, and I did it gladly.

Caius sat beside me on my left, holding my other hand. He constantly looked over to see if I was okay. His worry was worth more than a million spoken words of reassurance.

After a week passed, the shock remained. Caius took no chances; he posted his vampire guards all over the house. He doubled the vampires on duty outside, sending them to patrol as far as the wilderness beyond the manor's park. The key codes to the extensive alarm system were reprogramed, and security at Fluxx was amped up threefold.

It was during this turmoil that I finally began to understand the power and influence Caius held over the other vampires. I couldn't count the numbers under his control. They followed him loyally and respectfully. With that realization, I knew that we would win this war. There would be casualties, it was unavoidable, but I trusted Caius now. He would see us through. Eventually.

## CHAPTER 16

*O*f all ballets, love stories are my favorite. One of these, *The Talisman*, is about a beautiful young goddess who chooses love over immortality. Niriti is the daughter of Amravati, the queen of the heavens. She descends to earth with a guardian, the wind god, to see if she can resist the temptations of mortal love. Just before she leaves, her mother gives her a sacred talisman that will protect her, and enable her to return home.

On earth, Niriti and her guardian encounter a young maharaja who falls in love with Niriti. When the maharaja discovers the power of the talisman, he steals it so that she might never leave his side. He wishes to claim her as his wife and queen. Niriti and her guardian go to great measures to retrieve the talisman so that Niriti can return to her mother. Before it is too late, Niriti realizes that immortality cannot match the happiness that the maharaja offers her with his love. Ultimately, she chooses to stay with him on earth as a mortal woman.

The story of *The Talisman* always fascinated me. Niriti gave up all the celestial delights of immortality for one man's love. Instead of living forever alone, she chose to share a mortal life.

Before Caius came along, my experience in the realm of romance was rather pathetic. I only ever had one boyfriend, Simon, my first *pas de deux* partner. We never got past the kissing and touching stage, neither of which made me feel tirelessly aroused.

After Sophie's death, Caius presented me an open-ended invitation to enter his study whenever I wished. Sometimes I would sit cuddled up in an alcove reading while he worked at his desk, throwing me frequent looks. We enjoyed watching each other.

One afternoon, several weeks after Sophie's death, he found me in his study reading Shakespeare's, *A Midsummer Night's Dream*. He sat down beside me, putting his arm around my shoulders. I pretended to be entirely engrossed, acknowledging him with a mere, "Hello," as I sat reading.

He fussed over me, kissing the side of my head and rubbing my arm. "I have something for you."

That got my attention. I turned to meet his mischievous gaze. His wicked expressions were some of my favorite. It was better than seeing him angry or upset. Mischievous and wicked were his happy.

"Have you a kiss?" I teased. "I do love your kisses, Caius."

"Do you?" He placed his free hand on the side of my cheek and pulled my mouth to his. Heat erupted on my skin as our lips met. I kissed him back, losing myself in his taste.

"Mmm…" He pulled away from me. "I love your kisses too, Cece. Fortunately, I no longer need to *trick* you into them."

He would never let me live it down. "But, I have something else for you, something important. Come and see." He stood and held out his hand. I rose and took it, following him to his desk.

Much to my surprise, he presented me with a stunning pendant. It was the size of a quarter, and dangled from a delicate gold chain. "It's a moonstone." He held it up to the light. Its white moonlight surface glistened with shades of iridescent blue and pink.

"Wow, it's breathtaking." It reminded me of the moonstone talisman we used for Niriti in the ballet, except this one looked far more celestial, as if it had truly come from the queen of the heavens.

Caius smiled. "I'm not sure how much you know about the origins of your name, Cece, but *Celine* is French. It is derived from the Latin word *caelum*, meaning, sky or heaven. You are the heavens, Celine. As such, you are in need of a moon. This can be your moon." He unclasped the necklace and moved around me to put it on.

I was speechless. Where did he think this stuff up? But it was official—I was smitten. I loved vintage jewelry. "Thank you, Caius." My voice was thick with emotion.

"Never take it off, promise me."

"Never?" That seemed a little extreme. "What about when I shower?"

"Never."

Now I was curious. Why was he so adamant? I wanted an explanation, and so I asked.

"This isn't any moonstone, Cece. This is the first moonstone, carved from the moon by the moon goddess herself, Hecate. It is very, *very* old."

I never put much stock in folklore, including mythology. I'd heard the name Hecate, but I didn't know much about her. I highly doubted that this stunning jewel had truly come from the moon, or Hecate for that matter, especially since anyone could buy moonstone jewelry from a jewelry shop. Still, I humored him.

"So, is this like a magic amulet or something?" My mind jumped again to Niriti.

"It is, if you believe in magic. It will protect you from all those who intend to do you harm. You have my word on that. If you wear it, no one can hurt you."

"Is this because of what happened to Sophie? Are you worried about me?"

He sighed. "I simply wish to keep you safe."

I caressed the moonstone, smiling, before putting my arms about his neck. "I love your gifts Caius, your kisses, your attention. I won't take it off. I promise." He kissed me then, lifting me off the floor. Those were my favorite. I loved the kisses where he held me against him with my feet dangling, so that I looked down at his face rather than his usual towering over me. I felt most safe in his arms.

"Have you made up your mind about the ball?" he asked. He was referring to my hesitation about continuing with our plans. When Sophie died, I questioned if a ball was the right thing to do, given everything going on.

"I think I have decided to go through with it, but I cannot deny, it feels a little weird without Sophie. She oversaw all the decorations, you know."

"An important job. Tough shoes to fill."

I agreed. Very tough. "But, I think it will be good for us—a positive distraction to lighten our moods. I know Sophie will be with us in spirit."

Caius set me back on my feet. Then he gently kissed my forehead. "She will indeed."

I proceeded to update him on our progress. "Fredrick has successfully showcased nearly all the girls' gowns. He works fast." I was excited about this. I enjoyed watching him fit each girl with her respective gown. We treated it like a fashion show, *ooh-ing* and *ahh-ing* over every dress.

"Fredrick is a vampire, after all," Caius chuckled. "We can move quickly and efficiently. And your gown? Have you thought any further about my request?"

"About performing?"

"Yes. Is it wrong of me to show you off?" His question stole the words from my mouth. Was that why he wanted me to dance?

"I thought—" I cleared my throat. "I thought you wanted me to dance because your friends requested it of me."

"The truth comes out, I suppose. I've been bragging to everyone about the star that you are. Of course they want to see you, but I also want to show you off. Come now, you are leaving me in suspense. Will you oblige us? Oblige me?"

I smiled, relishing in his praise. "Well, I *do* know what I'm going to wear." I had already decided to take him up on his offer, though I hadn't told him yet. Fredrick and I spent nearly an hour talking about the perfect ball gown that would also serve as a ballerina gown, without being too restrictive. However, I didn't want to give any secrets away. I wanted to surprise Caius, and preferably, take his breath away like he did mine.

"And? Will you grace us *poor* vampires with a dance or two?"

I smiled mischievously. "On one condition."

A rumbling laugh sounded deep in his chest. "You are learning to play, Cece." He looked thoughtful. "What is your condition?"

"I want to go on a date with you. A *real* date, not one where I end up as food for a rogue." Caius cocked his head to the side. Perhaps he didn't realize that I'd never been on a single successful date. "Nothing serious," I added. "Just, maybe dinner and a movie."

The side of his mouth twitched. "A date…all right. Deal. A date for a dance."

"*Two* dances—two dates."

He sighed dramatically. "Very well, Cece. It seems you always get your way these days." I smirked. "And speaking of dates. What is the date you have settled on for the ball? Everyone is eager to know."

I had already picked a special date, though I was not sure if Caius would know why it was so. "Fredrick needs two more weeks to finish the gowns. We still have a lot of preparations. I was thinking in four weeks' time. Let's set it for Friday night, April the seventh, if that works for you."

He smiled wide. Maybe he did know. "Interesting choice, Cece. *Very* interesting."

"Why is that?"

"Is that not your birthday?" My surprise at his knowing was answer enough. "I looked at your driver's license when your purse was confiscated." Of course he had! My gaze narrowed at him. He merely chuckled. "Very well, Cece. April seventh it is."

I left his study grinning with excitement, full of ideas. There was so much to do, a ball to be planned, a gown to be made, dates with Caius. The first thing I was eager to tackle were my ballet solos. I wanted them to be special, and I intended to choreograph them myself. If Caius wanted to show me off, then I needed to be the star of that show. And so, I got right to work.

# CHAPTER 17

When a ballet cast list goes up on the wall, everyone in the company gathers around to search the names for their own. It's a tense moment. Plenty of members walk away upset. In cases like this, jealousy is unavoidable.

I once understudied Juliet for *Romeo and Juliet*, learning the role to perfection. The following year, I crowded next to the list and scanned it. To my great disappointment, I was set as understudy for Juliet *again*. I was instantly jealous. I threw furtive glances at the other three girls who got the role that should have been mine. After all, I worked hard; it felt deserved.

Ballerinas deal with envy and jealousy on a regular basis. We envy the beautiful leg extensions, the speed of turns, the graceful poise, or the flexibility displayed by our competition. We foster jealousy when that same competition is given the parts we want. Goodness, I've even seen girls get jealous of their classmates when their instructors don't offer them the same amount of critique. We've all heard the urban legends of vicious ballerinas putting glass in pointe shoes, and pins in dressing rooms.

As we advance in our careers, we learn to deal with it. You simply bite your tongue as you read the cast list. You wait to celebrate or weep until you're alone.

Learning to control jealousy as a ballerina did little to help me when I discovered that both drinking and letting blood was a sexual experience. This happened a few days after Caius gave me the moonstone necklace. I was working with Adel, drawing up more plans for the ball. We were going over the *hors d'oeuvres* menu when a stray thought suddenly hit me.

"Adel, do the vampires drink your blood?" My question was rather personal. Technically, I already knew the answer, Felix told me months ago. The girls provided blood for the vampires in the manor. Beyond that, I knew little else.

"Yes. The vampires drink my blood," Adel said. "When I allow." She didn't blush very often, but she did now. Her cheeks were bright red. I always suspected this to be a tender topic, though not in the way I imagined.

I assumed that the girls were taken advantage of. I thought the vampires were forcefully leeching off them. Before this, I couldn't bear to ask for worry of broaching a sensitive topic. In my mind, I'd painted this bloody feeding as a horrific picture, filled with pain and fear. It wasn't, it was the opposite.

Giving blood was a pleasurable experience, something the girls enjoyed, something they did *willingly*. The experience was nothing short of blood-kink. So you can imagine my surprise. "You like it when they drink from you?" My eyebrows rose.

"Oh, yes. It feel like…"

"Like what," I eagerly asked.

"Like sex."

My jaw dropped. "Sex?"

"Yes," she whispered.

I was wholly unprepared for this. The idea of Caius enjoying someone else's blood in a sexual way, sent my stomach plummeting. I was so jealous, that I excused myself from Adel's room in search of him.

As I walked through the manor, I was afflicted by an onslaught of emotions. I couldn't stand the thought of another woman giving Caius something I could. I was angry at both of us. I never considered offering Caius my blood. It always seemed like a heinous act. It wasn't, so why hadn't he said something?

I arrived at his study and slipped in quietly without knocking. Caius was deep in conversation with a vampire I did not recognize. This newcomer was dressed in odd clothing like something out of *Arabian Nights*. Their conversation came to a jarring halt as they turned to me.

I should have waited. I should have politely allowed them to finish their meeting. My emotions had already gotten the better of me. "Caius, I need to talk to you."

He gave me a brief nod and turned back to his guest. "Shahriar, please excuse us. I hope you will join us for dinner tonight. After that, we can continue our discussion freely."

Shahriar rose from his seat at Caius's desk, thanking Caius in a thick accent. As he left, his eyes raked over me with the same hunger I was used to. I waited until the door closed behind me before speaking, "Caius, I'm upset."

"That's obvious."

I crossed my arms. "Who are you getting your blood from?" He watched me without answering. As always, his face was too controlled. "Do you drink blood from the girls here in the manor?"

"What makes you think that?"

My eyes narrowed suspiciously. "Adel told me everything. Why didn't you—you didn't…" My emotions left me incoherent. Caius sighed, leaning against his desk as he watched me. "I want to know, Caius, who are you getting your blood from?"

"I do not get my blood from any of the girls here in the manor. I leave them exclusively for the others."

This was a relief. "Then who?"

He shrugged. "When I'm hungry I go hunting. I like to hunt. I'm picky. I find a scent that draws me in and I drink, males mostly, since they are easy to mind-manipulate."

I opened my mouth then closed it. I hadn't expected this answer. I'd pictured some seductive scene with a beautiful temptress in a red gown whose blood he enjoyed habitually.

"So, no women then?"

He afforded me a deadpan stare. I held my ground, glaring back at him until he answered. "Sometimes I bite women, but only if I'm confident that I can mind-manipulate one. I usually test that first. I'm not exactly keen on bringing more women here against their will."

"But, isn't it…" My face burned as I fumbled for the description I was both eager and nervous to discuss.

"Sexual?"

My eyes fell to the hand-spun Turkish rug beneath my toes as I nodded. Talking about sex with him intimidated me. I was convinced he would want nothing to do with me once he discovered my vast inexperience, as in, no experience at all.

"Cece, drinking blood is sexual in the sense that it feels much better than sex altogether. Humans possess many desires, but their desire for sex is their greatest impetus. Vampires only crave blood. So you can imagine, perhaps, what it is like when our thirst is quenched."

*Like having an orgasm?* I wanted to ask, but instead I merely gazed back at him. Even so, I couldn't really imagine, but I didn't admit this.

He crossed his arms and watched me. At last his facade shattered. He smirked. "Cece." His voice was rich with seduction as he said my name. "Cece, are you *jealous?*"

My skin burned as my heart rate increased. I cursed that heart of mine for betraying me. Was my jealousy that obvious? Silly me, of course it was.

I watched his expression turn tender. "Come here, Celine." His murmur was like a snare. I went to him. How could I resist? He didn't need to use his persuasion powers for my compliance.

As soon as I was within arm's reach, he stood and took hold of my waist, pulling me greedily to him. My body aligned flush with his. My muscles quivered in delight from his possessive touch. I was too embarrassed to look him in the face, so I pushed my forehead against his muscled chest. "Look at me, Cece."

I shook my head and pressed it harder against him, overly shy. He took his fingers under my chin and tilted my face up towards his. "Had I known you might be bothered by this, things would have gone differently. You were against me for so long. I didn't dare suggest it and risk further upset. But it seems your heart has changed. I must ask, are you open to the idea of letting me feed from you?"

My stomach clenched. "I—yes!"

His eyes glittered. "How about later tonight?" His whisper set my heart fluttering. "I must meet with Shahriar after dinner. Perhaps we can catch a late movie as our *first* date? After that..." He left the sentence unfinished. He didn't need to outline the conclusion.

"Tonight sounds..." It was sooner than I'd bargained for.

"Cece, I have lusted for your blood since you stepped foot in Anghor Manor. But I want you to be sure. Is this what you want?"

"I—I think so." Was I sure? Was this what I truly wanted? Yes. One hundred percent, yes.

"You must be sure. No indecisiveness. Once I have a taste, there will be no going back. Your blood will make me..."

My eyebrows knitted together and I pulled away slightly. "Make you what?"

"Different," he said. "I may become—well—not like myself. I cannot say with certainty."

"Haven't you ever had strong blood before?"

He chuckled. "Of course, my dear Cece. Of course I have."

"Then what's the problem?"

"The problem? The problem is, I've never smelled blood like yours. It drives me crazy. *You* drive me crazy with desire. The combination of both weaknesses could be dangerous. So I need you to be sure."

"I'm sure."

He gazed at me, searching my eyes. I suppose he wanted to see if I would recant. I had no intention of it. I was sure.

"Very well. No more jealousy?"

I smiled. "No more jealousy."

When I left his study shortly thereafter, my spirits were soaring. I'd never once felt so powerful over someone else. I affected him. He admitted it! And knowing that left me short of breath.

# CHAPTER 18

*T*rust was the first thing I learned in *pas de deux* class with Simon, and with each partner thereafter. When you dance with your partner, you must give yourself over to him. If you do not submit, then your partnership is a waste and you are merely dancing alone, relying only on yourself. How then can you let yourself go?

The prospect of submitting to Caius, allowing him to drink my blood, left my heart relentlessly aflutter. I was eager to give myself over to him. More so, I was dying to let go.

After leaving his study the afternoon before our first date, I couldn't help but repeat our conversation in my mind. His words left me beaming. And the anticipation created a nervous eagerness unlike any other experience, including my moments before performing on stage.

I hardly knew what to do with myself as I counted down the hours. During preparations for the evening meal, I told Adel everything. We whispered at first, but there was no keeping it from the other girls. The moment they found out, they all wanted to help me get ready for my big night.

"After dinner, can I do your hair, Cece?" Marie begged.

"Oh, you should wear your black babydoll dress," Kristi decided.

"No," Adel argued. "The white one she danced in with her red shoes. That one!"

The remainder of the meal prep went that way, with the girls arguing over how I should prepare, what I should wear, how to do my hair, and what I should talk about with Caius.

"You will like the *finale*," Marie hinted. "It's better than sex."

My jaw dropped, but I quickly closed it.

"No it's not," said Kristi, "but it comes close."

"Marie hasn't had good sex," Adel teased.

Dinner was a distinguished affair. There were quite a number of foreign guests staying in the manor, including the mysterious *Arabian Knight* (as I decided to call him), Shahriar. Adel insisted on sitting beside him, batting her eyelashes as she begged him for stories. He appeared taken by her too, supplying her with his constant attention. As often as I could without getting caught, I glanced at Caius. He was in a better mood than I'd seen him in a while. Somehow, I knew the prospect of my blood left him eager. He wasn't the only one…

After dinner, all the girls crammed into my room. "It's only a movie," I reassured them, grinning from ear to ear. I settled on a crop-top skirt set. The top was midnight blue with black beading. The matching skirt was tulle. It fell just above my knee. Its waist band was also beaded. Marie and Adel

147

curled my thick auburn locks, while Kristi and Valarie did my makeup. The others gathered around, picking out my shoes and admiring me from afar.

As I descended the stairs in the hall, I felt like a beautiful goddess. The look Caius paid me was all the reassurance I needed, leaving me entirely fulfilled. "You're glowing, Cece," he whispered into my ear as he took my hand.

The girls poked their heads out from the second-floor hall, trying to glimpse us, so Caius turned up the volume of his voice. "How very beautiful you look tonight, my dear. Stunning in fact." I heard a bunch of giggling responses. "The girls did a spectacular job," he added before escorting me out.

The drive into Vienna went quickly. Caius took me to a cozy theater near the outskirts of the city. We settled on an American action film with German subtitles. There weren't many choices, and the only romantic comedy had already started.

I don't think I stopped smiling once. We sat munching popcorn and laughing at all the unrealistic fight scenes. He kept his arm around me, regularly kissing my hair or my cheek as he cuddled up next to me.

"I can't take my eyes off of you," he whispered. His complement left me swooning.

After the movie, I knew the next step was close at hand. My mind raced, speculating over how it would happen. I couldn't seem to calm my heart, so I gazed out of the car window, watching the dark landscape roll by.

"Are you happy, Cece?" Caius asked, bringing my attention to the present. We were making our way up into the hills where the manor was nestled.

"I am," I answered. Of course I was happy. I'd just had a

successful first date. Not to mention, I was overly drunk on his scent and smoldering looks.

"But what about in general? Do you like your life at the manor?"

"I suppose so," I said, wondering what he was getting at.

"What if I allowed you to go home? Back to your old life? What if I let you leave? Would you?"

I was wholly unprepared for this question. My mind flashed to the conversation I'd had with my mom. I recalled the frantic worry in her voice. "Caius, are you asking me *hypothetically*? Or, are you actually offering me the option?"

He was quiet for far too long. "I'm offering you the option," he said at last. "I trust that you would never reveal our secrets. You may go home, if that is what you want. You once wished for it. You told me that you would do anything to leave Anghor Manor."

I became immediately frustrated. Why was he doing this? And, why now? Hadn't we already been over it in the ballroom the night of the red shoes? "Caius, I don't understand. Why are you asking me this?"

"Just answer the question, Cece." His tone changed to one of impatient demand.

"No, Caius, I don't want to leave. I already told you that in the ballroom."

He visibly relaxed, focusing once more on the road, but I was no longer at ease. His question came out of left field. I wanted to know why. "Are you—did you ask me this because you *doubt* me? Do you think that—"

"I asked, Cece, because I need to know that this is real—that what we have between us is real."

Is that what he thought of me?! Did he think I was *using* him as a pastime? Did he think I wouldn't want to be with him if given the option to return home? "Caius you've got it all wrong. You're charming, and handsome, and frustrating. You tease me all the time. You toy with me. Most times you make me both angry and crazy simultaneously. That's all fine and dandy, but the way I feel when you touch me, the way I feel when you're with me, I've never felt that way before. I wouldn't give that up for freedom. I wouldn't, because I'm already free."

I glanced over at him. He was smiling. Damn it all to hell! I had half a mind to smack him. He knew exactly how to get under my skin. I tried to relax, finally venting to calm my nerves. "You really are a pain sometimes, you know that?"

He smirked before reaching for my hand, which he kissed, before returning his own to the steering wheel.

When we got home, Caius led me to his study and locked the door. The instant the latch clicked, the gravity of the situation came crashing down upon me. Before this moment, drinking my blood was simply a prospect. Not any longer.

Unsure of what to do with myself, I stood near the edge of the room, watching Caius. He went to the large mantle and set his keys and phone there before stoking up a fire. Greedily, my eyes drank in his appearance: the black button down defining his muscular frame, the way he placed his hands as he lifted logs into the fireplace, his devoted focus on the task, the True Religion jeans hugging his body.

Reminded of his eminence, I became shy and nervous, and to

my surprise, slightly fearful. I didn't move. What was I supposed to do? Go to him? Wait for his command?

What I really needed, was for him to save me from the uncertainty. After all, was this not a *pas de deux*, of sorts? My trust and submission belonged to him.

As if on cue, he turned to face me. "Come, Celine," he commanded, gazing hungrily at me. I obeyed, closing the distance between us. His eyes stalked my progress.

Taking my hand palm up, he kissed it, keeping his eyes trained on mine. "Why are you nervous?" Unable to speak, I shrugged my shoulders, saving him from the many reasons why I could hardly breathe. His gaze continued to devour me. "Do you want to know something? A secret?" he asked. I nodded eagerly.

"One of the reasons I enjoy watching you dance is because of your inherent assuredness. When you dance, your confidence is absolute. Did you know that?"

"I—I suppose," I mumbled, having nearly lost my ability to communicate.

"I like that you are confident in yourself when you dance. Here beside me you are nervous, almost frightened, like a little bird, flitting and fluttering with no direction. Shall I tell you another secret?" His eyes glittered down at me.

I nodded, my own eyes wide with curiosity.

"The vampire in me derives pleasure from your unease."

"You…" I could no longer think clearly.

"Shh. No need to speak, my frightened little bird." He pulled me possessively against him, letting his fingers caress the exposed skin between my crop-top and skirt.

I trembled beneath the assault of his otherworldly gaze. In the depths of his eyes I witnessed the same hunger that every vampire displayed. The time for blood was near at hand. My heart stilled with unexpected fright. Why was I suddenly panicky?

"You fear what you do not know, Celine." Caius always read my deepest thoughts, my darkest worries. "I think more so than anything, you fear that you will *like* it."

My eyes were wide. I nodded compliantly. Yes, he was right, and he knew it.

Eagerly he buried his nose in my hair, inhaling deeply. "How intoxicating you smell." His grip on me tightened almost painfully. Again, he displayed his greed for my scent, dragging his nose through my hair and across my skin. It was beast-like the way he moved, exhibiting raw hunger, murmuring and purring as he tortured himself with my scent. My tummy fluttered with his yearning. Beneath his grasp, I began to quiver uncontrollably. I was caged. I was the prey he was eager to consume.

Our eyes met, and for an instant we were silent, frozen in the moment. Then his mouth was upon mine, claiming me with unrelenting kisses. His hands moved over me, caressing the small of my back, creeping beneath the hem of my top. I pressed my body eagerly against his, losing my mind in his kiss, feeling the heat of excitement expand within me.

More insistent he became, tugging and sucking at my lips, letting his tongue caress mine. Then without warning, he pulled painfully on my lower lip with his teeth. A coppery taste filled my mouth. My hands clutched desperately at his neck but I did not cry out. I enjoyed the pain.

Tasting my blood, he groaned deeply, pulling away to see me.

There it was on his lips—my blood—but it was his eyes that caught my attention. They were inhumanly dilated: the silver of his irises formed a thin, nearly nonexistent, glowing ring.

My tummy tightened eagerly. Was it time? Was this it? I tilted my head to expose my neck. In response, he clicked his tongue. "So *willing*. So impatient. I love the pain of torture too..."

Holding me tightly with one arm, he threaded his fingers into my hair with his free hand, which clenched into a fist. Hair pulled tight, I could no longer move. My neck was entirely exposed to him; and with the utmost torture to my senses, he began laying soft kisses along the exposed skin there. I cried out softly. My control was slipping. I willingly submitted.

Ever so slowly, he moved from one kiss to the next, *teasing* me, *taunting* me. He didn't stop there, he let his fangs graze my flesh with tantalizing promise, and each time, my breathing faltered.

His hot breath tickled my ear as he spoke. "My body is screaming for your blood, Celine. I'm not sure you understand. Perhaps you never will." Then he placed his teeth upon the lobe of my ear and pulled, but this time much harder than usual, making known the desperation he felt. It was deliciously painful. I cried out as my body clenched, needy with desire.

He growled in response; the grumble resonated through his chest. Still, he held me tighter. There would be no escaping. "I should ask that you consider with finality the offer you have made me, Celine. But I confess"—his breath came in heavy drags—"I am already too far gone."

So was I.

MELISSA MITCHELL

With no warning whatsoever, I felt a piercing pain on my neck. It was like that of a sharp prick, both brief and abrupt. There was only a moment of panic, which immediately transformed into blissful euphoria. It spread from my neck to the rest of my body. My knees grew weak and the world around me fell away leaving only Caius, supporting me within the strength of his arms, saving me from otherwise crumbling to the floor in ecstasy.

With every ravenous pull of my blood, my core thrummed like my beating heart. Numbing sensation spread from my abdomen to the peak of my thighs. Ever so provocatively, a tight frustration welled up deep inside of me. I tightened my hold on his neck, clinging urgently to him. Beneath my palms, his thick muscles flexed, pulsing as he drank.

A moan escaped my lips, long and drawn out. More followed the first, as my body slipped into an abyss of breathless yearning. There was no way to contain the rapture of feeling taking hold of me. I was stranded upon a precipice high above the depths of my undoing. I was utterly lost.

I couldn't have said how long it lasted—not long enough. I was almost angry when it ended. The sexual frustration from going unfulfilled was overwhelming. Were such experiences always so pleasurably vexing?

Caius pulled his teeth gently from my neck. I felt goose-bumps where his tongue licked me, lapping up the blood trickling from the wound. Like waking from a dream, my cognition slowly returned to normal.

I found Caius looking at me, staring into my eyes with a wild look. My hand went to my neck questioningly. I expected to find two gaping holes. There was nothing.

"My saliva healed you," he murmured, his voice gruff.

Without another word, he set me back on my feet and pulled my body against his, cradling me. He held me there for some time. "My sweet little bird," he whispered at last. "Can you imagine what I am feeling right now as your blood courses though my veins?"

I didn't respond. If it was anything like what I'd just felt, then I imagined it was pretty damn amazing. He looked down at me and smiled, exulted. His hand came to rest on my cheek as he tenderly rubbed my skin beneath his thumb. "Tell me. What did you think?"

I was still too euphoric to speak. I felt cheated, despite not knowing why. My body needed a release. Yet, that feeling was slowly receding as my high wore off. I was reluctant for it to depart. I'd never felt so pleasured and simultaneously frustrated.

"Was it comparable to sex? I'm told for some that it is," he said.

"I..." My stomach twisted nervously. "I don't know."

He frowned down at me. "You don't know?"

"I—well—no."

For a moment he was silent. Then his arms fell away from me and he backed up in confusion. "You're a virgin?"

My face burned red-hot with embarrassment. "So what if I am! Do you no longer want me because of it?"

His expression immediately changed to tender realization. He stepped forward, putting both of his hands on each side of my neck, gripping my head gently with his upturned thumbs. "I did not expect it, Celine—truly. It does not change the way I feel about you."

I relaxed, letting my tension fall away. "I thought maybe you might not—" I couldn't finish. His lips were on mine, crushingly intense. I responded in kind.

When he pulled away he kissed my cheek, then chuckled. "I look forward to tomorrow."

My brow scrunched. "What's happening tomorrow?"

"More of the same."

"Oh," I breathed with excitement.

"When you are ready, I hope you will come to me to alter the status of your virginity."

I gave a short laugh. "Who else would I go to?"

"No one, unless they wish to suffer my wrath."

"When I am ready, then." I agreed. The truth was, I was ready now. Except I was too nervous to admit this, so instead, he walked me back to my room and kissed me sweetly good night.

CHAPTER 19

$\mathcal{M}$any fail to consider the effort that goes into preparing for a ballet solo. Because a ballerina spends much of her time training for technique, it is often assumed she can simply walk on stage and thrill her audience with a beautiful rendition. But alas, we are always the perfectionists. A routine must be learned inherently such that it becomes second nature for our muscles.

Muscle memory is what allows a ballerina to immerse herself in the performance. If she spent all her effort concentrating on which movements followed the ones before, she would not succeed in portraying her character accurately. She would never deliver the emotions necessary to woo her audience.

In the weeks leading up to the ball, I choreographed each of my solos and practiced them unremittingly. One of them was my own rendition of *Cinderella*. I always loved *Cinderella*, and aspired to dance the role someday. In this version, I embellished many additional elements that most human ballerinas would struggle to complete. I planned to take advantage of the strength Caius provided through his blood.

In the ballet *Cinderella*, Cinderella's ball gown is often gold, and she's always masked. So I decided on a gown of white tulle delicately embossed with golden vines and leaves. The sequins used to create this art glistened spectacularly, starting on the bodice before traveling down to the midpoint of the skirt. Adel helped me dust my point shoes in gold glitter to match. I'd never worn golden pointes before. In leu of a gold mask, I would wear jewels glued around my eyes and face. I wanted to remain *mysterious*.

The second solo was meant to be more sensual. I wanted to depart from classical ballet and enter the world of contemporary. I was hoping I might entice Caius. I'd given it much thought, and I was strongly considering the night of the ball be the night I gave him my virginity. I hoped that my solo would bring him to me, needy with desire.

I pushed myself relentlessly over the month leading up to the ball. This was how I always prepared for my performances. Some days, I found myself dancing as much as eight hours intermittently. The experience was rewarding, but it also kept me occupied, otherwise I would have been obsessing over Caius with every spare minute.

I ordered all sorts of things in preparation, ballet necessities, props and decorations for the big night, accessories and favors for the guests. I think the delivery man was extremely curious. He appeared at the front door nearly every other day with lots of boxes.

The excitement didn't truly sink in until Fredrick finished my gown. I showed no one, not even Adel. It was to be a secret until my big reveal.

As Fredrick completed the final fittings in the privacy of my room, he admitted that this gown was the most magical piece he ever created. "I think if I were human," he declared in his thick French accent, "I would die fulfilled, Cece. Even Tisha agrees, don't you my sweet?" He looked over at Tisha the Sixth as she licked her paws atop my sofa. Bella the Fourth sat idly by, watching us.

Fredrick's gift with fashion wholly impressed me. I had already seen the other girls' dresses. They were all floor-length masterpieces, but this one was not floor-length. It came just a smidge above my ankles, the longest a tutu should ever be. Yet, it was a vision of perfection and elegance, and I felt stunning in it.

"There is no question in my mind," Fredrick said as he left my room, "you will stand out."

Caius usually held all the cards, so he wasn't used to me being the one with secrets. Sometimes like a child at Christmas, he would try to guess what my gown looked like, or what my solos would be, and I would purposefully lead him astray.

"You can't honestly be serious, Cece. You're not really going to dance *that* solo, are you?" Or, "How could you possibly think *orange* would be a good color for your skin tone?" His remonstrations always resulted in hysterics of laughter as I tried my best to tell him breathlessly that I was only joking.

I saw much less of him than I liked after we shared our intimate experience of blood. Following the night he drank from me, I was eager to relive the same experience over and again. He came to me the next day, as he'd promised, and every few days after that.

Each encounter was as exotic as the first. Yet, each time I was left feeling unsatisfied. For a time, I said nothing, but this turned out to be a bad idea, because with every incident, the desire in my body grew, making it more difficult to cope with the sensations I was subjected to.

A couple of nights before the ball, I came clean. Caius dropped by my room after dinner to see me. He spent some time pestering me further about my gown while trying to get hints about my solos. "If you do not show me your gown, how will I plan my attire to match to yours?" he complained. "Shouldn't Cinderella's prince be dressed to match?"

I refused to budge. I wanted everything to be a surprise. "I'm sure you will look great in whatever you wear, Caius." It was the truth; he could make a burlap sack look sexy.

He always kissed me sweetly after drinking from me, and usually he held me for a while, relishing in the way my blood made him feel, allowing me time to come down from my high. But this night, I decided to tell him how I felt.

"What do you mean, it frustrates you?" he asked when I tried to explain it to him. He looked at me curiously. "I thought you enjoyed it. You told me so."

"I—I do. That's not what I meant. It's just, well, it leaves me feeling *sexually* frustrated."

He fell quiet as he considered my words, then he said, "I see." I sighed with relief at his understanding. "I can't have you sexually frustrated, my dear Celine. The next time will be different."

My face burned, but still I asked, "How?"

His lips curled mischievously. "What does your gown look like again?"

160

I inferred his point. If I was going to toy with him, he would do the same to me. I had to be content with waiting.

The next few days were full of excitement. The girls and I worked tirelessly stringing garland for the staircases, placing ribbons throughout the dining room, and preparing the ballroom. There was to be a live, small-scale orchestra, and I'd already met with them well in advance. It took an entire afternoon to go through the music lineup for the big night—lots of classics like Mozart, Bach, and Beethoven. Vampires loved that stuff, and being a ballerina, I did too. I also had them perform for me both pieces I planned to dance to. Nearly two years had passed since dancing to live music. The prospect left me giddy.

The morning of the ball came quickly. It was the start of a day filled with many exciting moments. The first was with Caius. I came back from breakfast to find him sitting in my room—in the same armchair he always sat in—holding a square wooden box.

He rose when I entered. "Happy birthday, Celine."

I was happy to see him. His appearance alone was gift enough. He put an arm around me, kissed me on the forehead, then handed me the box. "It's your birthday gift. I was hoping you might wear it tonight."

I grinned widely. He was so sly! I pulled away from him so that I could open my gift, and gasped. "Caius! It's perfect." Inside was a delicate tiara. I'd completely overlooked the fact that Cinderella should probably wear a tiara for her dance, even if she wasn't yet royalty during the solo portion. Ballerinas often wear tiaras.

"Wow!" I exhaled as I took it reverently from the box. It

MELISSA MITCHELL

sparkled in the light as each of the little jewels changed colors. "It looks old, is it?"

"It is, but not terribly."

"What does *that* mean?" I still didn't know how old he was. He wouldn't tell me, so I wondered if the tiara was old by my standards or his.

"It belonged to the late Marie Antoinette."

I sucked in a breath. "Are you *serious?*" I was stunned. To wear something that graced Marie Antoinette's head before it left her shoulders was more than I'd bargained for.

"I thought you would like it."

"But, how did you—wait a minute. Did you two…" I scowled.

He chuckled, knowing exactly what I meant. "Good God, Cece. No. I only met the woman once. I happened to come across it in an estate sale. I enjoy collecting antiques."

"Aren't you yourself an *antique?*" I playfully nudged him.

"Very *funny*, Celine." He took my hand and led me to the love seat, sitting down beside me. "So, you'll wear it tonight?"

I continued to gaze at my new treasure in wonder. "Of course I will," I murmured as I rotated it back and forth, studying each of its little hidden mysteries. There were many diamonds along the edges, with several larger jewels, green emeralds and blue sapphires, that winked back at me.

"Good. And what of tonight's schedule? I assume you'll make your grand entrance after the party begins?"

That's what I was planning. I explained the details of the evening to him. While the guests arrived, the music would begin in the ballroom. There would be buffet tables in the dining room, and drinks in the large entryway—plenty of alcohol as vampires enjoy fine wines. I didn't expect to perform my solos until all guests were present, and I didn't want to make my entry too soon before that.

Caius reassured me that he would remain near the front door greeting guests until I was ready for him to escort me into the ballroom. There I would dance my solos. After that, I would simply enjoy the fruits of my labor.

"I do hope that you will grant me a few waltzes after your solos?" he asked. I agreed wholeheartedly.

As we sat together, enjoying each other's company, I was so close to telling him how badly I wanted him. If all went well, the night would end in either my bed or his. Did he have a bed? Vampires didn't sleep much, and I'd never seen his bedroom.

As inclined as I was to hint of my high expectations for the evening, I couldn't bring myself to do it. In the end, Caius left me to prepare for the evening while I scolded myself for my lack of boldness. I really needed Ginger to increase her sexy game tonight if things were to go as I wanted. And silently, I prayed that she would.

# CHAPTER 20

*C*inderella wears gold for her ballet solo, but I chose to go with white. I wanted a white gown for several reasons. The first traditional tutu was worn in the mid eighteen hundreds by the revolutionary Marie Taglioni. She was the first female ballerina to make *toe dancing* popular. Her tutu, the *romantic tutu*, was white, and fell just to her ankles to show off her toe work.

White was the color of my inexperience, my innocence. Moreover, it represented purity and perfection. I considered my own desire for stainless success. I am eternally a perfectionist when it comes to ballet. Most of all, for me, white represented wholeness, a direct reference to my humanity still intact. I was no vampire, not yet, though that option was still open. Finally, it signified completeness; for the first time in a long time, my life felt complete.

I thought of each of these aspects while I prepared for the vampire ball, speculating over the evening to come. To my relief, I was less nervous about the possibility of losing my virginity, than I was about giving my blood the first night

Caius drank from me. There was a chance it wouldn't happen; I would leave that to fate.

Nervous excitement buzzed through me as I attended to every detail of my toilette. I first curled my hair then twisted it up in a fancy messy bun, letting a few strands dangle about my ears. Then I did my makeup; I kept it simple since the rhinestones would add significant pizzazz. They were gold and varied in size. Before putting them on, I applied shimmer to the areas they would cover. The largest stones went closest to my eyes, and the smaller ones fanned out, such that they made the outline of a masquerade mask, almost butterfly-like.

By the time I finished, I heard violins drifting up to my room, their sounds airy and light. The ball had commenced. I quickly dusted my chest with more shimmer before getting into my gown. Caius's moonstone necklace came to rest just above my strapless, sweetheart neckline. I fondly attached my great-grandmother's pearl pendant to the front of my gown. *Grand-mère* would have been proud. The final touch to my evening attire was Marie Antoinette's tiara, which I fastened with dark clips into my auburn hair.

My nerves were beginning to rise as I slipped my golden pointe shoes on, tying the ribbons tightly into place. When I looked in the mirror, I stifled a surprised laugh. I was hardly recognizable. My exposed shoulders were sensual and alluring, glistening with shimmer. The gold vines on my gown complemented my auburn hair, as did the rhinestones. The tiara had me looking like a princess, but what I liked most, was the stark contrast between my heavily freckled skin with its darker pigments, and the pristine white tulle fabric of my gown. I felt like a radiating star. I was ready.

I strolled through Anghor Manor. I gave myself these

leisurely moments of privacy to collect my thoughts. Considering the way I smelled to vampires, I knew their eyes would be on me frequently for the remainder of the night.

My mood was electric, familiar. The many times I presented myself backstage before a performance came to mind. As I approached the second floor landing, the sounds from below grew louder. There were a few vampire guards in this portion of the manor. They each nodded respectfully as I passed.

Rich voices filled with joy and laughter floated my way. The full-bodied music from the orchestra saturated my being. It was intoxicating. I was beyond excited for the heavy moments to come, performing for the first time in nearly two years.

At the top of the landing I took a deep breath, relaxing my shoulders so that my arms gently rested at my sides. Grace settled over me. My movements henceforth would echo centuries of a perfected art.

The room below—part of *my* stage—was full of extravagantly dressed vampires carrying flutes of champagne and red wine. The ballet of *Anghor Manor* was about to begin, and it was filled with characters belonging to my *corps de ballet*. They all held masks to their faces. I felt as though I looked down upon a scene lost between the reaches of time. It gave me goosebumps.

Eagerly, I began searching the crowd for Caius. He was never difficult to locate. I turned my senses towards him, using his blood to feel him out. He stood near the front door, conversing with several distinguished individuals including Shahrair.

Caius was dressed in nineteenth century finery, all black

except for the white dress shirt beneath his tail coat. A pair of polished black dress shoes completed his attire. I liked every bit of what I saw.

As soon as he felt my gaze upon him, Caius turned and lowered his mask. Our eyes met briefly in a profound exchange of recognition. Then he looked me up and down, radiating with pride. His expression relaxed into a brilliant smile. Knowing I could elicit such radiant happiness left me breathless. Tonight was already going well.

The vampires around Caius fell silent, following the direction of his scrutiny to discover what held his rapt attention. Thereafter, the entire room watched me with hushed voices. I took a steadying breath, calming my fragile heart. Caius made me weak in every way, and yet, so powerful.

I descended the stairs, trailing my fingertips along the railing. All eyes followed me. Caius quickly excused himself to meet me at the bottom, sweeping me wordlessly into his arms with no care for his public display of affection.

"No wonder you wanted to keep this secret, Cece," he breathed. "You were trying to protect my now tortured heart." He placed his forehead against mine before setting me down. I took advantage of my pointe shoes to push myself closer to his face, lifting myself as high as possible. He held my hands cradled in his as he gazed down at me. "Your beauty hurts. How am I so lucky?" Like him, I forgot that we were surrounded by a room full of guests.

"*Who*, Caius, is this most stunning creature?" inquired a deep voice, smooth as chocolate liqueur. We turned. Standing behind Caius was a man of very dark skin dressed similar to Shahriar.

"Jafar, meet Celine. She is tonight's brightest star. Further-more, I boldly name her my greatest undoing."

"So, you have a weakness after all, eh, Caius?" Jafar's eyes sparkled as he looked from Caius to me. Then he reached for my hand, taking it to plant a kiss upon my knuckles. His eyes latched onto mine, boring into me with intense appraisal. I was used to the power of a vampire's gaze, so I did not look away. "Impressive," he said, releasing my hand. "Not many humans can look into the eyes of the great Jafar without quailing." I smiled, satisfied. "We are all eager for your performance tonight, Celine." Without another word, he slipped away into the crowd.

After Jafar, it was a whirlwind of confusing names and inter-ested guests. Many of them gave both Caius and I curious looks. Caius later said that it was because they weren't used to seeing him with a girlfriend by his side, let alone a human.

At last, Caius led me to the ballroom, which was already full of dancing couples. On cue, others followed us in, and as soon as the music ended, he took me to the middle of the room. The crowd cleared, stepping back to give us a wide berth. A profound hush fell, leaving only silence.

"Good evening." Caius's rich voice echoed from the walls. "Thank you all for joining us tonight. Anghor Manor is pleased, as am I, to host such *distinguished* guests." Polite applause followed. He squeezed my hand; I returned the gesture. "Many of you have heard the rumors: a talented ballerina has graced our halls. Tonight, she has willingly agreed to entertain us with not one, but *two* performances." There were a number of excited whoops, of which I was sure came from the vampires living in the manor, those who knew me well. I saw some of the girls gathered, each of them nearly unrecognizable. My eyes searched for Adel and found her in her burgundy gown. She gave me a huge smile and a discrete thumbs up.

"Without further ado, ladies and gentlemen, I introduce to you, Celine." The crowd murmured with excitement. Caius nodded a few times to acknowledge this before silencing them. "Her first number is—" He leaned down, whispering his inquiry into my ear. I answered quietly. "Her first number is *Cinderella*, from the famous *Cinderella* ballet. And—" Again he quietly inquired, whispering, "What is the second?" I gave him the name. "The second is *Seduction*, a ballet solo that, if I am not mistaken, she choreographed herself."

I nodded my confirmation. Cheers and clapping rang out into the ballroom as everyone welcomed me to my stage. I gazed around at my audience, finding myself surrounded by eager smiles.

Caius gave me a kiss on the cheek, whispering, "Good luck, my dear Celine," before moving away from me.

Like a wave, the crowd retreated further, leaving me a large space in the middle of the floor. I spent a moment flexing the arches of my feet. I never danced ballet without warming up, but Caius's blood would see me through. It almost felt like cheating.

Taking a dramatic pose in modified forth position *plie*, with one leg bent and the other held directly out in front of me, I waited for the orchestra. I'd already trained them for this cue. As expected, they took up their instruments. The ethereal sound of the first violin echoed into the hall, its tone bouncing gently from the walls and domed ceiling.

My face softened to reflect delicate tenderness, and I swept my arms downwards in front of me, spreading them wide before lifting them gracefully. My right leg followed, rising to my waist where it rotated into position behind me for a beautiful *arabesque*. Then I pulled my legs and arms downward to gather momentum. Dramatically, I rose onto my pointes, tiptoeing with finesse across the floor. The sounds of the other instruments followed me, slowly intertwining with the first violin.

I moved through the room portraying Cinderella, who at this point in the solo, had just arrived at the ball to introduce herself to the gallant prince. Guests gathered around to watch her dance, while her envious evil step sisters stood by angrily. I couldn't help but notice my setting was ever so realistic, minus the evil step sisters.

My crowd adored me. I could see the wonderment upon their faces. When you dance on stage the theater is dark, and you see nothing of your audience. Here, I saw everything.

I planned this solo to be the epitome of traditional ballet, cramming in complicated *fouetté* turns and jumps that would bring my piece to life. The best part was, I pushed myself without consequences. There was no pain from my left leg, no repercussions from jumping too high or over flexing my stretches. It was so good, it should have been illegal. If only ballerinas knew what vampire blood could do for their dancing.

As the music ended, the ballroom erupted into a chaos of clapping and whistles. I swept into a grand bow for my audience, and still, more cheers followed. Then I moved over to the orchestra to congratulate them on a number well played.

I would have been crazy to ruin my ball gown for my next solo, so I snuck out of the room for a moment. On cue, Adel met me. There I hid in a closet and quickly changed to my temporary, more contemporary outfit—a flesh colored leotard with a black chiffon wrap skirt. I wouldn't be dancing this solo in my pointes, so they remained in the closet with my gown. Instead, I wore cloth shoes. All set, I hurried back into the ballroom, ready to begin.

I named the piece *Seduction* for a reason. It was meant to seduce Caius, whether he put two and two together, I couldn't be sure. I think he did, considering the slight hesitation he made when announcing the name. I was dancing this for him alone.

With my light padded shoes secured, I moved back into the ballroom's center. The crowd clapped again to welcome me back. I smiled, curtsying with gratitude for their support. Then I took my position.

As the music started, I sank deeply into it, letting my body meld to the sounds of the instruments. Immediately, I felt the assuredness Caius spoke of. It claimed me, turning me into the sexiest version of myself. I moved my body seductively into each turn, making every leg lift alluring, and each pose tantalizing. As my body submitted to the melody, thoughts of Caius, his relentless desire for my blood, and my desperate need for fulfillment, erupted inside of me. It heightened my senses, drawing forth a most torturous temptress.

The voracious gaze of my audience stalked my every move, but there was one within the crowd wholly overcome by my directed assault. My lover watched me, entranced. He was locked firmly within my grasp, exactly where I wanted him.

The tempo of the music increased, prompting my first exciting stunt. I purposefully made eye contact with Caius, letting my regard impart upon him the deprived lust I felt. Then I moved quickly across my stage with increasing speed. I launched into a leap before throwing my body onto the floor with alluring hunger. The crowd gasped in excitement, unprepared for the sudden surprise.

As I crawled and danced, slithering along the marble tile, I knew I was afflicting Caius most tauntingly. At last, I lifted myself back onto my feet, and I glanced back over to my prey. I saw greed upon his face, and deep rooted lust.

I admit, this kind of dancing qualified more as contemporary jazz, than ballet. Many of the movements were done using the floor, and that added an unparalleled quality of sexiness. Thus, the reason for a different kind of attire.

The remainder of the solo was a frenzy of feeling and emotion, not just from me, but from Caius. He wore the same expression throughout, and for once, I knew exactly how to read him. As the music slowed, I knew that Ginger had delivered just as I'd hoped. I silently thanked her. Caius would never be able to resist me after such a show.

The crowd erupted into a tumult of praise and adoration. I took a sultry bow, studying their faces. Every one of them was aroused by my display. It would make for a most interesting night.

Caius rushed to me just as the orchestra took up a waltz. The crowd began to diffuse, filling the floor once more, chattering and laughing, many of them congratulating me in passing. They were impressed. I could hear it in their voices, and see it in their expressions. Several couples began to dance, motivated by the feelings I'd awoken in them.

"You temptress!" Caius swept me up into his arms laughing, spinning me around before setting me down and leaving me breathless. Then he guided me back to the closet where my gown hid. "You were beautiful."

"Thank you," I gasped, trying to breathe as we walked.

As soon as I emerged, once more Cinderella in my stunning gown, his smile greeted me. "Dance with me?"

I nodded taking his hand in mine as he lead me back to the dance floor. And so we danced, never once tearing our gaze from each other's. I couldn't have been prouder to be in his arms, circulating the ballroom in the breathless waltzes that followed. Caius was the finest vampire here. He was mine, and tonight, I wanted to be his. Completely.

CHAPTER 21

*T*here are moments in life so surreal, you find yourself having an out-of-body experience. The world around you begins to move in slow motion, and you no longer seem connected. This used to happen frequently while performing. It mostly occurred in front of my biggest crowds, theaters that seated thousands.

During these times, I would stand in the shadowed darkness of the stage's wings, preparing my psyche, flexing the arches of my feet, trying to breathe, all while attempting to control the adrenaline coursing through me. Not one bit of it felt real. And then, suddenly I would find myself on stage, dancing before an adoring audience. The world around me would blot out, and I would catch myself on the outside, as if watching my own body perform.

It's the strangest experience. I felt something very similar the night of the vampire ball, when I met someone I assumed to be long dead. We were well through the evening when Caius found me giggling with Adel. She'd just been dancing with Shahriar, and wanted to tell me every detail. He snuck up behind us, bringing our conversation to a halt. "Cece, It's time for your birthday present."

My face lit up. "But didn't you already give me my gift?" Was I to get another? Lucky me.

"Yes, but this is your *true* gift, the one most important to me. Come. There is someone I want you to meet. She has only just arrived."

He led me into the entry hall and brought me to a masked woman standing alone near the staircase. The first thing I noticed about this mysterious lady was her hair. It looked exactly like mine. As we approached, she removed the disguise covering her face to gaze upon us. I gawked at her with disbelieving eyes. It couldn't be. I knew this woman. I had seen many photos of her in black and white.

"Cece, I would like for you to meet Genevieve DuPont."

The woman stood silent for a moment, staring at me the same way I must have looked at her. This was one of those moments in life that can only be described as an out-of-body experience, and not simply because we were all but identical. It was surreal. Furthermore, there was no doubt in my mind she was a vampire.

"Cece?" she said in a heavy French accent just like *Grand-mère*. Her eyes traced my face then fell upon the pearl pin attached to my gown. "Mon dieu!" Hesitantly, she touched the pin that first belonged to her. Then she took between her fingers a lock of my hair.

"Caius?" She turned to him with utter disbelief. "Qu'est-ce que cela veut dire?" *What is the meaning of this?* "Dites-moi que ce n'est pas une blague malade!" *Tell me it is not a sick joke!*

*Grand-mère* had paid a pretty penny for my French tutors. It was important that I learn our native language. I spoke French fluently, though I am not sure Caius and Genevieve knew that.

Genevieve looked from me to Caius, very upset. *"When I last saw her she was safely in New York, dancing for the National Ballet. Now I find her in your clutches?"*

*"Much has happened, Genevieve, since you last paid your family a visit."* Caius answered back as though he'd been born French.

*"Explain!"* Genevieve demanded of him, failing to hide her anger. Her face was as red as her hair.

Caius explained how I was found with Thrax, how I was saved from certain death. Genevieve's face changed to one of shock. Despite Caius's best efforts however, Genevieve was still furious with him.

At last, it was time for me to interject. I put my many lessons to use. *"Please do not be angry with him, Genevieve. Caius and his vampires saved me from the rogues. They saved me from turning into a night-walker. I like it here. I am happy in my new life."* It took a moment for them to comprehend that I answered in French. Caius was certainly not expecting it. Genevieve looked pleased and proud.

At last, her face relaxed. Caius looked at me before his gaze settled on Genevieve. "I will leave the two of you to acquaint yourselves." He then took up my hand, kissing the knuckles the way a gentlemen ought. "You never cease to surprise me, my dear Cece. You speak French?" He smiled and shook his head before departing.

Genevieve and I toured the ballroom, walking in slow circles around the perimeter as we gazed upon the dancing couples. We had a lot to catch up on. Apparently, she had known of my existence since my birth, secretly checking in on our family from time to time, making sure that we were safe.

"I could never make myself known to you, dear," she explained in her heavy accent. "Part of becoming a vampire requires leaving your old life behind. The rules in place are meant to protect us. Besides, what would you have thought upon seeing your great grandmother stuck at the age of thirty-two?"

She was right, I wouldn't have believed it. "But what about *Grand-mère* Danielle? Your daughter?"

She sighed, squeezing my hand. "Hers is a sad story. She was the daughter I was never meant to have. I was young when I had her, many years before changing into a vampire. Once I did change, it became important to keep her at a distance. She hated me for it. I wanted to save her from the grief of abandonment that would soon come to pass. I knew I would have to let her go. After all, how could I explain the reason for my nonexistent aging? How could I show her that I would be young forever as she grew old and died? I did not want the life of a vampire for her. It was the only way."

"But why? Why did you choose to become a vampire in the first place if you had a daughter to look after?"

"Because of her father."

"Her father?"

"Yes. You see, in those days ballet was different—men were different. Well, some are still the same. But as a whole, it was a different time."

"What do you mean? Who was her father?"

"Her father was the artistic director of the Paris Opera

House, of the ballet company there. By no means was I the first girl he solicited himself to. Nor was I the last."

I processed her words, becoming disgusted. "He *raped* you?!" Her face darkened but she said nothing. "Genevieve, that's horrible!"

"Yes, well, he met his end."

"You—you killed him?" I looked at her with a newfound sense of admiration. A woman who could take revenge into her own hands was a fine lady indeed.

"Eventually, yes. It was an act frowned upon where vampires are concerned, but Caius made special circumstances for me."

"Wait, Caius?" What did he have to do with it?

"Oh yes, darling. Caius is the one who granted my immortality." Her words stunned me. How could it be? What had happened between the two of them? "He came to me when little Danielle was just thirteen. You see, ballet was nearing its height. Many humans and vampires alike took great interest in it. What could be more fragile, more delicate, than a ballerina? A ballerina has always been the epitome of grace since the days of King Louis XIII."

I was somewhat familiar with King Louis XIII. He was famous for making ballet into a matter of court during the early sixteen hundreds. He often danced the leading roles of his own ballets, going so far as to design the costumes. His interest in ballet was not merely frivolous. He made the act a matter of politics.

"Ballet is the epitome of beauty, dear, angelic in so many ways. You know this. Caius came to Paris eager to see what the fuss was about. In those days, I was in my prime."

Genevieve chuckled, growing reminiscent. "I was a true star of the stage, coveted by all when it came to parties and grand events."

"What happened? Did you guys? Did Caius—"

"Oh heavens, darling! Really? Me?" She appeared flattered by my suggestion. "No, I was never so lucky as to hold *his* affections, though he was fond of me."

"So, the two of you were never *intimate*? No sex or anything?" I would have been appalled had she said yes. Still, I needed to know for sure.

"*Sex*, darling?" She afforded me a look of kindness. "No."

I felt myself relax. I wouldn't have looked at Caius the same had she said yes.

"We vampires have *one* true desire. Caius is a vampire, he has no interest in sex. He derives pleasure from drinking blood."

Her words caught me off guard and left me thoughtful. Here I'd been entertaining the thought of making tonight special, of giving Caius my virginity. If he didn't care for sex, how could I seek something from him that he found little interest in? I pushed the displeasing realization from my mind, returning to Genevieve's story. "So, Caius turned you into a vampire?"

"Indeed, but it was contingent upon several things. He promised to provide me a means to seek revenge—revenge that I *so* desired—as long as I promised to follow the code of the vampires. I was more than willing. Besides, the code is not so bad. It is the only thing that distinguishes a vampire from a monster, from a rogue. But, he made one further request."

I stopped walking and turned to her, curious to know.

"He asked that I teach him ballet—probably out of boredom. I think he was eager to see if he had it in him."

"It was you?" I gasped, awestruck.

"Of course. I willingly complied, teaching him what I could and hiring male dancers to tutor him. Have you ever seen him dance, dear?"

I nodded, blushing.

She smiled. "He was my *most* devoted pupil, but that is neither here nor there. Come, tell me of your circumstances. Why are you *truly* here, Celine? If I know Caius, he has given you the option to return to your old life. Don't you miss ballet? Heavens, I certainly do."

I told her everything that happened since my injury. She listened intently, speaking at the right times. "Oh, that's terrible, dear." And, "Good for you, I'm sure Caius hated that!" It was almost like having *Grand-mère* back.

In the end, Genevieve admitted her surprise over how everything turned out. "As my great granddaughter, it is easy to see why Caius has taken an interest in you. But perhaps I speak out of bias." She fell silent. I watched her contemplative expression. "I can smell the scent of your blood. We DuPonts have always been strong blooded."

"Did he drink *your* blood?"

She shook her head. "Not for the sake of drinking. Only when it came time to change me." I was relieved.

We spent much of the ball together. Caius was nowhere to be seen, but I assumed he was socializing with his many connections—an important gesture since they were to be his allies in the fight against the rogues. Then, speak of the devil, he materialized before us.

"Caius, what's wrong?"

He looked upset. "Cece, Genevieve, I must leave the manor. A grave matter requires my attention."

"What can be the matter, Caius?" Genevieve asked.

"The rogues have set a large pack of night-walkers loose on the city."

"This is not another *diversion*?" Genevieve was referring to Sophie's death. I had already told her what happened.

Caius shook his head. "Not this time. I'm taking a number of my guards. Can I trust you to keep her safe, Genevieve?" Caius motioned in my direction.

"No harm will come to my own flesh and blood under my watch."

I could tell Caius disliked leaving me tonight of all nights, as it was my birthday. "I'm sorry, Celine. I did not wish for tonight to go this way." He took my face into his hands and gave me a gentle kiss.

"Please, Caius, be careful!" Apprehension latched itself onto my tummy.

"Always," he said. Then he took his leave, and I was left to finish out the ball without him.

# CHAPTER 22

*I* never danced the *Sleeping Beauty* ballet, yet the story always appealed to the romantic in me. A cursed princess who can only wake with her true love's kiss, must lay in wait. When her prince does come to her rescue, she wakes from her slumber helplessly in love. She is changed.

I wonder what it must have been like, opening her eyes to find a handsome man standing over her. Was there any recollection of the kiss they'd shared? Did she realize what it meant? I suppose in some ways I was like Aurora. Caius's first kiss awoke within me new possibilities, a new life, but that didn't mean I comprehended what it meant. And when Caius was forced to leave the vampire ball early to defend innocent people against night-walkers, I was almost relieved.

Genevieve opened my eyes. She helped me realize something I'd failed to consider. Vampires were creatures of blood. Blood fueled their passions, fulfilled their needs, and satiated their appetites. I spent the entire night hoping for an ending that seemed silly in the grand scheme of things. Yet, perhaps my prince wasn't as predictable as I believed...

Long after the vampire ball ended, while I slept, Caius came to me. Maybe he swept into my room the way Aurora's true love did. Although, he probably didn't sneak into her bed in the middle of the night for an alluring midnight rendezvous. At first, I thought perhaps I was dreaming. I soon became aware of the warmth of his lips upon mine, kissing me insistently, willing me to awaken from my slumber. A more pleasant way to wake could not be had.

His body stretched along mine, leaning against me. "I need you, Celine," he whispered against my lips, "I need you now..." He coaxed me from my sleepy fog the way the prince coaxed Aurora. I could sense his hunger—his desperation. "Wake up," he said before burying his nose in my hair.

"Caius, what—what happened?" I mumbled. "Are you okay?" He reeked of smoke. Had there been a fire? My worry ran away with itself. He'd never come to me like this.

His next words left me alert. "I need to feed. I am weak, Celine. Help me..."

"Weak? Caius, what's going on?"

He pawed at me, taking my nightgown into his clenched fist as he nudged my neck with his nose. "Please. Now, Celine." He avoided my questions.

At last, I nodded into the darkness, giving myself to him. I remained apprehensive. He swiftly pulled back the covers and slid beneath them, positioning himself atop my body, effectively pinning me. My gut clinched. I was immediately placated as I wrapped my arms about him. Perhaps he was simply hungrier than usual.

His fangs sank into my neck. I felt the familiar sting of his teeth. It lasted but a moment. Then he groaned almost at once, echoing his satisfaction as he relaxed against me. His weight was nearly too much. But I was distracted by the waves of intoxication already assaulting me. Each drag of blood greedily taken left me gasping. The burn of desire engulfed me.

Caius drank deeply, growling with enjoyment, twisting his fingers into my hair, pushing his hips against mine. He moved with tantalizing promise. I became keenly aware of the hardness of his length pressed against my thighs. I realized then that I was desperate for it—for him—for release.

"*Please*, Caius…" I whispered. If I didn't find relief this time, it would be torture.

He shifted his weight to the side of my body. The intensity of his pulls decreased, eventually slowing to a stop. I felt his teeth leave my neck, yet the onslaught continued. The sensation within my core was reaching unprecedented levels as the precipice of my passion increased. This time it was different. His hand was between my legs offering me the end I craved.

I opened my eyes briefly, questioningly. Caius's face hovered over mine. "Let go, Celine," he whispered urgently against my lips before taking them in his mouth. His tongue probed, finding my own.

His palm pressed against my body's most sensitive spot, massaging in circles, bringing forth raptures of desire, while his fingers pushed into me, quickening my undoing. My back arched away from the bed; I could no longer control myself. I cried out as the pounding in my core exploded, transporting me into a realm of exultation. Nothing else in the world existed except Caius, myself, and the bed that hosted us.

It was mesmerizing bliss. Caius kissed me as I drifted down from euphoria. I don't know why, but the moment I was able to speak again, I felt the need to thank him—perhaps because he'd given me something no one else ever had.

"Do not thank me for such a thing, Celine. I love touching you."

"But you wanted to, right? You didn't simply do it because it was—was needed?" My mind raced back to the conversation I had only hours earlier with Genevieve. Was sex a bother?

"Of course I wanted to, my sweet little bird." His fingers, I realized, were still in me. As if to make a statement, he stroked me there, bringing forth a soft cry from my lips. "If I didn't like being here, I wouldn't be." Then he slowly removed them. I felt strangely emptier. He playfully rubbed his nose against mine. "Did you like it?"

"Yes," I giggled.

"Excellent," he purred. "I like that I can make you feel good."

"It felt *really* good," I eagerly breathed. *Good* was an understatement.

"I thought so. Now, let's change the subject to one I haven't yet discussed with you."

"Oh, okay." I wasn't expecting his abruptness.

"Your dance tonight, Celine."

"My dance?" I whispered in confusion. His lips were still inches from mine, and I could hardly talk or think with him hovering over me.

"Yes, your dance, Celine. *Seduction* you called it. Fitting name."

"I thought so." I smiled against his lips.

He continued as if I hadn't spoken. "*Seduction* doesn't adequately reflect the torture you inflicted upon me, does it? That performance should have been mine *alone*."

"Yours?" I breathed.

"Yes, Celine. Mine." His hand moved to the back of my leg where he gripped my thigh tightly, pulling me against him. "I have half a mind to cancel Ginger's performances henceforth after that sexy little stunt you pulled—torturing me in front of an entire room of people, knowing they were watching, same as me."

Cancel Ginger's performances? "You wouldn't!"

"No, I wouldn't, not unless I want to submit myself to your wrath." He chuckled. "I suppose at the end of the day, it is my mouth that feeds from you, and my body that pleases you."

I'd never been spoken to with such passion. I hardly knew what to say. I did know that I wouldn't have minded more of his fingers, which wouldn't stop sneaking beneath the elastic of my panty line. He was doing it on purpose. If I didn't change the subject quickly, I was going to find myself consumed with renewed passion. I caught up his taunting fingers in my hand, lacing them through mine.

"Caius, tell me what happened earlier. Why did you come to me like this? You said you were weak. Was it the night-walkers?"

He groaned reluctantly, clearly not in the mood to talk about it, but that didn't cut it for me. "Is everything okay?"

He put his nose against my hair, kissing my ear. "It is now."

"Well yeah, now that you have my blood. But it wasn't before that."

He was quiet for a little while, laying his head on the pillow beside mine. I didn't push him any further. I waited patiently. At last he spoke. "When we arrived, the night-walkers were already rampaging the inner city. People were screaming and running. There were dead bodies scattered about."

I inhaled sharply. The picture in my mind was one of horror in a zombie apocalypse kind of way. I could tell by his voice that things didn't go well.

"We began staking night-walkers in the heart, trying to minimize casualties. Keenan—he was new to our ranks. He got distracted, overwhelmed. There were strong-blooded among the victims. He couldn't resist. I managed to pull him away from one, but I let my guard down." He shook his head in dismay. "At that moment, the rogues attacked us."

"No!" I gasped.

"Keenan died." There was remorse in his voice for the loss of one of his own. "We took the bodies out into the hills and burned them."

"Caius, I'm so sorry." I wrapped my arm around him. "Was it the fighting that made you weak?"

"Yes. I was wounded twice, but your blood has made me strong again. The fighting took much from me."

"My blood makes you strong?"

"You are strong-blooded. Your blood gives me a new kind of strength I'm unaccustomed to. I might go so far as to call it my own form of heroin."

His words made me feel special. I loved that I could give him something to make him stronger the way he did me. Most of all, I loved that he needed me.

After a few minutes of thoughtful silence, he changed the subject. "What about the ball, Celine? Did you enjoy your time with your great grandmother?"

"Yes, I did. Caius, I didn't get a chance to thank you. Genevieve has been the best birthday present. She reminds me so much of *Grand-mère*. Thank you."

"You're welcome."

"How long did you know she was my relation?"

"Since the pearl pin incident. The moment I beheld it, I knew. In truth, I should have recognized it immediately. The two of you are nearly identical in looks, not to mention personality."

"You knew for that long? Why didn't you tell me?" I was a bit surprised, and even a little annoyed. Months had passed since the pin incident in his study.

"I wanted her to come to you. That was the true reason for the ball, Celine. I knew it was the only way to get her out of her nest—the only way to persuade her to make the journey. I wanted you to see her in person before saying anything. I doubt you and Genevieve would have believed me otherwise. You are headstrong and stubborn—the both of you."

"I'm not stubborn!" I playfully slapped his arm. He made a sound of disagreement. "Caius, do you think..."

"Hm?"

"Do you think if she wants, she can stay with us for a little bit? Just so that I can spend some time with her."

"I think that would be a fantastic idea." He squeezed his arms around me with reassurance. "In fact, I was hoping you would want her to."

"I do." I cuddled my head into the nape of his neck, sighing contentedly, then I fell asleep.

When I woke the following morning, I was alone. My sleep was deep. I was left wondering if the night had been a dream, a delicious, tantalizing dream. If so, it was the best I ever had. I wonder if Aurora would have questioned things too, had the prince disappeared after his kiss.

I found Caius that afternoon in his study, deep in discussion with several vampires, Shahriar included. Jafar marched over to me with his usual air of importance. I should have been turned-off by his overly proud nature, but somehow it reminded me of Caius. I liked his confidence, it was reassuring.

"As-salaam alaikum, Celine." He greeted me with familiarity. "I never got to congratulate you on your spectacular perfor- mance. If ever you are in Arabia, you must come to my palace. Your presence will honor us, and we will treat you like the ballerina queen that you are." He then took my hand, kissed my knuckles, and left the room.

I heard Caius whispering; he was shooing the others away. Moments later, I found the room empty. He came to me.

"I probably don't need to say it, but you are a favorite among my guests, Jafar especially."

I gave him a pleased smile. "Does he really have a palace in Arabia?"

"*Saudi* Arabia. We vampires have trouble keeping with the times. And he does, a very fine palace at that. There are peacock statues made of solid gold littering the garden to his private quarters. I myself have seen them. Perhaps you and I should pay him a visit someday?"

"I would love that!"

He gave me an affectionate kiss on my forehead. "So, Celine, to what do I owe the pleasure of your company this afternoon?"

"Oh, I just wanted to tell you that I had the most spectacular dream last night." I stretched cat-like, my dress tightening across my chest.

His eyes followed. "Did you? What was it about?"

"I dreamt about this mysterious vampire who came to me while I slept. He was *so* handsome, with silver eyes that glowed. His hair was thick and shaggy, black as night, and sexy. His body—I've never seen someone so well endowed. Anyway, let's just say, he quenched my thirst better than water could have."

"And you certainly quenched his." He swept me into his arms, planting a gentle kiss on my lips.

"It wasn't a dream, was it?"

"No, Celine. It wasn't."

Thank goodness! Wrapping my arms about his waist, I pressed myself against him and exhaled noisily. Satisfied, I changed the subject. "I hope I didn't interrupt your meeting. Was it important?"

"It was," he confirmed. "But you didn't interrupt—we were just finishing up."

"What was it about?" I never involved myself in his business. I never asked him for information. What I knew, I knew because he willingly told me. But with the increase in attacks, I was growing anxious.

"Jafar has picked up a solid lead on the leader of the rogues."

"Their leader?"

"Yes. We may have a way of locating the one responsible for this whole mess."

"That's fantastic news!" The sooner he put a stop to everything, the quicker we could get to spending more time together, and me not stressing about him running off into the night injuring himself.

"That was the good news first."

"There's bad news?" My skin prickled with unease.

"I must part from you, Celine. The answers I seek lie away to the north, in Russia. I may be gone for some weeks, but I will try to hurry."

"You're leaving?" I dropped my arms from his waist, entirely dismayed. I tried to hide my upset, because I knew he needed to do this, but my heart hurt to know of it. How things had changed. Three months prior, and I would have been cheering. "Can't someone else go for you?"

"It must be me. I leave the day after tomorrow." He took my arms, which hung limply at my sides, and wrapped them back around his waist. "I'm sorry little bird. I do not *wish* to go, but I must."

I nodded, trying my hardest to appear resigned rather than heartbroken. He took my head in his hands and kissed me gently. It was a sad kiss, but meaningful. It held promise. He would return. Everything would be okay in the end. I simply needed to abandon the mounting worry in my heart. Something big was coming—something dangerous. We needed to be ready.

# CHAPTER 23

*A*t the end of every ballet, the cast participates in what is called a *curtain call*. This is our opportunity to come out on stage for the last time and bid our audience *adieu*. We bow and wave, they clap. In the end, it is bittersweet; after a job well done, we must take our leave.

When I left New York City bound for London, bag packed full of train tickets from my father, it was nothing like a curtain call. Saying goodbye to my family was the hardest thing I did next to quitting ballet. It was tough seeing my mom tearful. My dad struggled too, but he hid his emotion well. My little brother Austin took it the hardest. He didn't come to the airport to see me off. Instead, he shut himself up in his bedroom, angry at me for leaving him. None of that made things easy for me. I was already reluctant as it was.

Saying goodbye to Caius was just as difficult. The time leading up to his departure for Russia rushed by quickly. Before I knew it, I found myself alone in his study with no more than the echoes of our parting—our goodbye kiss in the entry hall, his whispered reassurances. With him gone, my brave face had long dissipated. I didn't feel so brave anymore.

Many evil thoughts crept through my mind. What if something happened to him? What if he never came back? With the increasing boldness from the rogues, I had good reason to worry. Yet, I didn't want to look weak, so I kept myself composed.

In the days following, Genevieve was a godsend. Not only had she agreed to remain in Anghor Manor for some time watching over me in Caius's stead, she facilitated preparations for my auditions with the Royal Vienna Ballet. It helped to have a cheerleader who understood what I was going through. She was a fantastic instructor. The best part was, she threw on a pair of pointe shoes and went through many of the exercises with me. I could see the same love of ballet I felt, mirrored within her. That alone bridged a deeper connection between us than the commonality of our blood.

Despite her true age, she was young and very much alive. I loved her fun, playful nature. I also understood her quite well. Caius was right, she was very much like me both with her headstrong personality, and her stubbornness.

A few days after we'd been working together, she stopped me in the middle of a declaration. "Why don't you call me *Gigi*, darling. Genevieve is too stuffy." In spite of being my great grandmother, she was beginning to feel more like a sister the way Adel and the other girls were.

Adel would often sit in the ballroom watching us, cheering us on. She even joined us at the barre for warm-up exercises. She caught on quick. Much to my surprise, the other girls in the house began sneaking in to watch. By the end of the first week, we had a full audience. All of them wanted to learn, and Gigi was thrilled to have pupils again. Needless to say, we had to order more ballet barres, leotards, and shoes. But it was fun, and their company helped pass the time.

I quickly learned from Adel that I wasn't the only one missing someone. She had formed an attachment to the *Arabian Knight*, as I liked to call him. She giggled every time I did. Shahriar was taken with her as well. He and Jafar had accompanied Caius to Russia. As it turned out, Jafar and Shahriar were cousins by blood. I was glad that Caius hadn't gone alone.

"I have not felt such passion, Cece," Adel told me one evening in her bedroom, practically swooning over her own words. We were sitting together while I taught her how to sew pointe shoes. I was going through pairs faster than ever before. She stuck her needle into its pincushion and looked at me. "Cece, after the ball, Shahriar and me..."

"What happened after the ball?" She had my full attention. I wondered if she had a similar happy ending like the one Caius had given me. My cheeks burned the moment I considered it.

"I let him drink my blood."

"And?!"

A slow smile spread across her face. "He like it! He ask if he can come next night."

We both giggled in delight. "You said yes, didn't you?" I asked. She nodded. "What happened then?"

"We kissed."

"Oh my gosh, Adel!" I tossed a throw pillow directly at her face. She caught it up, still laughing.

"I really like him, Cece."

"Wait! Did you guys"—my voice changed to an excited whisper—"have *sex*?" Her grin turned mischievous. "Adel!" I shrieked at the top of my lungs. "You guys had sex and you've waited five days to tell me this?"

After that, I demanded she tell me every single detail. She willingly did so, but not without significant giddiness and blushing. We were at that stage in our friendship where we could tell each other anything, and I mean anything. The best part was, before coming to Anghor Manor, I never had a friend like Adel, and now, I had the best kind a girl could want.

Sure, I had ballet friends, girls I saw on a daily basis, and sometimes spent time with in the evenings. Since ballet was our number one priority—and ballerinas are always the competitive type—we could never reach the level of friendship Adel and I had attained. I loved Adel for that.

After she went through each of my questions in the painstaking detail I required, I couldn't help but complain about my own predicament. "I'm seriously the only virgin in the manor," I half laughed, half grumbled. "I need to get a move on."

"Oh, Cece. Nothing wrong with being virgin."

"Yes there is." I fell silent. Was she right? Was there anything wrong with it? The real reason my virginity bothered me was because it made me feel young, almost childlike. I saw virginity as the barrier between being a girl and being a woman. It's kind of stupid, I know. Considering Caius's old age (he still hadn't told me how old), I wanted to be as much of a woman as possible.

Still, Adel didn't see anything wrong with it. "You just need right time," she said. I supposed she was correct. I was waiting for the perfect time—the perfect moment. "Beside, Caius love you. He make it special for you."

"He's never *said* that he loves me."

"But he love you, Cece." She grinned cutely. "I see it in his eye."

Her reassurances felt good, especially because I missed Caius so much. Fortunately, I got to hear his voice every once in a while. He didn't use his phone much; he told me that he needed to keep a low profile. When he could, he called Felix. We only got to speak for a few minutes, but those short instances made all the difference in the world.

When there was less than a week to go before my audition, he called. "Will you be back in time?" I asked, gripping Felix's iPhone tightly, nervous for his response.

"I am trying, Celine. Tomorrow night—if everything goes according to plan—will be our final day here."

"Okay," I whispered into the speaker, hopeful. "Caius, please be careful." I always told him to be careful.

"I will, Cece. I promise."

For the next few days I stayed positive, but the night before auditions, my mood plummeted. Caius still hadn't returned; Felix had no news. I know that the saying goes, *no news is good news*. In this case, it didn't seem like good news to me.

"Dear Celine," Gigi said to me that night in my room, "you must get your head under control. You know how much the mind influences the body. How can you dance tomorrow weighted down by such worries?"

She was with me under the pretense of helping me pack my dance bag, but really, she was trying to offer me moral support. I appreciated her company. "Did you get your extra leotard, dear?"

I had. She handed me a third one anyway, so I stuffed it into my bag.

"What about at least *two* pairs of toe shoes? Have you prepared extras just in case? And you borrowed Adel's sewing things to take with you?"

"I've got them all. I sewed four pairs last night watching *Vampire Diaries* with Adel."

"Oh dear! You don't watch that nonsense, do you?"

"What? I do! We like laughing at all the inaccuracies. Besides, Stefan and Damon? So hot."

She smirked. "I suppose I'll never understand today's youth. Now, let's talk about the ballet director. I've only heard snippets about him, but from what I gather, he has a weakness for graceful poise."

"Don't they all?"

"If the judges allow you to embellish the choreography, cater to the director's preferred style. Royal Vienna Ballet is *very* into contemporary right now. Keep that in mind."

"I know, Gigi," I groaned. "You've told me like a hundred times."

She chuckled. "I shall probably tell you again before you go into auditions tomorrow."

"Why don't you just try out with me?" I was partly joking and partly serious.

She laughed with feigned shyness. "Really, darling, me? Audition? At my age? Bah!"

"Come on, Gigi. You're what, thirty-two *forever*? But you dance better than any young prima I've ever seen."

"Oh stop it! Besides, I have no portfolio. What shall I tell them, dear? That I danced with the Paris Opera House in 1922?"

"Okay, point taken."

She smiled sweetly. "Ballet is your thing, Celine. I've passed my torch on to you. Did you remember to pack your pearl pin?"

"Yes. It's here." I showed her where I'd carefully tucked it away. It was my lifeline, that pin.

"Good. Then I think you are all ready for tomorrow."

I hoped so. Most of all though, I hoped Caius would be there.

## CHAPTER 24

When I first auditioned for the National Ballet, I was only sixteen, one of the youngest ballerinas they'd seen. Strangely enough, I had a bright-burning confidence that made me think I was ready for anything. How silly I'd been, small town girl coming to the big city. It was then that I was exposed to the real world of ballet. The rawness chafed me.

Girls can be cutthroat in the ballet world. They want to see their competitors fail, especially in auditions. Each of them smiles whilst secretly scorning your every move, whether out of envy or pure meanness, or both. In the end, I made it. I managed to hide my timidity and push through, landing myself the youngest ever company position in corps.

This time though, as I faced the Royal Vienna Ballet, I was ready. I knew what to expect. There was no stopping me.

I was up before dawn on the morning of auditions. Caius still hadn't returned, so Felix, Gigi, and Julia escorted me to the

Vienna Opera House. "We will wait for you here, Cece," Julia said, standing in the big entry hall.

I knew they were there to guard me, to make sure I stayed safe. It seemed a little extreme. What could possibly happen to me during auditions? After the night-walker scare a few months back, Caius took no chances. At any rate, I was happy to know they were there waiting for me.

In total, there were thirty females and thirty males participating in the morning portion of auditions. We began at barre, as is always the case, and we were each given a number to pin to our leotards.

This segment of auditions is always the easiest. You are expected to demonstrate perfect technique in your barre exercises. An instructor leads you through various warm-ups beginning with *pliés* and *tendus.* The time is used to prepare you for what comes next. On a regular training day, the morning always starts this way, so it makes sense to run auditions in the same style.

By the end of the two-hour session, ten males and ten females were dismissed as a judge silently walked among us. After this, we moved the barres aside to do floor work. These were the drills I'd been preparing for—fancy footwork and jump sequences across the floor. They are fast paced with only few minutes of rest in between each set. If you're not constantly breathless, then you are doing them wrong, but heaven forbid you show any signs of this breathlessness.

Every single moment of our performance was judged by a panel of judges set up at the front of the room. We went in groups of four. The pianist at his bench continued the melody without stopping. Neither did we. By the end of the morning, more hopefuls were cut.

I already knew I was on par with everything. I hit every movement with precision. Each turn across the floor, every jump sequence, each graceful pose, the judges watched me with impassive faces. That was a good sign. When they saw something displeasing from a dancer, they held nothing back. Two of the younger girls had already run crying from the room. I pitied them, having once been in their shoes.

By the end of the session, my competitors began throwing me looks of sheer envy. I didn't blame them. After all, I jumped a small fraction higher than everyone else; I turned a bit more gracefully; I displayed no discomfort after hours of pointe work.

I do not want you to think my work was easy. I wasn't impervious to pain or fatigue. Yet, Caius's blood certainly made me stronger. Even after nearly three weeks without him, the faint traces of it hadn't left me. And so, I pushed myself harder because of it, compensating such that I still felt strained.

We were given an hour for lunch. I eagerly rushed down to the lobby to tell the others of my good fortune.

"That's wonderful news, darling." Gigi swept me up in a big hug. I could tell she was proud of me.

"I believe I too have good news, Cece." Felix held out his phone. "Caius," he answered my questioning gaze.

I hungrily snatched up the phone, breathless. "Caius? I've been so worried! Is everything okay? You're safe?"

"Take a breath, Cece," Caius answered. Oh, how I'd missed that velvety rich voice. "Everything is well. I am safe. As a matter of fact, I'm heading your way this very moment."

"My way?" It took a minute to register his meaning. "To my

auditions?"

"Mm-hmm." He sounded very relaxed—opposite to how I felt. "Jafar is driving. We are about an hour and a half from Vienna. We will be there as soon as we can. I will be waiting in the lobby with the others."

Sweet relief flooded my body and the strain on my muscles calmed. I hadn't realized how perpetually tense I'd become on account of his absence. "I'm so glad you're okay, Caius. I was—I was really worried. Anyway, I only have a little bit of time for my lunch break, and then I have to go back."

"Everything is going well, I take it?"

"Yes." I proceeded to tell him every detail about the morning session. Our conversation lasted fifteen minutes. It was the longest one we'd had since his departure. My mood was completely altered afterward. Caius was alive and well. I could finally relax and focus one hundred percent on my performance.

The break went quickly after talking to Caius. I told the others how I'd done so far—they were eager for comparative information regarding other dancers. Before I knew it, I was back upstairs warming up. Only now, I was impatient to get through this portion simply for the sake of seeing Caius. Although these auditions were important to me, I couldn't help but notice how I was more excited by his return than by the opportunity to audition with the Royal Vienna Ballet.

"Congratulations everyone." The director stood before us as we sat scattered about the floor stretching. "You should commend yourselves for making it this far." I was impressed by his perfect English. "However, you have a long way to go yet. This portion of your auditions will be the most rigorous. We only have three company positions to fill in corps this year, one male, and two female. We cannot guarantee that any of you will be up to our standards. These openings do not promise you anything. If none of you has what we are looking for, the positions will go unfilled."

Everyone whispered, looking around. I kept my mouth shut. I didn't know any of my fellow competitors. I'd learned very early on in my career that one was better off keeping to one's self. Focus was key.

"Our brilliant choreographers will teach you a piece now. You will have one hour to learn it. After that, we will begin calling you into the audition room individually. If we like you, if you have potential, then you will be asked to remain in the hallway while the others have their turn. At the end of the day, we will make our decision."

More whispers followed.

When we began, I was very happy that Gigi had warned me of Royal Vienna Ballet's preference towards contemporary over traditional. I focused a lot more on contemporary technique in my preparations. This piece was a mix of traditional and contemporary, set to Chopin's *Nocturnes*.

The start was full of *pirouettes*, and *arabesques*. Not so for the middle and end. Those portions changed quickly, requiring an immense display of flexibility. I was eager to test my limits.

At the beginning of the melody the motions were delicate, requiring the dancer to take up a fragile ballerina bravura. Then they followed the evolution of tone on the piano, becoming more raw and primal, more contemporary. By the end, there wasn't a shred of traditional ballet left. Rather, exotically exaggerated movements requiring tightly trained muscles and flexibility.

I loved the piece immediately. In every movement, I found connections that brought the correct emotions to my surface. That's what dance is all about—emotion. It's about finding ways to connect yourself to every instance of your storytelling. I was growing quickly confident in each of my movements as my body memorized the choreography.

An hour is not very long to prepare. The individuals who were to perform near the end of the afternoon had the biggest advantage. One by one, our numbers were called in no particular order. As I waited, I continued to run through the piece with muted movements, quietly counting and coaching myself through it. Many were doing the same. At last, I resigned myself to a corner of the room for a few minutes of peace.

As I sat there watching my competition, my mind's focus waned. I couldn't stop thinking of Caius. Was he downstairs yet? Weeks had passed since I'd had any of his blood. Try as I might, I couldn't sense his presence.

It surprised me how much I missed him, how much I'd worried about him while he was away. The last few weeks of longing made clear to me how much I cared for him, how much he meant to me. I was left pondering all the many changing feelings I experienced over the last four months. I'd gone from hating his guts to loving them. Did I though? Did I love him?

Love was a foreign concept for me. Certainly I loved my family, but I'd never loved anyone besides. Frankly, I was more than a little scared by the possibility.

"Number forty-two?" My heart jolted.

"That's me." I jumped to my feet and grabbed my dance bag. The woman who led me down the hall was kind-faced and well past her prime. She held a clipboard with all our names, and waddled as she walked.

There were several men and women—contract hopefuls—loitering around the corridor. Some of them whispered to each other as I passed. It seemed that they had all performed adequately enough, else they would not have been asked to remain in the hallway.

"Just through here, dear. And good luck."

Within moments, I was ushered into a large, mirrored room. Ballerinas are obsessed with mirrors. We can gaze upon ourselves as we dance and re-establish our self-worth.

At the front of the room stood a table seating five people. The director stood off to the side, leaning casually against the mirrored wall as he scrutinized me. I judged him to be in his early fifties. He had good skin with minimal worry lines, and was very physically fit. Clearly he had danced when he was younger.

"Good afternoon, Ginger DuPont." One of the female judges greeted me. The others remained silent. They looked rather bored. I didn't blame them. They'd already seen at least twenty dancers.

Ginger DuPont had a good ring to it. I had taken a fake name as per Caius's suggestion. Gigi was flattered when I asked if I could use her surname. Caius didn't want me to risk exposing my true identity.

I set my dance bag in the corner of the room and went to stand before my panel.

"It says here that you danced with the National Ballet in America for a few years. We could not find any record of your having danced there. Please explain."

I cleared my throat. "That is correct. I danced with the National Ballet for four years, ma'am. Since moving to Europe, I changed my name for my own protection."

"I see," said the same woman with a deal of hesitance. She did not push the subject further. I was ready to explain an elaborate story about a witness protection program should she have asked.

"You began ballet at the age of"—she looked down at her fact sheet—"eight years old. Is that correct?"

I nodded.

"And you're twenty-three?"

"Yes, ma'am." There were a few whispers of approval. The other judges didn't have my portfolio in front of them, but they sounded pleased. I told them nothing of my earlier injury and how it crippled my career. My dancing would not reflect my past afflictions anyway.

"Very well. While we have no proof of your previous experience beyond your word, what matters to us today is how you dance your solo. We have looked over your scores from this morning—very promising." She glanced at a few of the judges before continuing. "You outscored most of the others."

I silently rejoiced.

"When you are ready, dear, you may begin."

Rolling my shoulders a few times in circles and loosening my neck muscles, I lifted my right foot onto pointe, taking up my starting position. Then I glanced up at the director; his face was impassive. Only then did I give him a brief nod. I was ready.

# CHAPTER 25

*S*elf-confidence is a ballerina's enemy. I'm most sure of myself when I dance. Even then, I'm constantly comparing my abilities to those around me. When I auditioned for the National Ballet, I started off with bright assurances, but after I saw my competition, all bets were off. Let's face it, at sixteen, the chance of landing a position with a company like the National Ballet was virtually impossible.

Fast-forward six years. At twenty-three, even with a healthy body made whole by Caius's blood, I still didn't bank on getting into the Royal Vienna Ballet. I had a great chance, but there was still that little voice in the back of my mind planting seeds of doubt.

At the end of auditions, as I thundered down the stairs into the lobby, I found myself pleasantly surprised. I saw the group of familiar faces long before I reached the bottom landing. I was so happy to have their support. Caius was there too. My heart leapt a little higher.

They turned to me, their expressions eager, ready for the

verdict I was to deliver. Caius didn't hesitate. He strode towards me with his long gait. "I got the contract!" I called to him as I closed the distance between us, nearly running. He smiled widely. The moment I reached him, he swept me up into his arms and lifted me off the ground in a huge bear hug. It made up for all the hugs I'd gone without over the last few weeks.

"Caius, I actually got it! I can hardly believe it," I cried with what little breath I had left.

"I am so proud of you. There was never any doubt in my mind." He twirled me in a circle before setting me down to kiss me. The others kept their distance, giving us a moment to reunite.

Shortly after, I was congratulated by all my vampire friends. "We never doubted you for a minute," they said, patting my back. "I'd better phone home." Felix winked at me. "Adel made me promise to call and let everyone know." He stepped away for a few minutes.

I wore my goofy grin for the entire drive home. Caius and I rode with Jafar and Shahriar, sitting in the back seat holding hands. They demanded every detail about my audition. My cheeks hurt from smiling so hard as I relived the excitement.

As soon as we walked through the front door of Anghor Manor, I was greeted by a loud cheer. "Surprise!" everyone shouted simultaneously. Adel tackled me, both laughing and crying. "I knew you get it, Cece! I knew it!"

Not only was the entire house downstairs in the entryway, but many vampires who did not reside in the manor had also arrived to join the fun. Everyone was eager to congratulate me. It was the perfect way to celebrate. In those moments, I had never felt so genuinely loved and appreciated.

There was a huge red banner with white lettering hanging from the second floor landing that said, *congratulations*, in bold. It seemed that the girls planned on me getting in. They'd prepared an entire party for the occasion, organizing this festivity with the *expectation* that I would make it. That kind of certainty, the confidence they had in me, was moving.

Not long after the party started, a pizza delivery guy stopped by to deliver *sixty* pizzas. He had them piled in his trunk and back seats. We all stuffed our faces and got drunk on champagne. By that time, after everyone demanded repeatedly to see my audition solo, I had no reservations.

I dramatically circled the floor, appreciating the support of my friends who had become more like family. Such a thing should never be taken lightly. I rejoiced in each *pirouette*, and relished in every *arabesque*; I delighted in jump after jump, savoring the new life I'd been blessed with. I pushed my flexibility, cheered on by *oohs* and *aahs*. When I reached the more contemporary parts, I heard Gigi loudly declare, "See? I told her they *love* contemporary. I'm so glad I could help her prepare." Goodness, Gigi was amazing; I was glad to have her.

Some of my greatest thoughts happen when I dance. It was in this time that I realized I was happier than I could remember. My future was filled with bright hope. I was going to work my way to the top of the ballet ladder with renewed fervor. I had more potential than ever. Not only that, Caius and I were falling in love. The prospect of sharing a happy life with him, possibly forever, set me free. This liberation seeped into my dancing, flowing forth for all to see.

I was truly becoming a new person—a better person than I'd ever been. The combination of Cece and Ginger was an unstoppable force within me, one that would carry me into any circumstance. Knowing that was worth more than all the riches in the world.

When my solo ended, there were simultaneous cheers and groans. "Give us another," someone shouted. "Come on, Cece!" someone else called.

"Now, now," I said, taking a very similar tone to how Caius usually mock-scolded me. "I'm a contracted dancer now, remember? You'll all just have to buy tickets to the Vienna Opera House if you want to watch me live."

I rushed over to Caius, breathless and eager to be in his arms. I half giggled half hiccupped, full of champagne, as he ran a finger along my neck.

"I want you to myself," he growled. We quietly crept away as the party continued. Halfway to my room, he swept me up and carried me the remainder of the way. With all the special treatment I was receiving, I felt like a princess. I wasn't used to this kind of spoiling.

Once in my room, Caius tossed me playfully onto my bed. I righted myself and scooted up against the pillows. He watched me as he kicked off his shoes. I'd already ditched mine in the entryway to perform my solo.

"I missed you, Celine." He moved around to the foot of the bed. There he stood gazing at me for several moments while he unbuttoned the top three buttons of his black dress shirt.

"I missed you too, Caius." My heart rate increased. We were alone. We hadn't seen each other in weeks. He was hungry for my blood. I was hungry for him. It was a dangerous combination. Only, I still wasn't sure if this was *the moment*.

He climbed onto the bed and crawled towards me on all

fours. His movements were primal as he ravished me with his gaze. My body was already clenching in anticipation. Stopping in the middle of the bed, he grabbed up my ankles and pulled them, causing me to slide towards him in one fluid motion. Then he laid his body atop mine and began kissing my chest, my neck, my jawbone.

I was still in my leotard, so I felt every touch of his hands on the fabric. "Mmm, this one-piece *what-cha-ma-call-it* is quite sexy on you." Caius's chest rumbled with approval. His voice was so alluring when he was near feeding. I suppose that was the point. How else was he to trap his victims? Well, I wanted to be trapped, quite desperately.

"It's called a leotard," I murmured incoherently, more focused on what his mouth and hands were doing. He took the neckline of the fabric in his teeth and pulled it. I giggled at his wolfish behavior. He slid the material of both the leotard and my bra back, exposing one of my breasts. There he took it in his mouth. I felt the nipple pucker as his tongue made contact with my flesh. Instinctively, my fingers twisted themselves into his hair, tugging gently as he did the same with his teeth.

A visceral groan escaped me. My body was fervently responding to his worshipful mouth. I squirmed beneath him, squeezing my thighs tightly against him.

He lifted his face from my chest, nuzzling his nose close to my ear. "Do you feel that? That longing? It's powerful, is it not?" I nodded. He inhaled my scent. "It is exactly how I feel every moment with you. Your blood drives me crazy, and I haven't had you in weeks." He had me hanging on to his every word. "Each time I fed during my trip, it was like stale bread. No one compares to you, Celine, no one."

I placed my hands on the back of his head and guided his mouth to my neck. He chuckled deeply in response, kissing my throat, planting eager hickies before finally taking what he really wanted.

After so many weeks without him, after my tense day, the experience was a sweet release. Once he had his fill, he finished me the same way he'd done before. I couldn't help but groan afterwards, "I don't know what it is you do with your fingers, but it's absolute bliss."

He settled down next to me, pulling me into his arms, holding me against him. We laid like that for several minutes as I regained my composure and found my breath again.

At last I asked, "What happened in Russia? You haven't spoken a word about it."

"Let us save serious talk for tomorrow. Today is *your* day. I want to celebrate your successes. Mine can be acknowledged after dawn." He turned his face towards mine, kissing my forehead. It was probably for the best.

After a while he asked me to tell him about my contract. It didn't begin until the fall for the start of the new season, so I had time to enjoy summer before I would begin the rigorous training that professional ballet required. After that, I'd likely be busier than him.

"I'm so glad to see you following your dreams, Celine. I am very proud of you." He sighed. "Did I tell you that already?"

I nodded against his chest. We lay together in each other's arms, happily content in one another. He stroked my hair, running his fingers slowly over my scalp. At last, I fell asleep, wondering what happened in Russia, and what kind of dangers the future would hold.

# CHAPTER 26

*T*he true history of ballet is not recorded in texts or scores, nor standardized notations or scripts—not the way music and theater are. Ballet's history is held within the bodies of its dancers. They are its scribes. Ballet's traditions are oral and physical, an art passed person to person, from master to student. This instruction is the only connection a young dancer has to the past.

At Anghor Manor, my connection to the past was through Caius and his vampires. Vampires have a rich history surrounding their existence, deeply rooted in tradition the same way ballet is. This is passed on each time a new vampire is made.

The day following my audition, Caius shared a little of this with me. It all started when I asked him about his trip. He explained that while in Russia, he tracked down an informant who was a rogue deserter. This vampire had been changed by one of the first. He was old.

As he explained this, Caius led me to a podium in the corner of his study with a large leather-bound book. A little gasp escaped my lips when he opened it. "We take our history seriously," he said. "The name of each new vampire is recorded within this book." I began flipping through its pages. Names were written in gold calligraphy with lines branching out to new ones. This was their version of a family tree, a web of immortality. As the pages flew by, the veins grew more complicated. "I have found that with each new generation, the blood has thinned. Younger vampires are nowhere near as strong as the older ones."

"But you're strong," I said.

"Very strong, Celine." There was a wicked gleam in his eyes.

"So, you have a maker?" I began flipping back through the pages to find his name, to see who had made him. He placed a hand over mine, stopping my search, then guided me back to the sofa. I was desperate to know everything about his past: what happened to him, how he'd become a vampire, how old he truly was.

"I do have a maker. Don't we all? Whether it be God, gods, or some other force of nature." His vague answer left me pensive. I considered the choice I'd been given. Before now, I'd failed to consider that he too probably wrestled with the decision to shed his human life and take up one of immortality.

"What was it like?" I asked. "Becoming a vampire."

"It is different for everyone. For me it was necessary. I am tempted to say I had a choice—like the choice given to you. In truth, there was only ever one option for me."

My brow furrowed. "How does someone—how does it work making the change?"

The corner of his mouth turned up. "I was wondering if you'd ever ask. Remember when I told you only the strong-blooded survive?"

I remembered. How could I have forgotten?

"To become a vampire, there must be an exchange of blood. If I were to change you, I would take a large amount of your blood. The moment it mixes with mine, a chemical reaction occurs. Your blood cells bind to mine. At that point, you would in turn drink from me. I would then give you much of mine, not like the small amounts I give you in your wine most nights. Much, much more. Enough for the newly mutated blood currently living in my body, to travel back into your body, and attack the remainder of your blood cells. It is a battle. If your blood wasn't strong enough, your cells would simply give up and you would die."

My jaw dropped. It sounded barbaric.

"As the days go by, as your blood fights, your blood cells die. They are replaced by the merged combination of mutated cells—your blood cells that bound to mine when I first drank from you. As the change completes, you have both my blood and your blood, permanently."

I couldn't think of anything to say. His explanation was thorough. It was a lot to digest.

"The offer remains open, Celine, if ever you should wish to become one of us. I know it sounds…"

*"Frightening?"*

"I suppose. You wouldn't have any problems. You've got Genevieve's blood, stronger even. If ever you decide, I will be here to help you make the change every step of the way." His gaze was earnest. "I will never let any harm come to you. Genevieve was the last vampire I ever made. Did you know?"

"No, I didn't know." We fell quiet for a few minutes. He traced the back of my hand with his thumb as I gazed at the dancing flames in the marble fireplace. "So, what happened with the rogue deserter?"

"Ah yes. Distractions are easy when there is much to be discussed."

I didn't mind. He'd given me a bit of his history. That was worth all the distraction in the world.

"The vampire we tracked down in Russia goes by the alias *Grip*. His true name, his birth name, is Agrippa. He was born in Italy—Roman—like myself."

"You were born in Rome?"

Caius frowned. "That was a long time ago, but yes, near Rome."

Something about his somber response left me wanting more. "We can talk about it if you want. I'm a good listener."

He gave his head a brief shake. "I would prefer not. Some things are better left buried." His eyes unfocused momentarily.

It was obvious that something happened in his early life, which etched him permanently. Every fiber of my body wanted to know what it was, except I didn't have the heart to press him further. "So, what happened with Agrippa, or Grip?"

My question brought Caius back to the present. "After we found him," he said, "Grip was not forthcoming. He was once a part of the rogue cause, so he wasn't eager to say anything that might expose his whereabouts or put a price on his head."

"But I don't understand, why did he leave the rogues in the first place?" The word rogue implied a misalignment of views regarding the vampire code. Did this man suddenly disagree with his crooked ways and wish for a new start? His desertion didn't make a whole lot of sense to me.

"He left because he did not see eye to eye with their leader."

"I see. So in terms of the definition, he's still a rogue?" It disgusted me that rogues didn't place any value on a human life, that they needlessly killed without a care.

"He is still a rogue in terms of the definition, yes. However, he has greatly assisted us. That is important. We are one step closer to bringing down the rogue regime."

"What did you find out?"

Caius shrugged. "He confirmed our suspicions—the leader is operating out of Vienna."

"Isn't it fishy?" I asked before he could continue. "You're living here in Vienna. The rogue cause could take place anywhere in the world. It could be headquartered anywhere. It just so happens to be here."

He grinned at my having made a connection. "Their leader wishes to prove a point to *me*, because I enforce the codes by which we vampires abide."

He picked up our wine bottle from the small coffee table and refilled my glass. I crossed my legs and got comfortable, taking my full glass from him before speaking, "If the rogues are only here because you are enforcing the vampire code, wouldn't that suggest..." My eyes widened. "Are you the designated leader of *all* the vampires?"

"I wouldn't say *designated*. My position came to me without appointment, but yes." He paused before saying, "Celine, I thought you already knew this."

"Well, I didn't realize you were the leader of *all* of them. Doesn't that make you like, a vampire king?"

He chuckled. "If you must label it, then yes. I'm respected. I'm old. I'm powerful. That is enough."

My eyebrows rose. "So, this rogue person, what does he have against you?"

"He? The leader is a she."

I choked on my wine. "It's a woman?" I hadn't expected that.

"Yes, their leader is a woman. I think she has it in her head to bring my regime to the ground. What better place to do it than right under my nose?"

"That would make sense. Did you find out her name? Who she is?"

"Her name is Delilah. I got a vague description of her features from Grip. She's about your height, with soot-black hair, and black eyes to match." His brow furrowed. "There's something else, too."

I questioned him with my gaze, only to find that he was reluctant to answer. "Is it something bad?"

His jaw flexed. "It's something I cannot decide if you should know. I don't want to cause upset, and really, it just happened the way it did."

"I'm not a child, Caius. Just tell me."

He sighed and took another sip of his wine before speaking. "Grip mentioned that Delilah has a lover, someone she holds very dear. I was interested when he told me this, so I pried a little. At last he told me who this lover was—a younger and very careless vampire. Only, Grip had not yet heard of Delilah's lover's misfortunes. I, in turn, enlightened him."

"What do you mean?" He was being too vague.

"I mean, Grip didn't know as much as I did regarding Delilah's lover. Yet, I hadn't realized the connection until he mentioned it."

"I still don't understand."

"Based on Grip's information, Delilah made, or rather, *changed*, a man into a vampire. This vampire became her lover. She held dominion over him since she was his maker. Young vampires can be controlled fairly easily by their makers. I'm not quite sure what kind of relationship they had. Grip said that she was extremely fond of him, that he did work for their cause. He's dead now, so that backstory is neither here nor there."

He was hiding something from me. I could tell by the way he avoided the details. What did any of this have to do with me?

A sudden name came to mind. Maybe I was just being paranoid. Yet, I asked anyway. "Who was it? Who was her lover?"

"Her lover was Thrax. The very same Thrax that nearly ended your life."

## CHAPTER 27

*I*t's rare for a dancer to encounter dance related guilt during his or her career. Although, I have heard of male dancers dropping their female partners during *pas de deux* practice and feeling guilty about the mishap, even if it was an accident. The thing about guilt is, it isn't a rational emotion. It doesn't necessarily take root at the correct time, or in the correct circumstances. It can be necessary when used as a push to overcome bad behavior. In other situations, it can become a weight, an albatross tied about your ankle.

The revelation about Thrax and Delilah became my own albatross. When bad things happen, we find ways of going about a situation wondering what we might have done differently to avoid it entirely. That pining can lead to guilt— guilt for not taking other roads.

I couldn't help but wonder, had Delilah traced her lover's death back to me? Did she hold a grudge against me for it? A woman like her—she would want revenge.

It's funny how we can trace the footsteps of an event, finding ways to relate it to our own choices, when in fact, our choices had little to do with the outcome. That is why guilt is a noxious weed. It is important to remember that no amount of guilt can change the past or quell anxiety.

The things that happened following the death of Thrax, perhaps they still might have occurred. Despite this, I found the connections strange. There was the suspicious night-walker attack when Caius and I walked together on the lawn. Then there was Sophie's death, which happened during that same time. And what about the attack on the city during the vampire ball—a vampire ball that I'd planned? In my heart, it felt related. To me, it was as if Delilah's aggression reached new heights simply because of Thrax's death, because of me.

I wondered over these things frequently in the weeks following Caius's return from Russia. I knew he was working hard to locate Delilah—to bring her down. The longer it took, the more my unease grew.

Despite the craziness taking place in the outside world, life in the manor continued normally as ever. If anything, it was better than ever, given all the good things to come my way.

I wasn't the only one in high spirits. Adel was head over heels crazy for Shahriar. He and Jafar had taken up temporary residence in the manor to help Caius. She couldn't go a moment without talking about him. I didn't mind it though, I felt the same way about Caius.

"When this war over," Adel said to me one evening, "Shahriar invited me to his palace." We were busy getting ready for another night at Fluxx. "He say I stay with him as long as I want. He like my blood."

"Adel, that's fantastic. Can I come visit?"

"Of course, Cece." Her face radiated pride.

With the way things heated up, it was obvious that we were at war. It wasn't so clear when I arrived. What was once a hushed topic, had become an unmistakable discussion among all. There were signs of it everywhere. The training room was always packed, vampires were constantly coming and going, and the amount of guards scattered throughout the interior of the manor had drastically increased. Caius could not bear another Sophie incident. Every vampire was tense, and constantly on edge.

The girls and I were the least involved. We were slightly removed. The girls especially because they didn't get the inside information I did. Yet, even they could tell things were getting serious.

"Shahriar is going tonight to Fluxx. He says he like to watch me dance," Adel informed me. She looked pleased by the idea. "Jafar will come too. They bored I think." Whether she realized it or not, Shahriar was using boredom as an excuse to protect her.

"I am so happy for the two of you," I said. And I was. I was glad Adel had someone to make her life better.

When it was time to go to Fluxx, we made our way through the hills and down into the city. I loved these rare little moments alone with Caius. He always escorted me to Fluxx, so I got six car rides with him each week. I'd missed that when he was in Russia.

"You know, you still owe me a second date," I teased, breaking the comfortable silence.

"So I do." His eyes did not leave the road. He seemed distracted.

"You'll just have to make it an extra good date to make up for it." I reached over and placed my hand on his thigh, massaging his muscles with my thumb. I could tell he was more anxious than usual, distracted from my company. "Another hard day at *the office*?"

He sighed. "I'm sorry, Cece. Yes. Another challenging day at the office." It was a little joke between us. I began to refer to his time on the job, which was nearly all the time, as time at the office. "Four in my city watch have gone missing—no one that you know," he added when he saw my look of surprise. No wonder he was unfocused. "They failed to report to me yesterday. We searched for them, but no sign."

"Rogues?"

He nodded. Goosebumps prickled my skin. I spent the remainder of the drive silent.

My night at Fluxx began normally enough. Caius kissed me gently before my platform made its way up to the club's dance floor. The other girls were lifted into place moments later.

Dancing something other than ballet was a nice reprieve. I'd been practicing a lot, even after my auditions. I loved the change in pace Fluxx offered; I enjoyed allowing Ginger to take over. The music was trance-like, and I let my body lose itself in the loud sounds and dark atmosphere.

When the first several screams rang out, they vaguely registered in my mind. I couldn't have said how long I had been dancing that evening. The blaring music drowned nearly everything out, so I was hardly aware of what was happening, but more shouts followed. Only then did I snap out of it.

I began looking around the dance floor. The other girls were doing the same. As if in slow motion, mass panic was breaking out, rippling through the crowd like a giant wave. The strobe light made it difficult to see what was going on, but a fight was happening on the dance floor, a big fight. It wasn't the kind of bar brawl that takes place between a bunch of drunks. This was a vampire fight. I panicked.

The screaming escalated as the fighting spread. Then the entire club erupted into chaos. Several bodies were thrown against the bars of my cage before dropping motionless to the ground. I cowered away and tried to locate Caius, but I couldn't find him. I did spot several vampires that I knew, and they were engaged in combat with rogues. Caius's vampires were powerful—evidence of many hours in the training room at the manor. The rogues they fought were ruthless, using humans as leverage. Bodies were dropping to the floor. What the *hell* was happening?

I lurched sideways as the floor beneath me moved unexpectedly. My platform was no longer stationary. I was being lowered. I breathed a sigh of relief, quickly looking around at the other girls. It took me a moment to realize that they were not following. Their platforms remained motionless. Was Caius rescuing me from pandemonium but leaving them to watch? It didn't make sense.

The last thing I saw before coming level with the ground was Adel's face. She'd witnessed a bloody fight at Fluxx a few years ago, resulting in her captivity. Our eyes met just before my head passed beneath the floor. Then my platform clicked into place. I turned, looking around the basement.

Fear flooded my heart. The usual guards that occupied the room were not there, but there were others, men with ill-favored looks on their faces. Suddenly I was ensnared. Tight arms latched onto me, and the cold metal of a blade pressed against my neck. I shrieked.

The pressure of the blade increased. "Cry out again and I'll slice through your precious little neck. Believe me, there are many hungry takers in this room." The voice was a woman's. That only made me further panic. I tried struggling against her, but the blade pressed in warning. So, instead I whimpered.

I could still hear the shouts from above. The music had ceased, allowing the sounds of the fighting to amplify. My eyes swept the room. There were six men. Only then did I notice several piles of clothing on the ground. My stomach churned. Caius's guards had been staked in the heart—all that remained were their garments. I felt bile rise into my throat.

Realization hit me. This had everything to do with Thrax. "What do you want with me?" My voice was weak and shaky, barely an audible croak.

The woman laughed. It was a sick laugh, an evil laugh. "What do *I* want? To kill *you* of course. And I will, soon."

In that moment, I knew exactly who she was. "Delilah?"

"Bravo!" she declared, as if guessing her identity was some impressive feat. "You'll pay for what you did, stupid little human." She whispered this quietly into my ear. I whimpered. "Your lover is busy upstairs. I should kill you here and now before he has any hope of interfering."

People appeared on the stairs. Delilah was holding my hair

tightly in her fist, so I could only see them from the corner of my eye, but it was not Caius, and that terrified me. Where the hell was he?

"Come now, Delilah." Another woman's voice sounded near the stairs. Her accent was similar to Caius's. "Why kill her and deprive the great Caius of witnessing her death?" I saw her approach from the fringes of my vision, heels delicately clicking across the concrete as she closed in on me. She walked in a procession, several men following behind—more rogues.

"How *thrilling*, is it not, Delilah?" Her tone sent alarming chills down my spine. "I never imagined that warring against the great *Caius* would bring me more sweetness than I bargained for. Here I have you in my clutches"—she stepped into view, taking my chin in her fingers and tilting my head up towards hers—"Caius's little bitch."

I gazed up at her, unable to look anywhere else. She was several inches taller than me, and built with muscle. Her face radiated evil and disgust as she looked down her nose at me. She had dark golden hair the color of beach sand. Her eyes were green, and they strangely reminded me of not just my own, but Titus's. Had she not worn such a nasty expression, I would have declared her beautiful.

She glanced behind me at Delilah, expelling a brief *huh* sound before eyeing me once more. "Personally, I'm disappointed. I honestly cannot understand what he sees in you."

There were thunderous sounds coming from the stairs. Distracted, she looked away from me, releasing my chin. I too turned my gaze in that direction as best I could, eyes straining at the corners of their sockets. Several figures appeared in the stairway. I expelled a gasp of relief. Caius was there, even if I couldn't see him clearly, I felt him. He'd come at last to save me from these psychos. There was no doubt in my heart where Caius was concerned, and in that moment, I realized something. I did love him. If I ever got out of this mess, I would tell him.

## CHAPTER 28

*P*erforming a ballet is like watching a movie. A fictional world unfolds around you, sets are constructed with elaborate props, dancers move into place, each with a specific purpose, and scenes are acted out. All the while you dance, but you are removed, as if watching something unfold from the outside. Sometimes the experience is so profound, you ask yourself if it's real.

That's exactly how it felt for me in the basement of Fluxx—unreal—not simply because I was being held captive, not because there was a knife to my throat, not even because I had a gallant knight to come rescue me. Caius was my prince after all. He was the prince who was destined to rescue the swan queen, Odette, from her horrible curse. All he had to do was fall in love with her, and earn her love in return. Caius had earned mine, that much was certain. Now he simply needed to save me from the lunatics holding me captive.

Like Odette, my future was entirely up to my prince. I was powerless to act. All I could do was remain within the clutches of evil while the scene played out before me. I was

229

watching a movie. Every moment of it felt unreal, especially what happened next.

The moment Caius and his vampires appeared in the stairwell, the green-eyed woman took control of the situation. "Don't move any closer," she called in warning, "or else Delilah will slit your little pet's throat." Delilah rotated me so that I could witness the scene taking place. The green-eyed woman sauntered towards my liberators. Caius was there, and Felix, and Marcus, and to my relief Titus, who was one of the greatest warriors I'd ever seen. There were others too, crowding in behind them.

They gazed at my captors in disbelief; their gawking betrayed them. Then Titus said something that quickly explained their shock: "*Sister*, you wound me deeply."

My eyebrows knitted together. I looked from Titus to the woman with the green eyes. It couldn't be possible. It made no sense. Sister?

My attention returned to Caius. Surely he would have an answer. Only, he looked just as stunned. "It cannot be!" he said. "Flavia?"

Alarm bells began blaring in my head. The name sounded familiar. Where had I heard it?

"Hello *boys*. Hello little brother." Flavia covered the remaining distance between them. "I'd say that I missed you, but…"

"You're dead!" Titus said. "You died. I mourned you. Yet here you stand before us."

Flavia waved a hand nonchalantly. "Deaths can be faked. Didn't you do the same after the *Third Servile War*?"

"That was entirely different, Flavia, and you know it." Caius spoke through clenched teeth. His tone was frigged. He wore this betrayal openly upon his face. "Flavia, surely this isn't so. Even *you* wouldn't stoop so low."

Flavia didn't answer, so Caius turned his gaze towards me. His eyes widened. "*You?!*" he said to the woman behind me. "You're Delilah? But that means..."

"Worked it out, have you, Caius?" Flavia sneered. "You thought *she* was leading the rogues? Delilah?" Her face changed into a sneer. "Oh! You did. You *poor* thing!" Her laughter gave me chills. As if she sensed my unease, she turned from my liberators and began walking towards me.

Her evil smile froze my blood. Suddenly I wasn't so sure of Caius's ability to free me, especially when Flavia removed a dagger from her belt.

"Why are you doing this, Flavia? What did we do to deserve it?" Titus did not hide his disbelief nor his sadness.

"You? What did you do? Nothing *directly* little brother. It was your idolized leader there. You can blame him." As she spoke, her eyes raked over my body, lingering on my face. "What I don't understand, is why Caius would want this little *whore*, when he could have had *me*. Perhaps, little brother, you can explain that?"

My insides squirmed under her searing gaze. Titus did not answer, so Flavia continued. "All of you follow Caius loyally, and without question. I have *never* been able to understand it. I decided early on that I wasn't interested in joining your little vamp club, not that I had much of a choice, did I, Titus? *Did I?*"

"It was the only way, Flavia."

"Oh?!" she screamed, rounding on Titus. "Is that so?" Her demeanor crumbled, only to be replaced with fury. "That's certainly what you used to tell me. That's what you tell yourselves to ease your guilt. You should have let me die with the rest of them!"

I looked from Caius to Flavia. What the hell were they talking about? I was lost in the plot of whatever fucked-up movie played out.

"You know I couldn't do that," Titus said. I was beginning to understand why Titus felt so wounded.

"I've heard plenty of your excuses, Titus, believe me. When it was clear that Caius would never stop loving his dear *Aurelia*, not even for me, I decided that I was done with the lot of you.

"Did you expect me to follow you *loyally*? No, I knew when it was time to get out. That's why I faked my death. I'll *die* before I'm forced to remain beside a man who never wanted me the way he wanted Aurelia. Bah!"

Flavia turned to me, still in a rage. She lifted the dagger towards my face, holding it there. "But this little bitch? She certainly hasn't had any trouble capturing the heart of the great Caius, has she? I've heard the rumors. What does she have that I don't?" Flavia shrugged. "No matter. This simply makes things more fun. I'm going to kill her and you can all watch."

"You don't have to do this, Flavia." Caius's voice was quiet.

"Oh but I do have to do this, Caius. I do. I owe it to myself to seek revenge."

"If you so much as touch her, I will make you suffer."

She guffawed, but her eyes remained fixed on my face. "You are in no position to make threats, Caius." As she continued to study my face, it was clear that she was trying to understand why he wanted me. Why *did* he want me, and not her? To be honest, aside from her nasty temperament, she had a point. In terms of beauty, she far outranked me.

"Besides, you can't kill me, Caius." Flavia finally grew bored with her scrutiny. She turned to face him. "Well, I suppose you can. I wouldn't recommend it. Do you know what lies within the city at this very moment?"

Caius, Felix, Marcus, and Titus exchanged perplexed looks.

Flavia snickered. "No? I didn't think so. Not that great at your job, are you?" She polished her dagger on her shirt, casually checking its shine. "You see, I've been a busy girl these last few years. My busy little bees are everywhere—all over the world. Under my orders, they've been collecting."

"Collecting?"

"Oh yes. At this very moment, there are caches of nightwalkers in pens throughout the city, hidden in warehouses, basements, abandoned buildings..."

"You lie." I could hear the slightly panicked edge to Caius's voice.

"You don't believe me?" Flavia waited a moment then shrugged. "Not my problem, but it will be yours when they are released. See, my keepers are in place, waiting. If things don't go according to plan, if something should happen to me, if they do not hear from me by tomorrow morning, by tomorrow night...I'm sure you can guess what will happen."

"I'd rather not guess."

"Well, should I not make it out of here"—she barked a laugh as if the notion was ridiculous—"my keepers will not receive my signal. If this happens, come dark tomorrow, you'll find thousands of *very* thirsty night-walkers roaming the streets of Vienna. I dare say your little coven, and even your reinforcements, will have a rough time rounding them up. I certainly hope you have enough weapons at your disposal. What do you think, Delilah? How many human deaths would you predict are in store for our little friends?"

Delilah spoke up behind me. "Thousands," she said sweetly. I could hear the nasty smile in her voice.

Flavia nodded. "Indeed. Our rogues won't go down without a fight." They both burst into fits of malicious giggles. It was obvious that Flavia was using all her leverage.

A black rage fulminated from Caius's eyes. "So, what are my options? Obviously you want to make a deal, else you wouldn't bother exposing your plans."

"The deal is as follows, you watch me kill your little bitch, and cease all opposition to my forces. If you comply, your precious city will be saved. If not, come tomorrow, you'll find quite an epidemic of death and turning on your plate. And that blood? That will be on *your* hands."

"Flavia, you are delusional if you expect me to side with *either* of those choices." Caius did not look happy.

Flavia ignored his reaction. "Rather funny, isn't it? All those deaths from your stupid little war. All those lives lost. How many was it? Two-hundred thousand? What about the remaining six thousand who were crucified along the Appian way? Did you go to see their bodies? Did you look upon their dead faces? Did you feel remorse for their losses? No? I don't blame you. I saw their faces—their tortured bodies. It wasn't pretty. Yet, they fought and died for *your* cause. Come tomorrow, your body count may grow higher."

The ground began to spin beneath me. I didn't want to believe a word Flavia said. Yet, I couldn't help but notice Caius failed to refute her. Was it true then? Was he responsible for the deaths of hundreds of thousands? That didn't seem like the Caius I knew.

I couldn't see her face, but I could tell Flavia was wearing an amused grin. She was evil, horrible, and I hated her like nothing else I'd ever hated. It's like she was purposefully doing her best to create rifts between us, to tear us apart.

She turned to me. "Oh look! Have I said something to upset you, dear?"

"I'm not your *dear*."

"Oh my! She's feisty, this one."

"Don't harm her," Caius commanded.

His warning had little effect. I flinched as Flavia bared her fangs. "I think I might have a drink from your little pet before I get to the fun stuff. She does smell *tantalizing*. I see why you want her."

"No!" Caius cried. His words stilled her. As if suddenly thinking better of it—she was likely doing this to frighten me —Flavia's fangs receded. "No? You *don't* want to share your precious *Cece*?"

I hated the way she said my name. She made it feel dirty, contaminated. I clinched my jaw tightly shut.

"Alright then. Let's just get straight to the death part." She lifted her knife, studied it for just a moment, and then thrust it forward.

# CHAPTER 29

In Act IV of *Swan Lake*, Odette and the prince die in each other's arms. Their death, their love, breaks the curse on the other swans, saving the swans' lives. Caius was my prince, but he wasn't in my arms for the final act. How could we finish our ballet? It was all wrong. Somehow I had diverged from *Swan Lake,* and entered Anna Pavlova's ballet solo for *The Dying Swan.* I was alone.

In those last few instances, when Flavia thrust her knife forward directly towards my heart, I knew I was going to die, just like the poor dying swan. I didn't spend effort struggling because I'd already done that. I didn't waste emotion panicking. I was resigned to die; I laughed at myself for it. All I could think was that I was going to die a virgin. Caius and I were cheated of our last moments together.

He was still restrained, forced to watch. I couldn't bear that thought. My eyes closed just before the knife made contact with my flesh. A white flash of light illuminated the darkness behind my eyes. It burned through my eyelids. Was this death? There was no pain.

My ears picked up Flavia's angry hiss. I opened my eyes just as her blade clattered to the floor. Had Caius saved me? I couldn't see anything as my eyes watered and blinked against the blinding white light.

As the glare receded, it was not Caius who stood before me. A woman had appeared. She could only be described as an angel. Her hair was black, darker than the darkest night. Her pale skin was smooth and flawless, glowing with a near-translucent radiance. Her face took my breath away.

The beauty of the world had combined into something unimaginably stunning. My gaze slid over her entirely, drinking her in. She was dressed as a Greek goddess, toga and all. Most assuredly, she was exactly that.

Her hand gripped Flavia's wrist. Flava did not fight her. She was just as stunned as me.

My gaze flicked around the room. Like me, everyone stood in disbelief. Even the rogues held their arms limply to their sides. The desire to fight had evaporated as quickly as this mysterious woman appeared.

My regard settled on Caius. He was the only one who didn't look surprised. Instead, he stepped forward and got down on one knee. My eyes narrowed and my eyebrows knitted together.

The goddess began backing away from me. She dragged Flavia with her. Flavia was too stunned to protest.

Once they were several feet away, the woman spoke. Goose-bumps prickled my skin as she addressed the room. "I have come to fulfill a promise." Her voice was pure like the trickling of a creek, or the ringing of silver bells.

"Thank you, Hecate." Caius bowed his head.

My eyes widened as my free hand jumped to my chest. I grasped the large moonstone medallion Caius gifted me with. I thought he was being metaphorical when he told me about the necklace. I never actually believed him.

"You may rise, Caius," Hecate said before turning to me. "Years ago, Celine, I was unable to protect that necklace's owner. It pained me deeply. A rare thing for the gods—pain. My rules are absolute, so my word did not allow for it. I am happy that I can mitigate such sad circumstances *this* day."

I saw Caius nod in acceptance. The others in the room remained still. Hecate turned her gaze upon Caius. "Tell me, Caius, what *was* the promise I made to you regarding that moonstone?"

"You instructed me to place it around the neck of the one whom I loved. You vowed that as long as she wore it, you would protect her from all those who would do her harm."

Hecate nodded. "You must love Celine greatly, else the power of the necklace would have never called to me."

Caius bowed his head, but not before his eyes locked on mine. A powerful emotion radiated from those eyes. My heart constricted. I looked away from him, back to Hecate.

The goddess continued, now addressing the others, "I am Hecate," she said. "I am of the moon and the stars. I am of the night. I am the crossroads to the world beyond. I am the key to magic within this earth. I rule the angels beside the other greats. I am, and always will be, the mother of vampires. You are all my children—my creation beginning with Caius. I never wanted this for you, this warring. Caius, what a mess this has become, would you not agree?"

"I take full responsibility, Hecate."

"Of course you do. That is your nature. Why else did I choose *you?*"

Caius did not respond. It was not a question seeking an answer. Hecate's eyes circled the room, pausing upon each of the occupants within.

"It is not my place to interfere," she said at last. "I am Hecate. I operate from a distance. You will fix this, Caius, but I will make good on my promise." She released Flavia, who remained dumfounded, and then moved over beside me.

"Your name, *Celine*, is one of the heavens. Did you know?"

I nodded, having lost all control of my voice. I was as dumbfounded as everyone else.

"Do not be frightened. Take my hand. I will bring you to safety."

My face screwed up. Bring me where? I looked from her to Caius. Caius nodded reassuringly, urging me with his gaze.

"What about—what about the rest of them? Can't you see what is going to happen here?" My voice was raspy. Not everyone was going to make it out of the basement alive. Hecate's appearance did not magically erase the war.

"Of course, Celine. That matter does not concern you or me. Let us go. I haven't all night."

"Go, Cece," Caius called softly. At last I nodded to him and placed my hand in Hecate's. Her skin was soft and warm, and her body radiated comfort, which was quickly enveloping me with calm. The last thing I saw before shutting my eyes was the same blinding light present during her coming. It was so bright, it glowed through my eyelids.

My body was overcome by an odd tingling sensation. I felt light like a bird, yet, I was free like the wind.

"You can open your eyes now, Celine," Hecate said beside me. "Welcome to the dominion of the gods." She still held my hand. I didn't mind, considering the relief it gave me.

I followed her suggestion and opened my eyes. My jaw dropped. We stood in the middle of a decadent garden. The color green, in its varying shades, was overwhelmingly present. Green was accented by a vivid array of other colors, purples, blues, pinks, yellows, oranges. There were trees in vast shapes and sizes. These were laden with blossoms. Bushes and shrubs were also covered in blooms. I beheld the most luscious flowers imaginable. They were all open.

"In the garden of the gods, every moment is spring. Every living thing shall never face death. There is no change here, no sadness, no darkness. Come." She led me through the aisles of flowers first, and then through the trees.

I was overcome with bliss. Had I lived any other life than this? I could not remember. In my mind, there was only now, just as is the case for all ballerinas.

Hecate led me to a bench before a fountain. We sat gazing at our surroundings. Birds flitted and fluttered in and out of the water of the fountain, chirping gleefully.

"Tell me, Celine. Are you happy in your life with Caius?" Her question brought me back from my trance.

I nodded, not really thinking about my answer. I was still too distracted. She gently placed her finger beneath my chin, turning my head towards her. My mind immediately cleared. "I—I'm happy."

She nodded, waiting for me to say more, so I did. "After

tonight, I have so many questions. There's so much I don't understand. I thought…"

"You thought you were finally beginning to understand the world, yes?"

"Yes, I suppose so. After Caius told me about the vampire war, and about how vampires were made, I thought I was beginning to understand. I never imagined that he was…"

"He was the first—my first—my only."

"So, you *did* make him?"

She smiled sadly. "I suppose I was too selfish. Even two thousand years later I find it difficult to admit to my folly."

My eyes widened. "He's—Caius is two thousand years old?"

Hecate shrugged. "He is the first. They are not *all* as old as he. And if you think two thousand years is old, please refrain from asking me *my* age." Her joke lightened the mood.

I was quiet for a moment, thoughtful as my eyes slid back across the garden. This time I was too deep in contemplation to be tempted by its lush beauty. "Hecate, you said Caius was your *only*. Does that mean you didn't make any other vampires?"

"That is correct. I made Caius because times warranted my interference. Problems in Rome were mounting. I needed a way to fix them. Caius was my solution. He elicited quite a rebellion. Many lives were lost, but for a cause that was great."

That must have been what Flavia referred to. "What cause?" I asked. I prayed that it was something worthwhile and not simply a petty whim. I wanted to believe that Caius was good, that he was genuine. If it were anything shameful, I would have lost my faith in him.

"At the time, Rome was a society that functioned upon slavery. It was a republic, but not all peoples were free. They needed a wake-up call. There were already several slave rebellions, but none made its mark. In fact, the Roman heartland paid them no mind whatsoever. It was time for something greater, something that would bring about awareness and trigger a reform."

I breathed a sigh of relief. "So Caius fought for a good cause."

"He fought for the truest cause one can fight for. Humans were never meant for slavery. It is their greed, and ultimately their entitlement, that led to such practices. Enslaving their own kind is an atrocity."

"But, Flavia said it was Caius's fault so many died."

"No, dear. If any blame is to be placed, such blame lies with me. Don't *all* wars result in the deaths of thousands, whether the cause is just or not?" That was true enough. I nodded.

"Some of the most crucial moments in humanity's history are the result of wars and thus, thousands of sacrifices. Do not think negatively on Caius's actions. He has always possessed a true moral compass. I would not have chosen him otherwise. He was merely acting out of love and genuine goodness."

"Love? What does love have to do with this?"

She squeezed my hand. "Love, dear, is often at the forefront of all actions. I think perhaps it is best if I show you. Come."

I hesitated. "Shouldn't I be getting back? Caius will worry."

"Oh," she waved her hand in dismissal. "Caius is busy with Flavia at this very moment, fighting her to the death."

"What?!" I ripped my hand from hers. How could she speak about something like that with ease? "You're not going to help him?"

"You need not worry on his behalf, child. He is more than capable. I have never doubted him, and neither should you."

"But, you said they were *your* children."

"And so they are! Why then should I take one life to save another? I love my creation, as monstrous as it turned out. I do not deny there are problems, which Caius must fix, but he is capable. He will do that which needs to be done."

"So he's not—he's not going to die?"

"No my innocent beauty, not today. Not for a very long time. See, it is like I told Thetis when she made Achilles. A man with a single weaknesses will fall. But a man with many weakness surrounded by hundreds like him won't fall so easily. Wasn't I correct? Didn't Achilles fall when his heel was struck by an arrow?"

My eyes bulged. Was this for real? It was only starting to sink in, the mention of Achilles, Hecate's existence, the Greek gods, and mythology. I never put any stock into such things, but now I had a reason to.

"Come now, I can see that you are overwhelmed. I will give you a choice. I can return you safely to Anghor Manor, or I can show you the answers you seek, returning you once your questions have been met." I considered my choices, but I already knew what I wanted.

"Either way, I shall time it such that you arrive after the

fighting at Fluxx is finished. Neither of us will be any help anyway."

"I have so many questions," I sighed.

She held out her hand for me. "Come then, Celine. For I have the answers. I will bestow upon you a gift that in all the ages, I have never given, but only because you wear my necklace, and only because Caius loves you. I love him, and so I love you as well."

I took up her hand. Once more she led me through the garden of the gods. I was finally going to get answers.

hen Caius gave me the moonstone necklace, I saw new parallels with *The Talisman* ballet. The moonstone necklace became my own talisman. Like the goddess Amravati, queen of the heavens, Hecate was the mother who rescued me from harm, bringing me into her dominion. Somehow, everything had come full circle.

Being in the garden of the gods was nothing short of extraordinary. It was exactly how I'd pictured the Garden of Eden—peaceful, innocent, breathtaking. If I could have forgotten about my life, I might have stayed with her forever, never returning to Caius. Instead, I had so many questions— questions Hecate was going to answer.

After she led me through the garden, Hecate stopped before a fountain, a wall of water. There was a small pool beneath it, extending several feet outwards. A sheet of water cascaded down from the stone fountain, which towered above us as we stood before it, hand in hand.

"I call this my mirror of memories. Is not an accurate name, not really. It shows me the past, true, but also the present, and even the future. Time does not move in this world; I suppose past, present, and future, are all relative."

I looked upon the mirror of memories. It appeared harmless, merely a wall of water. The sheet was smooth as glass, and landed with a small splash in the pool at its base. It was ethereal in its beauty.

"I think we should begin at the beginning, don't you?" Hecate asked. I agreed, gazing fixedly at the fountain. "Excellent. Since you don't speak Latin, you will hear English in your mind."

She waved her hand before her, and the sheet of water rippled. The ripple started in the middle, traveling in waves across the surface, until it reached the edges. A moving picture formed. It was so crisp, so clear, that it looked akin to a high resolution television. The images zoomed by, too fast to follow, until they slowed and settled upon a marching army. Armor-clad Roman soldiers were trooping in unison, throwing up plumes of dust as their feet struck the ground.

Hecate spoke, "I had my eye on Caius long before I revealed myself to him. Here, he is a soldier in the Roman army." The image zoomed forward, abruptly zeroing in on a man amidst the ranks of many. There he was—Caius. My heart skipped a beat as I beheld him. He looked slightly younger, but also human. He was dressed identically to his comrades.

"During his time in the legion, Caius was a distinguished fighter," Hecate explained as I watched. My eyes remained hungrily glued to him. "He came from good stock. Thracians were of a strong build. They made ideal soldiers." I wasn't sure what a Thracian was, but I didn't stop her explanation. "Caius was already in love at this point, engaged to be married. Here he is returning home to Rome, finishing his tour. The woman to whom he is promised, eagerly awaits him."

The image rippled and new images flew past. Again they slowed, settling on Caius. He remained dressed as a soldier, with the exception of his plumed helm, which he held under his arm. His cuirass was tight against his muscled body, and his sleeveless arms spoke of many hours under the sun. He approached a flat within the outskirts of Rome. The houses, most of them, looked the same—rundown, blocky, and white —with wooden doors and square windows. They were recognizable facades in Roman history. Night was falling so Caius knocked quietly.

A young woman answered. She had dark, curly hair, which was tied at the nape of her neck, and reached her lower back. Her soft brown eyes sparkled when they caught the waning light. The instant she beheld him, her expression radiated with excitement and joy. He too cried aloud, dropping his helm to the ground. He lifted her into his arms, kissing every inch of her smile and face.

"This is Caius's first time seeing Aurelia after his return to Rome. They have been apart for nearly three years."

It felt wrong to watch such an intimate moment. Yet, Hecate wouldn't have shown me if it wasn't her wish for me to see it, so I did not turn away. The scene continued as he carried the woman, Aurelia, inside. Though I felt the need to, I didn't hide my eyes when Caius began playfully removing her belted overdress, laying her down upon the mat in front of the fire to make love. At last, the moment became so tender that my cheeks burned. I was forced to look away.

The picture flickered, recapturing my attention. The room

remained the same, but the scene changed. There was only Aurelia now. She was sitting at a small table, sobbing.

"Aurelia has just killed a man," Hecate said. "He is there by the door—a prominent city official."

I studied the room, locating the man she spoke of. He was dressed in his stola, but he lay in a pool of his own blood. My stomach dropped. What had happened?

The door opened and Caius entered. His eyes widened as he looked around him. Aurelia rushed to him.

"What is the meaning of this?" he gasped, taking her into his arms. His voice was muffled, almost as if it came from beneath the fountain's water. I knew exactly what it felt like to be in those arms.

"He tried to rape me, Caius. I did not know—I did not know what to do." Caius was not angry as he comforted her, murmuring into her hair. "He came in search of you. When I told him that you were away…"

I looked at the scene in horror, now understanding what had taken place. Pity welled up inside of me, for her, for both of them.

The scene changed again. This time I wasn't ready for what I saw. Caius was in a cell, looking weary. The conditions were horrid. There were other estranged men around him, sitting on the dirt floor. My heart tightened, and I could hardly look upon him. The scene flashed once more, showing Aurelia in a different cell with several other women, all wearing torn, squalid tunics.

I glanced at Hecate. She was watching me intently. I opened my mouth, but she answered my question before I could ask. "They were unable to disguise the death. The man was important. Eventually, their crime was discovered. Both await trial. The price of murder in Rome, especially the murder of a city official, is death, unless you have a healthy sum of money to bail yourself to freedom."

I was disgusted. Caius was too poor, lowly plebeian soldier that he was, to afford their freedom. It was heart-wrenching to realize.

When my gaze returned to the mirror of memories, the picture changed. Caius stood in a ring, dressed identically to the gladiators I'd seen on the hanging tapestry in the dining room at Anghor Manor. Suddenly, the art piece made sense. The relic meant more to him than I realized, but now I understood.

Caius held a sword, and couched in a fighting stance. There was a large, cheering crowd. Big gates opened, and two men sprang forward. I couldn't look away. My heart pounded forcefully. I nearly forgot that this was merely a memory, and not currently happening in real time.

"Caius's name is *Spartacus* now—a name given to him by his new owner. Perhaps that name is familiar to you? Here he has been sold into slavery. His purchaser paid a high price to add a new gladiator to his collection, taking him from the cells beneath Rome. Thracians were highly coveted for sport. They always made the best gladiators in those days."

The scene advanced to show Caius fighting ruthlessly with the two men, both of whom he killed. It was barbaric. "He had no choice," Hecate said. "It was fight, or die trying."

"What about—what about Aurelia?"

"That comes next. Here—" She waved her hand and the scene changed. This time Hecate was *in* the scene. She looked exactly the same, unchanged by the ravages of time. Caius slept in a cot against the wall. She moved to his bedside and woke him, putting her finger to her lips to signal silence. She led him out of the small locked room he shared with several other men. The picture changed, and they stood alone in a corridor.

Caius wore an expression of pure wonder. "Surely, I am dreaming," he whispered. "Are you not a goddess?"

"You do not dream, Spartacus, or should I say, *Caius*." His eyes widened at the use of his true name. "I have come to save you."

"Save me?" A fleeting expression of hope appeared on his features. Then his face fell. "I care not about my life, only of Aurelia's. What good is my freedom while she rots in a cell awaiting judgement—awaiting death."

"I can offer her freedom and protection. In return, you must serve me until your task is complete."

"What task?" His eyes were so youthful, so eager, so *human*.

"How would you like to bring about an end to slavery?"

His brow furrowed. This woman was toying with him, surely. How could he, Caius, do such a thing?

"I can offer you a way to free your wife, to free Aurelia, and to protect her against those who would do her harm. In return, I ask that you lead a rebellion against the masters. Free the gladiators from this school, and begin an uprising that will make a statement, the echoes of which will last an eternity."

He was aghast. "I will be killed!"

"Not if I make death nearly impossible. What do you know of

Achilles?" Caius opened then closed his mouth. "Achilles had but one weakness. Likewise, you will have a weakness—a number of them—but you will also have the ability to make others strong like you. In so doing, you will select a group of men whose loyalty is absolute. Together, you will escape and bring about the uprising. Do we have a deal?"

"You offer me a way to free Aurelia, a way to protect her." His face hardened with resolve "The rest does not matter. Where she is concerned, I have no other choice. I must do that which you ask. But, I have another question."

Hecate nodded.

"How long must I serve you?"

"Until your army is depleted."

"I have no army." He clutched at his coarse chiton, fit only for a slave.

"You will."

The Hecate beside me waved her arm and the scene changed. Aurelia stood haggard and frail upon the grass near a small cottage. She was crying, her body shaking with sobs. Caius was with her, urging her to be calm. Hecate stood in the shadows, watching.

"I did not show myself to Aurelia," said Hecate beside me. "Caius is the only person to ever see me. I chose it to be that way."

"What is he doing?" I asked.

"He is reassuring Aurelia that she must stay here with her sister and her sister's husband. They live twenty miles outside of Rome. He is telling her that she must never return to the city, or risk discovery. There will be a price on her head once the guards realize her disappearance. She does not wish for him to go. He is doing his best to explain himself, who he is now, and what he must do."

"Wait, did you—"

"No, he is not yet a vampire."

I turned back to the mirror of memories. Caius took from his pocket the necklace that was now upon my neck. My eyes widened. "It was meant for her?" I whispered. The sudden realization hit me full force.

"It was my way of protecting her from those who might do her harm, just in case she was discovered." Caius put the necklace around Aurelia's neck. "I think that's enough there. Let us move on." The goddess gave another regal sweep of her hand.

The next view was back at the school of gladiators. Caius was once more in the corridor speaking with Hecate.

"A week has passed," said Hecate. "I am visiting Caius to see how his rebellion progresses."

I gazed into the mirror, watching eagerly.

"I have found many hopefuls," Caius said to Hecate. "Not just males, for several female gladiators wish to take part."

"Have you told them about the promise of immortality?" Hecate asked. He shook his head, looking worried. "Very well, Caius, that can come after. Are you ready?"

"Now?" He asked, looking unsure. "Is it truly necessary?"

"It is necessary. You will die, otherwise. You will never see your beloved Aurelia if you are dead," she warned. At last, he was resigned to nod. "Good. Close your eyes."

He followed her orders. A moment later she was upon him, her mouth at his neck. He screamed, eyes opening wide with shock, a look of utter betrayal upon his face.

"You did not explain to him what it entailed, did you?" I was hardly surprised by what I saw.

Hecate shook her head. "It was better that way."

And so I knew, after all that time spent wondering about Caius's beginning, the truth was laid bare for me to see.

Once he recovered from the initial shock, Caius agreed to feed from Hecate. In the days to follow, the change occurred. It was a slow process, though Hecate rushed us through it.

The others were soon changed too. One by one, he built his coven of vampires. They all believed themselves monsters at first. Each was reluctant to feed, afraid of the death they might cause. Despite the lives they took in the ring, their new strength scared them.

Caius guided them, showing them how to stop before the human body became entirely depleted. He taught them how to manipulate the human mind. In the end, they began to appreciate their increased strength.

For a while, they decided to bide their time. They became recognized gladiators of that era. I saw many faces that I knew. That was a strange experience, witnessing Titus, Cato, Nero, and even Julia. In one memory I saw Flavia, and my blood boiled. She was a good fighter too. I watched her practicing with her brother Titus. Flavia's dedication to gladiator life, to the ring, to fighting, and even her green eyes, were all similarities that Titus had once seen in me. It was only natural for him to miss his sister.

Eventually the scenes changed. A large fight broke out at the school, marking the start of the slave rebellion. The masters of the school were slaughtered. Seventy gladiators, even those who had not become vampires, escaped. We followed Caius's trek through the Roman countryside as he gained followers, thousands upon thousands of them, which he freed from households.

The scene changed again. It grew dark. I found myself gazing upon a large battlefield hosting the bodies of the dead. "This one did not turn out so well, as you can see," Hecate said. The view shifted to Caius. He sat crouched upon a hill, over-looking the bodies beneath him. I couldn't mistake his look of defeat, of regret. This was his doing.

"This was his first loss." Hecate sounded mournful. "It was a big shock to him. You are seeing him a year after his change. Yet, he is merely halfway through his campaign."

"How many died?"

"Fifty thousand here. They were met with much success before this, raiding and pillaging the countryside. They gained a reputation—a name for themselves. Eventually they turned enough heads, as I hoped. This is the first formidable wave of legions sent to stop to the slave rebellion, which by this time, was being called the *Third Servile War.*

"Unfortunately, there were many losses to follow. It was a very hard journey for Caius. He owed me a debt. Everything he did here, he did for his love, and for the people, so that Rome could begin the journey to end slavery."

"So much death," I sighed. No wonder he never wanted to discuss this with me.

I felt as if I finally understood Caius in his entirety. He'd been through more than any man ever should. Yet, he maintained his dignity. I admired him all the more.

"Let me show you the battle that ended it all," said Hecate, bringing my mind from its thoughts. "This battle freed him from my service." Hecate moved time forward. Flickers of fast moving pictures raced across the water's surface. At last the images came to rest on a new battle field. This battle wasn't finished like the last. The fighting was in full swing. It was gory, Caius was outnumbered.

"The Roman legions you see here are under the order of Marcus Licinius Crassus. He became a vampire some time later, you know, serving Caius. Ironic, is it not? You will see why shortly."

I looked upon the man she mentioned. My heart leapt into my throat. I knew Marcus, but he was fighting on the wrong side! The scene panned out. Caius's rebels were being *slaughtered*.

"This was the last time I ever spoke to Caius, not in human form, for he did not see me. He only heard my whisper," said Hecate.

Caius was fighting. I'd never seen him fight anywhere but the training room, and a few memories of him in the ring. On the battlefield, he was a force to be reckoned with. In the few seconds I watched, he managed to fell four Roman soldiers. Suddenly he stood, alert, motionless.

"I have just told him that this is the end, that he is released. I never told him to fake his death. That plan was his doing, put in place with the other vampires. See there? He's sending out the signal."

Sure enough, Caius gave a strange call. In response, I saw

groups of men sneaking away from the field. "But, they are leaving the others!" The human slave rebels did not notice their comrade's silent retreat.

"Sad, is it not? He never forgave himself for that. He had no other choice. His numbers were not great enough to conquer the twenty thousand Marcus Crassus brought forth. He would have died, vampire or not."

The scene flickered and died. We moved to the city of Rome. There was a big celebration taking place on the streets near the Coliseum. Roman legions were marching, people were throwing flowers at their feet, petals drifted down from open windows.

"Rome has won the war," said Hecate. "The people are celebrating. The rumor went out quickly, encouraged by the leaders of Rome, specifically Marcus Crassus, that Spartacus fell valiantly in war, slain by Marcus himself. There were no survivors. Those who did survive were hunted down and crucified. I believe Flavia mentioned them already, lining the road known as the Appian Way, which traversed Rome to the city where Spartacus's gladiator school was, in Capua."

I nodded, watching the happy people in the streets. "I don't understand," I said at last. "It doesn't look like much has come about from all this. These people are *celebrating*."

"The rebellion had very significant far-reaching effects. It triggered the eventual transition from the Roman Republic, into the Roman Empire. Rome saw nearly fifteen hundred years of political stability after that. Out of fear, the Romans began treating their slaves less harshly. Before that, they were considered mere property. An owner could kill a slave without any consequences, but that changed after the *Third*

*Servile War.* Eventually, larger numbers of freemen were employed."

I tried to process her words. I knew little about Rome or its history. "Change takes time, Celine. Without the proper catalyst, it would never happen at all."

At last I nodded, accepting her explanation, though I'd hoped for more drastic effects.

"There is Marcus Crassus now, riding among his men in the procession. He claimed to have singlehandedly ended the war. In history, he is remembered for such. That was why I always found it ironic that he now serves Caius with undying fealty. He owes Caius many debts."

I had too many other questions to focus on Marcus. "What about Caius? He faked his death to get away. Did he get his happy ending? Did he return to Aurelia?"

Hecate looked at me sadly. "I am afraid not, Celine."

My eyebrows knitted together. "He did this for her. What happened?"

"Hers is a rather sad story. Do you truly wish to know it?"

Fear was creeping into my gut. Somehow I'd known since the beginning that things wouldn't end well for Caius, yet, I so desperately wanted them to. "I want to know."

Hecate nodded. The scene changed to a familiar one—the cottage I'd seen Aurelia at. A man walked towards it, his shoulders slumped. He was burdened.

"That is Aurelia's brother-in-law. He has just come from Rome, where he heard about the death of Spartacus."

"But, Caius isn't dead."

The man entered the cottage where Aurelia and her sister were cooking. They both looked up with excitement. Aurelia's sister went to her husband, hugging him and kissing him happily. "What news?" she asked, only then taking in his grim mood.

The man looked from his wife, to Aurelia. "The war is over. Rome has won." His words left Aurelia pale. I saw the color drain from her face. Her sister went to her, whispering reassurances. "There is more," the man said. "They are shouting the news through the city streets—Spartacus is dead."

"No!" Aurelia screamed and fell to her knees, wailing. I watched the scene in horror. I felt the same tears forming in my eyes. She put her face to the ground and began beating her fists upon the dirt floor.

I too could hardly breathe. A stifling sadness took hold of me. My heart ached for her deeply. I wanted to shout at the mirror, "He's not dead!" It wouldn't have done any good. Tears began pouring down my face.

Time sped by as the hours of that wretched day stretched on. Aurelia sat motionless in a chair, crying without ceasing. She heard nothing of the words spoken by her sister, who continued to throw worried looks at her husband. Without relinquishing it, Aurelia gripped the moonstone necklace. I realized that I too was gripping that same necklace.

As the hours stretched on, her sister and brother finally retired to their small bedroom, leaving Aurelia alone. Once she was alone, she rose and began moving about the living space with lifeless motion. I watched, growing more sickened as she found a rope and climbed atop the table. There, to my revulsion, she tied it to the rafters. Then she made a noose.

I began shaking my head, reaching for the sheet of water with an outstretched hand as if to stop her. "No!" I whispered. "No, Aurelia. No…"

Hecate took hold of my wrist before I could touch the water. Aurelia placed the rope around her neck and stood for several minutes, eyes wide but unseeing, still grasping her necklace. I held on to a faint glimmer of hope. Might she come to her senses? Might she think better of what she was about to do?

"Where the hell is Caius?" I whispered.

Aurelia stepped off the side of the table. Her body fell and her neck broke. She went limp.

"No!" I screamed. My feet no longer carried me. I sank to my knees, sobbing into my hands. "I can't…" I gasped. "I can't watch anymore."

Strong arms lifted me to my feet, but my legs could hardly support my weight. "You wanted this," Hecate reminded me. "You must finish."

"But, she's dead! You were supposed to protect her! You promised. What have you *done*?" I looked at Hecate as if she were a monster.

"My necklace was never meant to protect her from herself."

"But…"

"You see now the error of my promise. How was I to know she would take her own life? I was too focused on my own work to look ahead. Even we gods are fallible."

"But, but everything Caius did, he did for her. His entire life was taken from him. She was all he cared about. Now he won't get his happy ending!"

"He will. In time." She gave me a sad, knowing look. "You must finish the scene that you have agreed to watch."

The pictures changed. It was day now. Aurelia's pale body rested upon a cot. Her sister wept over her. The image panned out. I saw a man on a horse. It was Caius. He was racing towards the cottage, spurring his steed onward. He was coming home to his wife, but he was too late.

"No, please. He can't see her like that." I cried, shaking my head back and forth in disbelief as I spoke to the mirror.

Aurelia's sister came out from the cottage minutes later to see the approaching traveler. The moment her eyes fell on him, it was as if she'd seen a ghost. She collapsed onto the ground, finally realizing what had happened: her sister had taken her life for naught.

Caius knew something was wrong. He probably smelled the scent of death pervading the dwelling. Without a word, he sped into the house. The moment he beheld Aurelia, he cried out. It was the most heart wrenching, agony-filled cry I ever heard. He rushed to her body, shaking her, kissing her dead lips, massaging her fingers, as if any of it might wake her from death.

At last, he sank to his knees while laying his upper body across her midriff. I'd never seen him cry. I never imagined that he could, but there he wept, reduced to grief.

It was too much to watch. I turned away, squeezing my eyes tight. I felt the momentary halt of my tears as my eyelids held them in place, allowing them to pool up, until even that could not stop them. I couldn't bear to witness his pain. I would have given *anything* to heal his woes, even my life.

"You see now why Caius is the way he is. He is the man he is today because of what shaped him." The light behind the sheet of water faded. I was left with a final scene of Caius digging a grave in which he gently laid to rest Aurelia's body. Only then did he remove the moonstone necklace.

The wall darkened and turned to water once more. I turned to Hecate, not sure if I should hate her or thank her for what she'd shown me. I was so wrecked. How was I supposed to feel? All I wanted was for someone to tell me, because trying to work it out for myself was more than I could handle.

"I'm ready to go now," I announced through my tears. "Take me to him."

CHAPTER 31

*I*n the final scenes of *The Talisman* ballet, Niriti regains her stolen talisman from the maharajah. He'd stolen it to keep her from returning to heaven. After some pleading, Niriti takes the maharaja's knife and threatens to kill herself. Seeing this, the maharaja relents and tosses the talisman at her feet. Niriti picks it up and is faced with a choice: she can return home to her mother, to heaven, or she can stay on earth with the man who loves her and wishes to make her his queen.

At first, her decision is easy; she will return to heaven. Yet, when she bids farewell to the maharaja, she looks into his eyes and sees his hurt within them. She too is overcome with sadness. How can she leave the man who offers her such a love? What celestial delights could ever be worth more? Her will is set. She drops the talisman and throws herself into his arms.

Like Niriti, my place was not within the dominion of the gods, but rather, Caius's arms. For months, I had already considered Anghor Manor to be my home. Even after I decided to stay, it took time to sink in. Home didn't truly hit me until Hecate returned me there, depositing me in the entry hall.

My eyes were closed when her voice whispered in my ear, "Goodbye, Celine." Without seeing, I knew exactly where I was. This place was familiar and warm. It smelled of safety. Warm scents met my nose, cinnamon from the candles that burned in the evenings, and fresh flowers abounding in their vases near the stairs. Yes, I recognized the calm serenity enveloping me. The next instant, I knew Hecate was gone.

I opened my swollen eyes to find the hall a rush of activity. It was so busy, that no one noticed me standing alone, tears streaming down my face. My body was still shaking with grief.

I needed to find Caius, the one whom I loved, the one I'd chosen. I needed to see the man who suffered so much hurt and disappointment. "Caius," I called, not very loud, my voice was too weak for that.

Only then did the room fall still. "Cece!" someone gasped.

Strong arms closed about my waist as Caius pulled me to him. His touch was equally familiar, intimate, soothing, comfortable. He stood behind me, his body pressed to mine, his nose buried in my hair. "There you are," he whispered. It was impossible to quantify the relief in his voice. "Where have you been? I looked everywhere."

"Caius…" I cried, turning in his arms to face him. The moment he saw my face he was immediately alarmed. I wrapped my arms around his waist, buried my head in his chest, and began weeping anew. I cried so hard that I could no longer breathe—no longer think. Everything that I'd seen in the mirror, every bit of revulsion I felt watching Aurelia take her life, and every ounce of sadness at seeing Caius mourn, closed in on me. I was suffocated under the weight of those harrowing scenes.

Caius was confused. Questions began tumbling from his lips. Where had I been? What was wrong? Had Hecate harmed me? "Please, Celine. What is the matter? I cannot help you if you don't tell me."

"Caius, I'm so, so sorry!" was all I could manage through my gasps, repeating the words over and again.

"Sorry for what?" he whispered. "You look like you've seen death."

"I did," I mumbled into his chest before pulling away to look at him. "I saw *her*, Caius. I saw you. I saw all of it."

"I do not understand. Saw *what*, Celine?" His sudden hesitance told me more than his feigned misunderstanding did. He knew immediately.

"I saw *her*. Aurelia. I saw her die. I saw you try to save her. I watched you become a vampire. I witnessed the war, her death, *everything*."

His body tensed. I felt the breath leave his chest as it deflated against my own. Then his arms fell away from me. Instinct told me to give him space, so I did. I stepped back from him several paces to look at his face. He shook his head in disbelief.

"I know I probably shouldn't have watched," I said. "But Hecate showed me. She showed me all of it."

His lips were pursed. Before I could say anything more, he turned away from me and I found myself looking at his back. Was he afraid to show me his sadness? His anger?

"Caius, please…" I begged, moving forward and linking my arms around his chest from behind, hugging him to me.

"You should not have watched any of that, Celine." His tone was unreadable. He kept his voice low.

"I understand why you didn't tell me," I said. "Please don't be angry with me."

His shoulders dropped and he turned back to me, putting a hand on each side of my face, looking deeply into my eyes. His were depths of grief. "I am not upset with you, Celine. I'm not happy with what you have witnessed. What's done is done." He fell quiet for a moment. "All that matters now is your safety. Now, come along. I'm in the middle of a meeting. Moreover, we've got something else that requires your immediate attention." Just like that, he swept everything away, as if it were no longer important.

"But—but we need to talk about this, about what I saw." I wasn't ready to simply drop the subject. I needed to get it off my chest.

"Celine, there is a time and place for everything. Now is neither. Come." His mood had changed abruptly to business. I wondered if he was doing it to hide his hurt. Taking my hand, he led me up the stairs to a quiet corridor. Then he stopped and removed his iPhone.

"I promised your parents you would call them as soon as we found you safe."

Sadness momentarily forgotten, my jaw dropped. "My—my parents?" When I didn't take the phone, he put it in my hands.

"Genevieve insisted. I relented. They know you are here, though they do not know where *here* is. I promised them that they may see you when this is all over, in exchange for their silence. They agreed. They need to know you are safe—say nothing else."

I continued to stare at him with wide eyes. Had hell frozen over? He gave me a stern look that silenced all further questions. I dialed my parents' number. Mom answered before the first ring finished. "Cece?"

"Yes, Mom, it's me."

"Thank God you're okay." She was already in tears. I could hear it in her voice. "What's going on, Cece? Who is this Caius person? Are you, are you tangled up with some kind of mafia? I don't understand. He didn't answer any of our questions. Do we need to call the police?" Words were tumbling out of her mouth. "I've got you on speaker so that your father can hear."

"Mom, I'm fine. I promise. I'm safe. I can't talk right now. Caius said we can see each other when everything calms down."

She was quiet for a moment. I so desperately wanted to keep up my reassurances. I wanted her to hold me like she used to, to comfort me, but Caius was right, there was a time and place for everything, and now was neither.

"What happened, baby? What kind of trouble are you in?"

"I can't talk about it right now, Mom. I have to go. I promise I'll call again when I can. I love you."

"I love you too sweetie. Promise me you will do what is right."

"I will try. Tell Dad and Austen I love them."

"I will." The quiet dejection in her voice left my chest painfully tight. I was too emotional for this.

"Bye, Mom." I hung up the phone before my tears got the better of me. I'd never cried so much. Caius pulled me against him and we were quiet for several minutes. My exhaustion was catching up with me, so I didn't bother asking any more questions.

"Before you arrived," he said, "we were in the middle of a meeting. The others are waiting. Will you join us?"

I pulled away to look at him. "I would like to, if that's okay."

He nodded and stepped away. Taking my hand, he led me to his study. As we walked, I began to look around. It was still dark out. After being away for what seemed like an eternity, I felt out of sorts. "What time is it?"

"A little past three in the morning."

"What happened with Flavia? Is everyone alright?"

"We will discuss that in my study, but yes, we are unharmed." He walked quickly.

When we entered, I found his study full. There were a number of vampires gathered around his desk, all of whom were speaking in hushed whispers. As I glanced about, I recognized most of them. Caius didn't drop my hand as he led me to his position behind his desk.

Then I saw a face that brought anger to my exterior. A sudden need to place blame arose within me. I snatched my hand from Caius's grasp and walked over to a blue-eyed vampire. "This is all *your* fault, Marcus Crassus!" I spat, punching him as hard as I could in the chest. It probably hurt my fist more than it did him. Marcus looked a little stunned as his eyes went from me to Caius, not understanding. "How could you, Marcus? I saw the *Third Servile War*. How can you even *stand* here in their presence!" His mouth opened, but he said nothing.

"Cece," Caius called in warning. "Cece, come here."

"No!" I cried, keeping my gaze on Marcus. "I trusted you, Marcus. I've been your friend. But I saw you leading the legions of Roman soldiers, countless legions. I saw the thousands of lives taken under your command on the battlefield. I saw you parading in the streets of Rome, claiming all the credit for your victory."

"Cece," Caius drawled. "Marcus has recognized his wrongs. He is not that man anymore. Come here." Caius was short on patience. I turned to see his hand outstretched for me to take. The other vampires watched us silently.

I felt childish acting this way, but after what I'd seen, all the deaths Marcus had caused, it was difficult to stop myself. Worse still, the rumor he created that Spartacus was dead, which led to Aurelia's death, infuriated me.

"We'll talk about this later," I muttered to Marcus, glaring at him before walking back over to Caius. Marcus was speechless as he gazed back at me.

As soon as I reached him, Caius took my hand and pulled me close him. "Marcus has long since repented," he whispered into my ear. "What are we if we do not forgive?"

"I'm sorry," I mumbled, trying to calm my frazzled nerves.

It turned out that the vampires were in an important meeting to determine a solid plan of action for the night to come. "We do not know how many night-walkers we will encounter when the sun sets, but we must be ready none-theless."

"Flavia wasn't bluffing?" I suddenly recalled her threats.

"No. We must plan for the worst."

There was a large map on the desk. Felix was standing over it with a Sharpie. He was marking places suspected of hiding night-walkers.

"Caius, what happened with Flavia? Is she dead?" I asked quietly so as not to disrupt the other low conversations around the room.

"As soon as you left with Hecate, we took advantage of her lingering surprise. The fight was short lived. I took the opportunity to kill her myself. I cannot say that I relished in her death. I made her, after all. I have never killed someone of my own blood before. I couldn't have asked it of Titus."

My head snapped up to look at Titus. He was standing at the opposite corner of the desk looking devastated. I got his attention. "Titus, I..." I hesitated, unsure if he wanted to hear my apology. "I'm sorry for your loss." He thanked me with a brief nod of his head.

Jafar stepped forward. "Caius, I just got off the phone with my connections in Arabia. They are on the first jet over. They will be here by mid-day."

Caius nodded. "Thank you, Jafar. And thank you again for allowing Gigi to use your private jet as well." Jafar nodded then moved away to join in conversation with a few others.

"Where is Gigi?" I asked.

"She's on her way back to France. She left shortly after we got home. She will bring as many from her coven as can be spared. I sent my call for reinforcements around the world. Those who can come in time will be here."

I quickly scanned the faces in the room. "What about Shahriar? Did he leave too?"

"No, he is with Adel, calming the girls."

I hadn't given a single thought to my friends, my sisters, and that left me feeling guilty. Everything was so overwhelming. I just wanted it all to be over. "Please tell me that this is the final assault," I asked.

"I believe so." Caius squeezed my hand.

I looked down. I was still dressed in my club lingerie. "Caius, I should go change."

He pulled on my hand, holding it against his thigh. The look he gave me said, *you're not going anywhere*. Perhaps he was afraid to let me out of his sight. I suppose he had every reason to feel that way.

So I stood by his side for the remainder of the meeting. It was mostly a brainstorming session. The vampires went over numbers, logistics, and their plan of attack. As looked from face to face, I realized that these were Caius's closest companions. Nearly all of them had been in various memories I'd seen, most from the gladiator school near Capua. Caius was the first vampire, and he'd changed each of them. They had stayed with him all this time. Loyalty like that was irreplaceable. Surely we would get through this final stand. I couldn't guarantee everyone would make it out alive, but I trusted them.

# CHAPTER 32

*B*allet is too contrived to be sexual, even when one's limbs are wrapped around another, joined in a passionate embrace. The level of technique and concentration required does not allow for arousal. Yet, ballet can still be erotic. I once heard a choreographer say that he could watch a dancer for a few minutes, and tell how she made love, simply by her movements. There is something sensual about putting the body on display, exposing it at its most vulnerable. Few things in life are more beautiful than vulnerability.

Seeing Caius in Hecate's mirror of memories allowed me to see him at his most vulnerable. I'd seen him as a human, making love to Aurelia. I'd seen him become a vampire. I'd seen him kill, lead men into battle, to victory, and to death. Moreover, I'd seen him lose the one he loved most, and mourn over her body. His beauty went beyond his surface; it lay deeply embedded in his tortured past. I was desperate to unlock that part of him and share in his vulnerability.

When the first rays of sunlight cast themselves upon Anghor

Manor, Caius broke up his meeting and sent his vampires to their assignments. It was the moment I longed for. We could finally be alone.

I was too afraid to bring up Hecate, so instead I tried something different. "Caius, I wanted to thank you." I sat perched on the corner of his desk, my legs dangling casually off the side. He sat in his desk chair, pouring over his map of Vienna.

When I spoke, he set his Sharpie down and turned to me. "Thank me for what, Celine?"

"I wanted to thank you for protecting me, for giving me the moonstone necklace. I know now what it means to you. If not for that necklace, I can't imagine…" I pictured a gruesome image of Flavia grinding her dagger into my flesh. "I'd most likely be dead."

Caius placed his hand on my leg and massaged my muscles with his thumb. "Even the recollection of that situation pains me deeply. It shouldn't have come to that."

I shrugged. "Shit happens."

"Verily. It was scary for all of us, you most of all."

"I really thought I was going to die," I whispered, my voice growing hoarse. "It sounds funny now, but at that moment, I was mad about dying a virgin." I snorted. Of all the things to cross my mind. "I suppose people think crazy things when they're close to death."

I expected Caius to laugh. He didn't laugh. Instead, he abandoned his chair to face me. "Cece, it's been months since we discussed your virginity. I have waited for you to seek me out, but I did not realize you were already ready." He gently nudged my legs apart, moving between them before placing a hand on each side of the desk. Then he leaned towards me. I had to lean back to maintain a clear view of his face.

"I think I'm ready. I mean, I want it. I want you. I was thinking about telling you at the vampire ball. It just didn't feel right *asking*—not for my first time. I choreographed *Seduction* hoping you would want me badly enough to come to me. After that I met Gigi. She told me vampires don't desire sex."

He sighed. "I wish you would come to me with your worries, rather than speculate. It's true, we vampires do not *crave* sex the way we crave blood. I have told you this. That does not mean we refrain."

"I know but, are you able to enjoy it? You know, the way a human does?"

"Yes. We can come, if that's what you mean. In my case, sex lost its luster long ago, replaced by my desire for blood. I am old after all. Even a good thing can get boring when something better exists."

My brow furrowed. His words confirmed my suspicions. Blood would always win over sex.

"Cece, sex with you would never be boring."

"It—it wouldn't?"

"God, no." His voice was a deep growl. "The effect that I have on you is arousing. Watching you flush beneath my touch only makes me want you more—it makes me feel powerful. In the grand scheme of things, when I have power like that, who the fuck cares if I get off or not?" He hovered inches from my lips.

"But I care! I want you to get off, and I want you to *want* it. I want you to be selfish, at least just a little."

"Oh, I am very selfish, Celine, and yes, of course I want to get off. That simply is not my chief motivation for pleasing you. Does that make sense?"

I thought about it, finally nodding.

"Good. Now then. I think it's time to make good on my promise to you. Where would you like it? In here on the couch? Or in your bedroom? Or anywhere else you can scheme up."

"Wait—like—like right now?" My eyes widened, and my pulse leapt into action like a horse from the starting gate.

"There is no time like the present." He didn't bother hiding his devilish grin. "I'm suddenly in the mood to be...*selfish*."

"But..."

"But what?"

"It's too planned. It's so *contrived*," I argued. His sudden suggestion gave me no time to mentally prepare.

"Did you expect it tonight?"

"Well, no."

"Then it is spontaneous."

He moved forward putting his mouth close to my ear. "You want me to be selfish. I'm going to be selfish. I'm going to take you right now."

Before I could protest, he scooped me up, forcing me to wrap my legs around him. My arms coiled instinctively about his neck. His abrupt acquisition of me brought about a fit of nervous giggles. He carted me away to the leather sofa and stretched me across it. I suddenly found him on his knees, leaning over me. His face was close enough to see the bits of dark stubble growing along his jaw.

I gazed into his silvery depths, allowing the nervous tension within me to build. My mind raced. What was I supposed to do next? Lay here and watch him? Unbutton his shirt? Kiss him? I bit at the skin on my bottom lip.

Caius looked me up and down. "You're perfect, Celine." His low murmur was honey to my ears. He ran his fingers across my bare skin, across my ticklish spots.

I laughed and flinched, capturing his hand. "Please," I gasped. "Don't torture me."

"Is someone ticklish?" His eyes sparkled.

"Too much for my own good," I breathed.

"Very well. No more tickling." He brought his mouth nearer and I released his hand. There he hovered above me, gently brushing his nose against mine. Before kissing me, he splayed a hand across my tummy. I felt the warmth of his palm radiating through my skin. The slit in my lingerie top was already separated, leaving my stomach exposed to him.

As soon as he kissed me, his tongue began teasing mine, but it was his hands that were truly provoking. One grasped the top of my head, thumb stroking my scalp. The other trailed up my midriff imparting gentle caresses as it went. When he reached my breasts, my nipples puckered in anticipation. Once there, he gripped my breast through the fabric, massaging it with his thumb. My breathing hitched, and I sighed into his lips.

"See?" he mumbled. "This is what I enjoy, making you want me."

"I always want you," I whispered back.

He chuckled. I felt a snap against my skin as he undid the front clasp holding my lingerie top together. A rush of air against my cleavage left me holding my breath. His hand slid beneath the fabric, and the heat of his skin left goosebumps on my own. I couldn't bear his teasing. My heart was sure to betray me.

Caius exhaled, turning his gaze back to mine. His eyes were filled with unspoken promise. My core clenched in anticipation. I would have rather he kissed me, so that I could hide my eyes. Instead, he gazed upon me to watch the desperation he inflicted.

The moment his hand began traveling downward, I squeezed my legs tightly, rubbing my thighs together, squirming with delight. When I felt his fingertips trace the lace of my boy shorts, I sighed, closing my eyes in delight. His hand continued to tease, and my legs now having a mind of their own, fell open for him.

"Celine," he whispered. "Please don't hide those stunning green eyes from me." My eyelids flew open. I found his silver gaze once more. The corner of his mouth turned up before he planted a tender kiss upon my lips.

"Do you want to drink first?" I asked, eager for the pleasure of it. His hand still stroked the fabric between my legs. Every so often, a finger would creep just beneath the elastic and I would stop breathing entirely.

"I *do* want a drink, but not first. Everything you feel from this —from me—I want it to be real. My feeding can wait until later." His finger slipped beneath the elastic seam of my panties again, but this time it found its mark. I gasped. In response he groaned, moving his mouth over mine and taking hold of my lower lip, pulling gently with his teeth.

When the tension between us became unbearable, he stood. I watched him as he removed his dress shirt, and then his T-shirt. He had the chest of a god! toned and broad, with a bit of curly hair across his pecks. The sound of his jeans zipper brought my gaze south.

I had to be the luckiest girl alive. Caius was offering me a strip show with the firelight dancing behind him. Better still, he was revealing himself to me first. This was the vulnerability I craved, and he was giving it to me.

Without any warning, off went his pants. He stood up and remained motionless for me. I looked him up and down. When he noticed my captivation, he said, "Breathe, Celine." I released a huge breath, betraying my delight.

Without wasting another moment, he laid himself on top of me. Our lips met, both of us hungry for the other. I loved the way his tongue explored my mouth. I couldn't stop thinking about the hardness pushed against me, painfully pleasurable as he ground his hips hypnotically against mine.

I moved my legs to get comfortable, wrapping them around him. Only, that angled me just right, to my own delicious torture. I groaned into his mouth, greedy and expectant.

He moved off me and took hold of my lingerie bottoms, tugging them ever so slowly down my legs. He was doing it on purpose. My eyes were glued to his every movement.

With my panties gone, I became suddenly shy. Heat spread from my face, down my neck, through the rest of my body, pooling at the apex of my thighs. He didn't bother taking his eyes off me. I watched as he took me in. His regard turned hungry, like how he looked before feeding. He ducked his head between my legs.

I gasped. His tongue was on me, ardent and passionate. My body pulsed in response to the fire stoked by his exploration. His hair was silky and thick. I ran my fingers through it, twisting and pulling at the curls as I guided his head against me. Every time he stroked me, I clung to fistfuls of it, crying out.

I could hardly keep still. The muscles in my core clenched and released, threatening to come apart. My body was climbing a familiar pathway, one he was leading me to the top of. If he didn't stop, I would come undone, but if he did stop, I would shatter. My breathing came in gasps, as I tried to get air and cry out, all at once.

At last, to both my relief and deprivation, he pulled away. "Don't—please don't stop," I cried. He kissed my bent knee, locking his eyes onto mine.

"No stopping, Celine," he said. "I cannot wait any longer."

He positioned himself atop me, stretching his body along mine. I gasped at the sharp pain I felt as he filled me. He stilled, waiting. Then, agonizingly slow at first, he began to move, increasing his tempo. Each movement left my core clenching against him.

He was the antidote to my bursting affliction. I was already so close to the height of my mountain, impatiently waiting at its peak. I needed his push, and he gave it, grinding his hips into mine. I cried out. Again, he moved, and again, offering and then taking away the finish I needed. My nails dug into the flesh of his back with satisfied frustration, holding onto him as if my entire being depended on it. Then at last, the stones beneath my feet crumbled. My body took its plunge. I cried out in triumph, my voice husky and sensual. He growled deeply, calling my name in supplication.

The world through my eyes was nearly dark as I fell. I could only feel. My body was a mix of sensations and emotions. Caius was still moving, but slowing as he brought me down, catching me at the end of my descent. It was pure ecstasy—nothing compared.

"Breath, Celine," he reminded me again, his voice a low rumble. I could hardly gasp as my lungs labored. One of his arms was underneath my neck, supporting my head, and the other was still cupped against the back of my thigh. As he shifted, my body clenched again. "Caius," I murmured, sated. "Is it always like this?"

I felt him chuckle against my neck. His head was hidden there. "No." He too sighed with satisfaction. "Only for the lucky ones." The gruffness in his voice, the contentment I heard, was sexy and fulfilling.

I was almost reluctant when he removed himself from me. "Can we do it again?" I begged.

This time he laughed outright. "Yes, Celine. As many times as you desire."

I smiled. "Good. But first, I need to use the ladies' room."

Caius led me to a wooden panel on the wall at the far side of his study, which turned out to be a hidden door. I was shocked to discover an elegant bathroom hiding behind it. The bath tub was the size of a Jacuzzi, and everything was white marble and iridescent tile.

"I may not have a private bedroom, but I do have this."

For some time, I had wondered about his bedroom. I finally had my answer. Still, the notion surprised me. "No bedroom?"

"This is my bedroom." He spread his arms wide to include his study behind us. "I don't sleep much. I spend most of my time here. It's pointless to have a room with a bed that I'd never use." As he finished speaking, he looked me up and down, taking in my naked body. A familiar heat returned to my skin. "I'll leave you to it, then." He walked away, a pleased smile on his lips.

After splashing some water on my face, and taking several deep breaths in front of the mirror, I finished my business then returned to the sitting area. Caius sat naked on the sofa, arms outstretched as he leaned back to watch the fire. I watched him from behind for several moments, appreciating him for the god that he was. Then I sat down beside him, nudging myself under his shoulder where I comfortably leaned against him.

We sat content in our silence. I listened to the crackle and pop of the flames in the grate. Our little world felt so peaceful, so perfect. Outside, the world was anything but; danger waited, but it would have to wait a little longer; I wasn't ready to give this up just yet.

After a time, Caius broke the calm silence we shared. "I once promised myself that I would never love another," he said. "When I lost Aurelia, I vowed to steer clear of this afflicting emotion. In that, I have failed. My love for you frightens me."

I turned my gaze upon him. His face was impassive. The reflection of orange flames danced within the slivers of his eyes. "You were right, Celine, when you said that we should talk about what you saw with Hecate, and we will, just not yet. I don't think I'm ready."

He turned to me, capturing me with his regard. I swallowed and nodded. "I will be here, Caius, whenever you are ready."

"Thank you. Now, I believe there is a certain matter you wished to repeat?" He did not wait for my answer. He took my arm and gently pulled me atop him such that my legs straddled his. As I gazed into his eyes, eagerly anticipating what was to come, I felt his hand slip between my thighs. Of its own accord, my head fell back, and I groaned. Caius guided me down upon him until he filled me.

As made love again, we sank deeply into the leather sofa; Caius sank deeper into me, and I sank deeper into the abyss of my own happiness. This time it was even sweeter than before, with his arms wrapped around me as he held me against him. His love for me was enough to frighten him, and that left me aroused.

When we finished, I expressed the same sentiments. "I promised myself that I would tell you how much I love you the moment I got back."

"Is that so?" he murmured into my hair. His arms remained tightly wrapped around my body as I continued to straddle him. "And how much do you love me, Celine?"

"So much that it hurts." I recalled seeing his pain in the mirror of memories. "So much that I would give my life to heal your woes and make you happy."

"That is a love I will treasure forever." His use of forever resonated within me the way it ought. Forever was no small matter to an immortal vampire. Forever was a concept we ballerinas could merely dream about, and I understood well the gravity of his meaning. If only our morning could have lasted just as long as forever.

As it faded, and the sun rose higher in the sky, we were resigned to end our blissful moments together. The heavy realization of what was to come grew stronger. Neither of us could hide from the approaching danger.

Each kiss we shared, we treated as the last, letting our lips linger longer and longer. I placed my arms around his neck, reluctant to let him go. He nuzzled my cheek with his nose, sighing and saying, "The time I have spent with you has been a gift. Thank you for giving yourself to me—for offering freely both your heart and your blood."

"You don't need to thank me, Caius."

My words earned a brief peck on the cheek and a smile. "Run along now and change, my sweet little bird. My afternoon meetings will begin shortly. Return to me when you are ready."

I shared one last kiss with him and then left, retreating to my bedroom. It felt as if I had been away for an age. In a way, I had. Two thousand years into the past I had traveled. I half expected to find my surroundings covered in dust. They looked the same as before.

As I showered, I couldn't help my smile. Caius had given himself to me. He'd offered me the vulnerability I craved, and I returned my own to him. Not even my apprehension could stifle my joy. I was thankful for the small moments Caius and I had stolen amid chaos. What we shared was truly magnificent—perfect in every way. No matter what was to come, no matter what we would face in the night following, I would carry our memories with me, even into death.

CHAPTER 33

*T*he biggest sacrifice a ballerina will ever make is the sacrifice of a personal life, or what outsiders call, "living." Waking up late on Saturday morning to enjoy a plate of French toast and syrup, staying out till dawn with friends, or enjoying a three-course meal with a glass of wine. That is what we call living, and we sacrifice it. To us, living is dancing. There is nothing else.

There are a few who *try* to balance dancing and living. They find themselves in constant conflict, struggling every time they dance, knowing that each step of their choreographed routine is a step away from living. Then there are those like myself, who simply accept the sacrifice and make peace with it.

When I returned to Caius's study after our incredible morning together, I never imagined I would need to make a sacrifice of a new kind. This one would be selfless, unlike ballet, which is always a selfish endeavor. I found Caius's study packed. Even the hallway outside was lined with bodies. Vampires from around the world had been arriving

283

all afternoon. The manor was now bursting at the seams. One thing was certain, our numbers would not match the thousands of night-walkers we would face.

I pushed my way through Caius's study to his desk, where he and many others were heatedly discussing a plan of action. Marcus was there; I avoided his eyes. I still didn't know what to make of him. He was my friend; I'd known him for the entirety of my time at the manor. He'd protected me during the night-walker attack on the lawn, and often escorted Sophie to Fluxx before her murder. If Caius had already forgiven him, then I needed to too.

Everyone fell silent when I stepped up beside Caius. "What's the matter?" I looked from Caius to the others.

"Cato has presented a new plan. It is both reckless, and dangerous. I dislike it immensely."

"Oh?" I looked from Caius to Cato.

"Half of us agree with it, the other half of us disagree. Unfortunately, I cannot think up anything better." Caius frowned.

"What's the plan? Maybe I can help tip the balance?" I very much doubted my power since I knew little of vampire politics, but I was curious.

"Cato proposes that we use bait to lure the night-walkers into the city's center. This way, we will have an easier time grouping them together, detaining them."

I considered the idea for a moment, then shrugged. "It seems reasonable to me. The night-walkers are drawn to blood. If there are bleeding humans, they will be inclined to go for them, rather than going after others." An image of a bleeding human in shark infested water came to mind. That's when I realized that the plan was slightly barbaric.

Caius remained thoughtful as he spoke. "Yes, Celine, but it may not have much of an effect overall. In fact, it will probably do more harm than good."

"Well, people are going to die regardless, aren't they?" It felt a little heartless to admit this, but it was true. Flowing blood would entice them.

"Yes, many humans will die regardless. How do you choose which people to offer up?"

It was a good point. I certainly wouldn't want to oversee a decision like that. "How come you don't think it would have much of an effect overall?"

"Because the average person doesn't smell as appealing as you might think. For it to work, we will need good blood—tempting blood. Even then, it would take a true strong blood to lure the night-walkers on the outskirts of the city to the center."

"How strong?"

"Very strong," Cato answered from beside Caius. His eyes were glued to me, as if inviting me to make an important realization. That discovery took but a second. Before I could think better of it, it was out of my mouth. "I have strong blood—the strongest. I've seen the way all of you look at me."

Caius rounded on me. "Are you *insane*, Celine? Absolutely not." The room fell silent.

"She's got a point, you know." Nero caught my eye. He was smiling devilishly. An image of him in the gladiator ring flashed through my mind. He was a strong warrior like the others. I smiled back, thankful he was on my side.

"There's no way in hell I would put Celine in danger." Caius looked at each of the others.

"But I'll never be in danger," I reminded him. "The necklace, remember?" Instinctively, my hand clutched the moonstone pendant to caress its smooth surface.

Caius sighed. At last he admitted that he couldn't argue, albeit reluctantly. My point was too true. "I doubt Hecate will be eager to aid you twice in one day," he murmured. Still, I could see that he digested my idea, mulling it over.

"It doesn't matter what makes her happy," I said. "She promised. What choice does she have?" I felt a little manipulative using Hecate in this way. "Besides, it may not come to that. I have an idea."

I realized that the room was still silent. All conversation had ceased, and everyone's attention was on me. I looked at Caius, waiting for his permission. This was his meeting after all, and I didn't want to impose.

He considered me for a moment, caressing my hand as he held it in his. "I suppose even the littlest bird can have the loudest song. Very well then, what do you have in mind?"

After selflessly sacrificing myself, I quickly formulated my plan. I went through the details with the vampires, reassuring everyone that if all went well, I'd be long gone by the time things got too messy. "And if anything goes wrong, if my guards fall, or if I don't get out in time, then Hecate will appear and sweep me away from the fighting. It's foolproof."

"Hecate is a god," Felix reminded me. "She can refuse if she so chooses. Are you sure we should count on her?"

I nodded. I was sure. "She made a promise, Felix. Gods don't back down on their word."

Caius sighed beside me. I gave him a sidelong glance. I could tell that he was torn. He had every reason to be. I squeezed his hand reassuringly.

"Are you sure you want to do this, Cece? I cannot stop you if this is what your heart desires."

"I—I'll do it. I don't know if it's the correct solution. Maybe we should take a vote?"

He nodded. A vote was taken. Nearly every hand went up —*nearly*—Caius, Titus, Felix, and Julia did not raise theirs, but I knew it was their feelings for me that kept them from it. They cared too much about me.

Majority ruled, so it was decided. After that, the meeting disbanded and everyone began final preparations. It was nearly four in the afternoon by the time groups of vampires began departing from the manor, eager to get to their positions around the city.

When Gigi arrived with her coven and discovered what I'd done, she made a huge scene. There was so much shouting between her and Caius, that the girls crept from their hiding places to see about the racket. "If you allow this, Caius, if you allow her to do this, I have half a mind to withdraw my forces *and* my great granddaughter," Gigi snapped. "I'll take everyone straight back to France."

I could see that she was both anxious and stressed. My volunteering had pushed her over the edge. "Please, Gigi. I want to do this. I want to help." At last, after much reassuring on my part and Caius's, I convinced her to leave me be.

Still, she insisted on guarding me. "I'll not have it said that my great granddaughter came to harm under *my* watch," she muttered as she led her vampires from the house to make her way into the city.

No one was taking cars. Vampires could cover short distances with great speed. The trek into Vienna wasn't much of an obstacle for them. Longer distances were tiring, but they'd all made sure to feed that afternoon.

I spent the last few minutes in privacy with Caius, insisting that he feed from me once more. "Please," I begged him. "I need you to be at your strongest tonight. I would die if anything happened to you."

His face softened upon hearing my words. Finally, he took a little. He'd already had plenty that day, but it felt safer this way. At his strongest, he'd be most capable of overcoming anything.

We were the only ones driving, so we did not linger. It was important for me to have a safe getaway vehicle, and Titus's giant black Hummer was a worthy choice. "He's quite fond of this thing, you know." Caius helped me into the vehicle. "He asked that we keep it dent and blood free."

"I have a feeling it will need replacing when this is all over." I plastered a smile on my face, but the atmosphere was charged with danger. We both knew that tonight might be our last.

"I hope you are wrong, Cece."

As we drove into Vienna, the sun was already sinking low. Caius began going through the logistics of my plan with me. I listened silently, allowing him to run through it repeatedly. He needed to distract himself, and this was the best way. "Our safest bet is putting you in the middle of the city. It will draw the most attention with bystanders, but the night-walkers will flock there anyway."

Buildings were beginning to materialize as the countryside grew sparser. I kept my gaze upon the scenery, but I didn't see any of it. I focused on Caius's voice.

"I've assigned many guards to you. As soon as I give the signal, I want you out of harm's way. Do you understand? No protesting. You'll get in the Hummer with your driver, and you'll leave. You'll go straight back to the manor."

I nodded. I'd already agreed to this earlier.

"Marcus will drive you the remainder of the way into the city after we meet at the rendezvous point. Are you okay with that?"

I was silent for so long that Caius said, "If you are still angry with him, I will understand. I can have someone else. I want you to feel comfortable and unafraid. Do you trust him enough for the job?"

Of course I did. "Marcus is fine."

"Good. I trust Marcus with my life. You should too."

The rendezvous point, it turned out, was Fluxx. I wasn't used to seeing it in the setting sun. It looked almost mundane, like a celebrity out of costume.

We went inside. I was led to a room I had never seen. My jaw dropped; this room was full of weapons, but mostly boxes of wooden stakes. All the walls moved as buttons were pushed, bringing forth trays and shelving, laden with every imaginable device for killing.

Caius noticed my expression. "It never hurts to be prepared." Vampires were all around us, stocking up on supplies, filling backpacks and duffel bags. Caius lashed a sword to his belt. It looked very old. "I've had it for thousands of years." He answered my unspoken question. "I always keep it sharp."

I nodded, suppressing my increasing nerves. At last, Caius handed me a loaded revolver and a holster. "This is for you. Just in case. It's filled with wooden bullets."

"Will it kill them?"

He shook his head. "No. But it will buy you time. There is more ammunition in the back of the Hummer."

When we emerged from the building, our huge team of vamps was already heading to their separate posts. They went in smaller groups. We had no real idea where the caches of night walkers were hidden. It was best to spread out and cover all outlets.

"Cece?" I heard Marcus's voice from behind me. "Are you ready?"

I was. Caius turned to me, squeezing my hand. "I'll see you very soon, okay? I just need to close up shop here."

"Okay," I whispered, reluctant to leave him.

It was a short drive to the middle of the city. We passed all sorts of cute little coffee shops and book stores. I found myself silently letting my eyes slide over them. I tried my hardest to keep scenarios of what might happen from afflicting me.

"Cece?" Marcus was speaking to me. I'd zoned out without realizing it.

"Sorry, Marcus. What did you say?"

"I said, I wanted to apologize to you for what you saw of

me, for what Hecate showed you. I am not that man anymore. I was only doing my job, one I mistakenly believed to be a good calling. The things I did—I must live with them for an eternity. Not a day goes by that I do not think about all the innocent lives I took—the innocent lives my men took."

"I'm sorry too, Marcus. I shouldn't have snapped at you like that." Our petty squabble seemed ridiculous now, with all that was going on.

"I need you to understand that I feel remorse for what I did. I need you to know that I would do anything for Caius. I owe him numerous life debts. When I was young, when I held my position in the Roman army, the name Spartacus was nearly legend. Everyone knew it—parents told their children stories. I never succeeded in killing him, to my own disappointment at the time. Because of it, I felt myself to be the world's biggest failure. When he disappeared from the battle, I believed that proclaiming his death was good enough. I encouraged the rumor to help my own political position in Rome. I made many foolish decisions when I was young. I hope—can you forgive me?"

He glanced anxiously at me as we drove through each of the stop lights, steadily making our way deeper into the city. We were near its heart. At last I nodded. "None of us are perfect, Marcus. I forgive you."

"Thank you, Cece. I would give my life for Caius if it came down to it, and for you."

For the last few minutes of the drive, we remained silent. I knew that it was important for Marcus to get that off his chest before the fight. I was glad that we were good again. The last thing I wanted was for something to happen to him, especially if we ended things on a bad note. I never would have forgiven myself.

At last he pulled the Hummer to a stop and parked. We were in a large cobblestoned square surrounded by older buildings. There were tourists meandering about the tall buildings towering over us. When we pulled up, they looked at us strangely for parking illegally. We ignored them.

The sun was at the horizon now, casting its golden rays everywhere. Marcus was thinking the same thing I was, as he followed my gaze to the setting sun. "It will be dark in twenty minutes. Caius will meet us here shortly. Your blood, it will be tempting enough for them. You need not worry about me or any of the others. We are strong, and we've all been fed."

Thanking him for his reassurances, I followed his lead, climbing out of the Hummer to circle around back. Marcus began removing supplies from the hatch.

"I saw you on the battlefield," I stated matter-of-factly. "You're a strong fighter."

He paused. "Thank you, Cece. That was before I was a vampire. Let us hope that tonight my skills are enough. The night-walkers are not mere humans like those men I slaughtered back in Rome. My guess is, they will be very hungry."

I imagined he was correct. Our enemy had likely been pinned-up for a long time, deprived of blood. They would be ravenous.

"Celine? Are you ready?" Caius whooshed up behind me, placing a hand on my shoulder. I nodded. "Good, then come."

I followed Caius, hand in hand, over to the passenger side of the Hummer. We had a few moments together. He kissed me sweetly, looking into my eyes. "We will be by your side the whole time," he reassured me. "I won't let anything happen to you."

"Caius." My voice was barely a whisper. "I'm more worried about you than me. Promise me you won't do anything stupid. I can't lose you."

His mouth turned up at the corner. "You won't, Celine. Hecate owes me a happy ending, I think." It was true, but the gods were known to be fickle. "Now, are you ready? This will hurt a bit, bleeding freely."

I knew what he meant. This time there would be no pleasure to follow his bite. That only came when he drank, but I already understood this—it was my sacrifice—the cost of helping a good cause. "I'm ready," I whispered.

He took my hand, lifting it to his mouth. I watched him and he me, his eyes never leaving mine. Just as the sun set, just as the world around us fell into darkness, I felt his teeth sink painfully into the flesh of my wrist. My blood poured forth. It was time.

# CHAPTER 34

*B*efore the curtain rises at the ballet, there's this short span of silence that at times, feels like an eternity. The calm before a storm is a curious thing. It's so peaceful, so quiet, yet you can sense the impending chaos stretching out before you. Vienna was like that. The city around us was almost frozen in time. The short minutes before our battle seemed to last an eternity.

After Caius bit me, my wrist bled freely, blood sliding down my hand, and finally my fingertips, where it slowly drained onto the ground in a pool. Caius was right, it hurt like hell. My pain let me know I was alive. My scared, beating heart made the throbbing worse. I did not have to wait long before sounds of chaos began ringing out into the city.

I knew something was happening when the sirens started screaming. They echoed through the streets one after another, all coming from different directions, some far away, others nearer. All were repeating with various tempos and different pitches. I realized then that the night-walkers were free. Up until this point, I held fast to the hope that Flavia was bluffing.

My guards were whooshing in from everywhere as they began gathering around the square. Some gave reports to Caius, who remained by my side. From the sound of it, night-walkers were already rampaging the outskirts of Vienna, working their way into the center of the city.

"They smell her blood," Cato said the moment he arrived. "They move with a purpose, and all of them are coming here. I could smell her too, the moment you bit her."

"Good. It is working," Caius replied. "What about the humans? What does the death count look like? Any sign of the rogues?"

Cato glanced briefly at me before answering. "No sign of rogues. The death toll is rising, but not as quickly as I would have expected. Cece's blood has them distracted." He then gave me an apologetic look. "How are you holding up, Cece?"

"I—I'm fine," I squeaked, trying to mask my pain as I stood, grinding my teeth together.

These few minutes following my bite were the calmest. Caius didn't expect me to bleed forever, just enough for the night-walkers to pick up my scent. When the time was right, one of the vampires would close my wound with their saliva.

Gigi appeared by my side, placing a wooden stake into my hand. "Don't you drop this." She gave me a stern look, kissed my forehead affectionately, then sped off to stand guard at the perimeter of the square. The humans that occupied the area had mostly dissipated into the buildings. Many were alarmed by the sounds of sirens echoing around the city. Some of the braver ones remained out of doors to point and whisper at us. We must have looked quite strange to them. Caius was too focused to bark any orders at them—to warn them.

The moment the first night-walker arrived at the scene, it was staked so quickly that I hardly noticed. Then came another, and another. At first I believed that we stood a good chance. Caius's vampires were efficient. Each enemy fell as another arrived. But, I was so wrong.

Soon they were coming in droves, pouring in all at once. That's when I began hearing the gunshots. Like Caius warned, wooden bullets wouldn't do more than stun them and slow them down. I knew that these were sounds of desperation—last minute resorts.

After that, everything exploded into mayhem. The night-walkers converging into the square had one desire—me. Each was trying hard to feed this desire while my guards did everything in their power to keep them at bay. I could hear shouts as vampires called out commands to each other, working as a team. I caught a glimpse of Gigi as she plunged a stake into one of the night-walkers while it tried to get away from her. Others used wooden spears, swords to lop off heads, and exploding arrows, which I thought was the most effective method, but also the most dangerous.

Caius's coven of vampires fought exactly like the gladiators I knew them to be. Their weapons moved with deadly efficiency. Unfortunately, we were so terribly outnumbered. It was probably a good time to get out. Yet, if I left too soon, not enough night-walkers roaming the city would move into its center. I waited for Caius's command.

My eyes went to him. He handled his blade efficiently, removing one head after another. I watched him for a minute, gripping my stake, hoping that I wouldn't have to use it. With the speed at which everything happened, I struggled to process what was taking place.

Vampires move with extreme speed, especially when they are hungry. The night-walkers were no different. When I volunteered, I didn't have a clue what I was getting myself into. I initially believed this would be similar to the battle I witnessed in Hecate's mirror of memories. Instead, it was completely different than I imagined. Many of the movements from the vampires were so rapid, they blurred together. I was forced to watch everything in fast-forward.

Then came the moment I needed to retreat. I realized it at the same time Caius did. I saw him glance back at me. Our eyes met briefly, exchanging silent understanding. He couldn't come to me, he was surrounded by night-walkers. Although he handled them efficiently, we were cut off from each other. I began frantically looking around. The sounds in the square grew muffled, like being underwater. I was losing too much blood.

Once more, my gaze went back to Caius. A fresh wave of night-walkers converged upon him. I called out in warning, "Caius!" The sound of my cry echoed around in my head. There were too many! He would never manage them on his own. I had to help him. I pulled out my gun with sluggish movements as my vision blackened at the edges. I fired the entire round of bullets in an attempt to hit the night-walkers surrounding Caius. Not a single one fell.

I struggled to breathe, blinking against my vision. If I could just hang on for a minute longer, I told myself. Suddenly, Jafar materialized before Caius and began lopping heads off, clearing the space around them. In the same instant, two night-walkers latched onto Caius, feeding from him as he attempted to fend them off. Shahriar appeared, rescuing Caius as he pulled the two feeders away from him. Jafar covered their backs. "I'm fine!" I heard Caius yell, giving Shahriar a nod of thanks.

The night-walkers continued to come. In a flash, a cluster of them pounced simultaneously on Shahriar, bringing him to the ground. He cried out in agony. I did too. I could no longer see his body beneath the pile as they began ripping him apart. I only saw the gore that went flying. My stomach churned. I leaned against the Hummer while keeping my hand closed around my bleeding wrist. Caius and Jafar began detaching the night walkers from the pile, but it was too late. Shahriar was gone—dead. The *Arabian Knight* was defeated. I stifled a horrified sob.

"Cece! Get out of here!" Caius yelled as he spun around with his sword, slicing through the nearest night-walker. He wore the same look of defeat I saw when he lost his first battle in Hecate's mirror.

"Marcus!" I called, feeling faint. Marcus appeared at my side an instant later. He grabbed hold of my wrist and ran his tongue along it to seal the wound. His eyes were wide. The frenzy of battle was upon him. "I've got to get you out of here, Cece! Quick, into the Hummer!"

I didn't need telling twice. I moved to the passenger door just as three night-walkers detached from the bunch and threw themselves at me. Marcus cried out in warning. It wasn't enough. The two he wrestled left the third unoccupied. It grabbed me.

I screamed. Pain erupted in my neck. I knew the feeling well. Euphoria took me as it began to feed. For a few seconds, I was too paralyzed to fight back. It was the stench of death that brought me to my senses. Remembering my stake and the many lessons from Titus, I stabbed forward with all my strength. The stake sank into flesh. The night-walker's teeth freed themselves as it cried out. I hadn't gotten its heart, but I'd stunned it.

I didn't need to think twice as my instincts took over. Grasping the stake with both hands, I ripped it from the night walker and thrust it into the vile thing's heart. It screamed in fury, withering into ash and disappearing before my eyes.

More of them appeared before me. They began fighting each other over me, each trying to win the prize. A moment later, Caius appeared at my side. Without warning, he thrust something into my hand. It was another gun. Then he leaned over and closed the wound at my neck.

"Get into the Hummer!" Right as he said it, the mob of night-walkers threw themselves at us, eager to get Caius out of the picture.

I didn't hesitate. I began pulling the trigger, clearing a path as they clawed at me. As soon as I could, I opened the Hummer's door and got in, closing myself within. It felt like the only safe place within a raging sea of danger. Marcus was not long behind me. He slammed his door shut, panting.

"Shahriar!" I cried, hardly recognizing my voice as I spoke. "Shahriar is dead!"

Pain reflected in Marcus's eyes. "Look." Marcus pointed over to a cluster of buildings at the corner of the square. "The rogues are here." My eyes followed his finger. My breath caught as I saw Titus and Julia, busy with rogues who'd just arrived.

"We can't—" I struggled to speak.

"You don't look so good, Cece." Marcus looked me up and down. Without wasting time, he bit into his wrist and shoved it into my face. I turned away at first. "You've lost too much blood, Cece. You must drink. Hurry!"

After his prompting, I didn't question him. Caius trusted Marcus with his life—so did I. I took his wrist and pulled blood into my mouth. It was coppery and stung my tongue. I took several drags before he pulled away. It coursed through me the same way Caius's did. Immediately thereafter, I felt better, stronger, heartened.

Once more, I tried to speak. "We can't leave them, Marcus. We can't run away to safety." Our team was too outnumbered. "Aren't there other vampires—the ones around the city?"

"They are working their way in." Marcus struggled to breathe as he answered me.

"We need all of them here, not just some. Marcus, we can't leave them like this!" Neither of us were cowards. "We've got to do something."

"All right then, put the window down, Cece, and keep shooting. We're going to plow us some night-walkers."

Excited and relieved. I shouted in triumph, "Yee-haw," picking up a country accent from God knows where. The Hummer's engine roared into life. I rolled down the window as Marcus put the beast in gear. Taking aim, I began firing and Marcus began driving. For a fleeting amount of time, I felt productive, but the gun quickly ran out of bullets.

"There are more in the back, but you'll have to climb." Marcus motioned with his head to the back. We were moving out of the square, down one of the side streets. Every thump I heard, every bump we went over, was a night walker caught off guard. The hits would hardly injure them, but they would slow them down. So much for no dents and blood. I doubted Titus would complain.

I monkeyed my way to the back and rustled around in the big boxes for more bullets. "Which one do I use?" There was more ammo than I knew what to do with.

"The nine millimeter," Marcus called. I looked around for the box, finding it at last, shouting with triumph when I did. I scrambled back up to the front seat.

We worked our way up another street, heading back towards the square. "What's all that screaming?" I'd only just heard the anguished cries.

"The humans in the buildings."

I shuddered.

As we approached the square, bodies slammed into Titus's Hummer. Just as we reached the cobblestones of the square, my gun was reloaded.

"Can you drive?" Marcus asked.

"What?" I shrieked.

"Do you know how to drive?"

"Um, yes, I remember, but—"

"Good. Switch me and take the wheel. Give me your gun."

I followed his orders as we stalled our progress to flip duties. Then he was at the window with the gun. He was a better shot than I was. Most of *my* bullets missed their mark, but not so with Marcus.

"Drive!" he ordered. "Drive now and hit as many as possible!" So I did, putting my foot to the floor. We made a good team, clearing a path as we went. It wasn't enough.

It soon became clear that we needed a miracle. The fighting in the cobblestoned square stretched on for hours in stalemate. Marcus and I did our best, me piloting the Hummer and he, the trigger man, while our vampires resorted to every means possible to do theirs. Defeating our enemy was harder than everyone anticipated. The night-walkers were just too quick and too frenzied.

Midnight came and went. By then, Marcus had several guns in his lap, which he procured from the back. He must have reloaded them a hundred times or more.

We both knew we couldn't go on forever. At last, the Hummer puttered to a halt when it ran out of gas. We were forced to abandon it.

Caius was too exhausted to be furious when we reconvened in the square. Marcus led me there, protecting me along the way. We stumbled over bodies. I slipped a few times on the blood that pooled up around them. The air smelled metallic, with the stench of pervading death.

Once we got into position, Gigi was there beside me. I never saw her so exhausted until now. Everyone around me was covered in blood wearing the same looks of fatigue, of defeat. Still, we fought on. I began grabbing up wooden stakes off the ground from vanquished night-walkers. No one protested when I joined the fighting. Titus would have been proud, but I didn't see him anywhere.

The missing faces from our group left me worried. How many from our side had died? Our numbers were dwindling, but so were theirs, only, at a much slower rate.

Night-walkers began to close in around us, packing us tightly together. Eventually, less than a hundred vampires bunched around me. We were trapped.

There was only one thing left to do. Putting my hand on my necklace, I called for Hecate. I put everything into that call— my sense of exhaustion, my growing hopelessness, my fear. A gentle whisper responded, soothing and recognizable. "Hold on a little longer," it breathed, riding the breeze.

My stomach dropped. Hold on for what? We were all going to die. Hecate had abandoned me.

I glanced at Caius, remembering how he looked the time Hecate told him to retreat from his battle in Rome. He looked much the same. Only, there would be no retreat. We couldn't have escaped had we wanted to. We were condemned to our little circle.

I looked everywhere, trying to come up with a solution, anything that might help us. Isolated, there were no other options to be found. "Look to the sky," another whisper called. I felt Hecate's breath on my ear. "You are saved."

I turned my gaze skyward. The horizon shed its dim light upon our little slice of the city, but that dim light was growing brighter. Dawn approached!

"Caius!" I cried triumphantly. "The sun!"

My words pulled him from a trance. He stopped fighting for a moment to look up. His demeanor changed immediately. There was hope. "Keep them busy until the day comes!" He rallied everyone together.

Our vampires attacked with renewed vigor, bringing down many more night-walkers as new courage took hold of us. I began keeping count, staking eleven to the heart as the sun began to rise. With each kill, I saw a little more of my surroundings with clarity.

Just as I staked the twelfth, the sun peeked up from behind the first tall building, sending its rays of warmth down on the fringes of our little square. It took but a minute for its rays to fully bathe us in light. The night-walkers, oblivious as they were, distracted by their desire to defeat us, had not considered the growing light.

Harrowing shrieks went up around us. Seconds later, the cobblestoned square was alight with fire. Hundreds of night-walker bodies burst into flame, turning into ash as they disintegrated, to be carried off by the wind.

Our depleted group looked around in shocked silence. We were too overwhelmed by our own luck to respond. It wasn't until Marcus shouted beside me, "Habemus victoriam!" that our shouts of victory followed his, echoing around the square. It was over.

Hecate had saved us, after all. She'd known. The moon goddess had called forth the sun when we needed it most.

Caius took me up in his arms, kissing me deeply, laughing with frenzied relief. He didn't need to say a word. We felt everything in our emotional exchange. I could only smile, unbelieving, up into his beautiful eyes. We were alive. We were together. Death had tried to take us, but we kicked ass!

Our celebration, though short lived, was jubilant. Before I knew it, Caius was in command once more, calling out orders to the others. There would still be night-walkers hiding in the dark places. He held fast to my hand all the while. "I need to get you home," he murmured at last.

"But what about everyone here?"

"Do not concern yourself with that, Cece. You have sacrificed enough."

I wanted to protest. There was still so much work to be done. I glanced around at all the human bodies. Some hadn't been fully drained. The ones that were would need to be burned. The few that were still alive were crying out for help, fully traumatized.

"We will do what we can to save them," Caius spoke, answering the question I hadn't asked. "I will see to it as soon as I get you home."

As I nodded, a horrifying realization flooded my mind. "Adel!" I cried, stifling a sob.

"Yes, I will get you to her." Pulling at my hand, Caius led me away. It didn't take long to find an abandoned car. Most had been left unattended to during the turmoil. We drove back to the manor in silence. As we made our way, the sun's welcome warmth radiated through the windshield and comforted me. Never again would I take its rays for granted.

I felt several tears slide down my cheeks. How was I going to tell Adel? I was sickened by the thought.

After pulling into the circular drive, I climbed out of the car. Caius followed me to the door, taking one of my hands in both of his. "I can tell her if you need," he offered, seeing how pained I was.

I shook my head. "No. It should come from me."

After kissing me goodbye, Caius left me there. I took several deep breaths, collecting my thoughts. Then I stepped through the doors of Anghor Manor.

# CHAPTER 35

For a long time, I believed the suffering I experienced after my leg injury would be the worst phase of my life. When a ballerina isn't dancing, she often wonders if she is a dancer at all. We are so tied to the stage, that every moment away, we struggle with our identity. I felt as if I'd lost myself. I couldn't have imagined anything more terrible than losing my ability to dance. It was to be the darkest, bleakest chapter of my life, or so I thought.

That changed after the night-walker attack on Vienna. I knew the attack trumped all, because I would have relived my injury over and again if it meant eliminating Flavia's existence and the heartbreak she brought us. All our lives were a mess after she wrecked us. Some lost more than others, especially Adel, who lost both Sophie and Shahriar in the span of a few months. But, we'd all lost someone, and that brought us together, lending us the strength we needed to pull through.

When I entered Anghor Manor after the fight in Vienna, I was greeted by a few of our vampire guards, each questioning me with their intent gazes. These were the ones forced to remain behind to guard the manor.

"It's over," I said. "We did it." I hadn't the energy to run through the events of the night. "Where are the girls?" I asked.

"Sleeping in the television room," one of them answered. I nodded and made my way there.

I was relieved as soon as I saw them, smiling at how sweet and innocent they each looked. They had pulled out blankets and sleeping bags, clustering them together in the middle of the room. There they huddled together, fast asleep. I didn't want to wake them. So instead I tiptoed into the room and plopped down on the floor before the couch, leaning my back against it. The guards followed, remaining in the doorway to watch me.

Marie stirred first. She yawned and blinked several times when she saw me sitting there. I must have looked like a mess to her. "Cece?!" Her declaration quickly woke the other girls. As soon as they saw my face, they knew something was wrong.

I had no idea what our overall losses were. Too many faces were missing when I left Vienna, but I held fast to the hope that they'd simply been separated from our main forces, especially because several of my closest friends hadn't been among the final count. The thought of losing them was devastating.

Adel quickly stood and came to me, taking my hands in hers. "Cece. Tell me. What happen?"

The way she asked—there was such worry in her voice. I could see the bags under her eyes. She was desperate for news about Shahriar. A fresh wave of tears freed themselves from my eyes.

"What happen, Cece?" she asked more frantically. I saw it then in her expression. It was almost as if she knew. "Shahriar?"

I gave my head a little shake and shut my eyes.

"He's—he's dead?" Marie choked, scooting close to us from her spot on the ground. I nodded because I couldn't speak.

"No!" Adel gave a pitiful wail as she fell into my arms. I caught her up and pulled her to me as her body began to shake. She clung to me. "Please, Cece! It can't be true! Please!" she begged.

All I could do was rock her back and forth, cooing. The other girls looked distressed. "Who else?" Marie asked. I knew she was worried about Cato.

I began naming the names of those I was sure were alive. The girls breathed a sigh of relief with each that I gave. When I glanced at the doorway, all the guards in the manor were gathered there. They looked just as upset.

"I cannot answer for those I did not see. But," I paused to swallow, "I hold fast to the hope that they were simply separated."

"But, you don't *know*?" one of the vampires asked from behind me.

I shook my head. "Caius brought me home before I could find those who were missing." Julia and Titus had been among those missing faces. I silently prayed that they were okay.

"I can't—" Adel was trying to talk as she took great gasps. "I can't breathe."

"Take deep breaths Adel." I wiped the remaining tears from my face. I could no longer cry. I was too numb now—too exhausted. I'd lost so much blood, and then physically worn myself thin fighting, so I did my best to comfort her.

"First Sophie, now Shahriar," she cried. I felt my heart break again as she said this. All the girls were crying.

We stayed in the room like this for a long while, hours perhaps. One by one, vampires began returning. They all looked like hell. Some said nothing as they silently passed to their quarters. I didn't blame them for wanting to be alone. I knew that those returning had lost at least one vampire they cared about.

When Jafar came back, I went to him. His face was blank. I knew out of everyone, that he would hold himself accountable for his cousin's death. He wasn't close to anyone else here, only Shahriar, so I did what I could to offer him condolences.

Taking his hand in mine, I looked into his eyes. "I am so sorry for your loss, Jafar. I won't ever forget what Shahriar did for Caius. If you ever need anything from me, please ask. I am in your debt and his, for as long as I live."

Had it not been for Shahriar and Jafar, who came to Caius's aid when he was surrounded, when he was trying to protect me, Shahriar wouldn't have died. Had I not been there at all, his death might never have occurred.

Almost as if he read my mind, Jafar answered. "Do not blame yourself for his death, Celine. He fought bravely, but your bravery, your sacrifice, will be remembered just as heavily. I thank you, Celine, for your condolences and your sacrifice. Tusahibuk alsalama." He then dropped my hand and moved away into the shadows.

My shoulders fell and I expelled the breath I was holding. I wanted so badly to do as he did—to escape away into the depths of my room. In there I could shut the world out, try to forget what had happened, try to ignore what I'd seen, but Adel needed me. So did the others. Most of all, I needed Caius, and I could not hide away until I saw him safely returned to me.

In the hours following the big attack, I desperately looked upon each face returning to the manor, counting those I recognized. With every recognition, I breathed a little easier. Yet, my heart grew desperate as I searched for several people I wanted so *badly* to be alive. As every hour ticked by, when they did not return, my spirts fell deeper into despair.

When it was nearly dark, Caius came home. I rushed to him, begging him to tell me where the others were—those who were missing. I knew he did not want to answer. His jaws were clenched tightly, and it took just a brief glance into the depths of his eyes to know that he'd lost a great deal more than the rest of us.

"Felix is with Cato, comforting him in his sorrow," he replied at last. I spent the span of several heartbeats analyzing his words before breaking down. "We lost Vivian?" I was in shock. Vivian was Cato's sister.

"Cato saw her die."

"No!" I cried. "But what about—"

"Titus and Julia are dead."

The first sob slammed forcefully into my chest. My legs gave out and I nearly collapsed to the floor as Caius caught me up in his arms. Images of Titus and Julia flashed through my mind. I loved Titus! He filled a gaping hole in my life by allowing me into the training room to spar. And Julia had always been a favorite.

My sobs ripped through my body. "Are you sure you looked for them?" What if they had simply gotten separated?

"I am positive, Celine. They are dead." His words held finality, and I knew better than to argue. The hurt was too heavy. I cried for a long time, and Caius held me all the while.

Most of the days following the attack brought a fresh wave of tears. Reminders of the ones we lost could be seen in everything. Such sorrow pervaded the manor, it seemed that a blanket of darkness had settled over our little corner of the countryside. Everything was deathly silent, day after day, month after month. It was as though Anghor Manor itself wept for the inhabitants it lost.

I spent much of that time hiding away, as did we all. Caius still had a lot to do. So much harm had been done in the city. There were many memories to erase. Moreover, plenty of night-walkers who'd slipped past us still needed a stake to the heart. It would have been a headache for anyone. Caius threw himself into the work in an effort to escape his torture. In his eyes, this was all *his* fault.

Conversation between the two of us was rocky for a while. Talking to him was like walking on broken glass. He was so torn up. I knew he saw the loss of every vampire as a personal failure. I also knew that losing Shahriar pained him the most. It was during this time in particular that I discovered it was best if I didn't speak at all. It was better to simply *be*, *be* with him, *be* there for him, *be* the strength he needed.

It hurt me see him in this phase of his life, just as much as it hurt me to see him lose Aurelia. He'd already experienced so much loss in his younger days during the *Third Servile War*. He didn't deserve this.

I often woke in the middle of the night to find him wrapped around me. He'd taken to retreating into my bed each night, albeit in the predawn hours. Most nights he was out hunting the remaining night-walkers, but he always came home to me. He always needed to feed. For those nights when he wasn't hungry, he cuddled up next to me to watch me sleep.

Nearly two months after the attack, Caius and I finally had the second date he owed me—that was the first step and the first instance I saw an improvement in him. I knew that it would do him good to take an evening off. He'd been working relentlessly, and the time came for me to insist upon it. So, we spent a romantic dinner in the city and got drunk as skunks on expensive wine, talking about anything and everything that would distract us from our deep wounds.

Slowly, the spring turned into summer. It took a long time before any of the girls wanted to dance at Fluxx again. In fact, Caius didn't re-open the club until late July. The vampire community worldwide had been rocked by what happened. Those who couldn't get to Vienna in time for the fight eventually made their way across the world, some from the most remote reaches, to pay their respects to those who had fallen.

I spent most days during that summer sunning myself with Adel out on the manor's large terraces. Sometimes we'd stretch towels out on the back lawn and lay out for hours, lathered up with sunscreen. The warmness was a good anti- dote to the chill that saturated our hearts. Ever so sluggishly, our souls began to thaw—to heal.

I never stopped dancing. I used my pain to express my deepest emotions. I made it a point to practice every day. Caius told me that if I didn't feel up for it, I could cancel my contract with the Royal Vienna Ballet, which was quickly approaching as the fall season drew near, but I couldn't do it. Dancing was an ever-present pillar in my life. It was all I had known since childhood. I needed ballet to make sense of the new status quo.

At long last, the summer slipped by. As promised, Caius and I did eventually discuss Aurelia. The need to talk about what I'd seen wasn't as strong by the time we got around to it. I think after having time to digest what Hecate had shown me, some of the questions answered themselves. Regardless, Caius told me the entire story from his point of view. It was hard reliving it that way, for both of us.

I expected the talk to upset him. Surprisingly enough, he held himself together. I admired that about him. He was so strong—stronger than I could ever hope to be. Given enough time, even the deepest scars fade a little.

When it came time to begin my contract at the Royal Vienna Ballet, things were already getting better for everyone except Adel. My being gone more often than not, training and working extensive hours with the *corps de ballet*, took a toll on her. I hated to see her so depressed, and I did what I could when I could, to spend time with her. Cheering her up was a challenge, understandably, but I never gave up on her. After the club reopened, she opted out of dancing at Fluxx. I held on to the hope that someday, she would change her mind. Like the rest of us, she just needed to heal, and eventually, she would.

## CHAPTER 36

*B*allet season runs from fall, until the end of spring. Performances kick off with numerous evenings of the *Nutcracker*, which has become a staple in the ballet world. As the season progresses, the mood changes. Various ballets are performed, some well-known like *Romeo and Juliet* and *Giselle*, and others more obscure, like Balanchine's *Le Tombeau de Couperin*.

The end of ballet season is bitter-sweet. It is a time to rejoice and relish in accomplishments. It is a time to mourn the coming loss of our stage presence. It is the end of a phase, the end of one life, and the beginning of another. It is our chance to begin *living*.

Opening night at the Royal Vienna Ballet was a big deal for everyone in Anghor Manor. The holidays were upon us at last. The manor was decorated with big boughs of pine garland, Christmas trees, and tinsel. Better still, Adel's mood had improved greatly. She was as excited as I, for my first performance.

Caius purchased all the best seats in the house, bragging to all who would listen, that I was to be one of the snowflakes. He'd given tickets to everyone in the manor. Moreover, he hinted that there would be a big surprise to follow the performance. How he loved surprises!

That night I arrived early to the theater, chatting backstage with many of the corps members I befriended. We would never truly be friends the way Adel and I were, but I did my best to be cordial and friendly towards them. Each of us plastered our faces with make-up, hiding all our human blemishes, working hard to achieve the appearance of immortality. We were ballerinas—we lived to dance and nothing else.

Moments before I went on stage, I stood in the left wing waiting for my entrance, flexing my toe shoes, arching my feet to keep them warm. Others waited around me. Everything seemed to stop as I counted down. My adrenaline raced as I listened to Tchaikovsky's music. The mood of the evening was infectious.

Then it was time! We rushed onto the stage one at a time, each of us tip toeing and frolicking back and forth in our white tulle. We assembled, bursting with energy as we threw our bodies into the choreography. I forgot everything but my movements. There was just me, the stage, and the audience.

Dancing as a snowflake is magical, especially to Balanchine's choreography. As you perform your movements on stage, snow flutters down from above, covering everything. It gets everywhere—in our hair, our cleavage, our eyelashes. This time was no different, but I didn't mind it as I once did, for it reminded me of so many past memories. I would never again take dancing for granted. I would savor every second, every instant, the good and the bad.

I was invigorated as I danced. I'd never felt so at home in my own element. With all my friends there to watch me, it was truly ideal. How lucky I was to have all of them. How lucky I was to be alive!

I danced better than I could ever remember. Everything that made up my past was funneled into my movements, into my facial expressions. I danced for those I had lost. I danced for those I loved. Each experience made me a stronger dancer, as did Caius's blood.

At last, when the curtain fell, we dancers congratulated each other and giggled as we tried to be heard over the thunderous applause of the audience. Linking hands and taking our places, we waited for the curtain to rise again. When it did, we bowed not once, but twice, bidding our audience *adieu*. Then we rushed backstage to prepare for the reception.

I wiped off my makeup and went for a fresh face, leaving my hair in its ballet bun. I didn't sweep away the little snowflakes that covered my hair. I looked too magical. Instead, I quickly threw on a little black dress and a pair of strappy heels. Together, the other snowflakes and I rushed out to greet our friends and family.

The entry hall of the Vienna Opera House boasted of dark marble floors and great jeweled chandlers. Sweeping staircases led to the upper floors of the theater. The hall was already packed with guests when we entered through a side door. The crowd immediately noticed and broke into another round of applause. Then they parted for us, and we began to mix.

Caius quickly found me, taking my hand as he kissed me. "You were brilliant!" he cried. "Absolutely brilliant." I squeezed his hand and thanked him. I was so happy, that my smile refused to depart. "Are you ready for your surprise?"

"Yes!" I was breathless. Guiding me through the sea of bodies, he led me to a cluster of people. I stopped dead in my tracks before we reached our destination. Standing with a group of vampires and friends—Felix, Adel, and Gigi included—were my dad, mom, and Austin.

"Caius?" I turned to him with wide eyes.

"I promised your family that they could see you when the excitement died down," he explained. His smile melted my heart.

"Do they—do they know?"

"I told them enough—they know that we are vampires."

My jaw dropped. "You did that for me?"

"I would do anything for you, Celine. Anything." I threw my arms around him. He held me tightly before setting me down. "I think it is time to go and greet them, don't you?"

I nodded, turning my gaze upon them. Just then, Felix noticed me. He elbowed my dad, who turned. Right when he saw me, his face lit up. He and my mom ran to me, followed by Austin. As they crowded around me, kissing and hugging me, I burst into tears. It was all too much.

"Oh Cece! Caius told us everything," my mom said as she buried her own sobs in my hair. "I have never seen you dance with such happiness. We missed you so much."

"Your performance was truly spectacular," Dad said, keeping his arms around me and Mom. "We are so *proud* of you. But you've got a lot of explaining to do, Kiddo."

I nodded and smiled. At that same instant, my tearful eyes met Gigi's. She was beaming.

Shortly thereafter, others began gathering around us, vampires and friends, to wish me congratulations. I had flower bouquets thrust into my arms until I could hardly support my spoils. Caius stayed beside me all the while, grinning and silently enjoying my special moments.

The reception was in full swing when I caught Adel chatting with one of the male dancers. She winked at me when she caught me staring. I couldn't help but smile. My heart soared to see her happy and mingling.

It wasn't until later during the party that I realized my happy reunion was only the first surprise of the evening. When Caius disappeared from my side, I thought little of it as I continued to mingle with my well-wishers. It wasn't until I heard the clang of cutlery on crystal silencing the hall, that I realized something suspicious was happening. All eyes traveled to the top of the staircase where Caius stood with my ballet director.

"Ladies and Gentlemen," my director said. "Thank you for making this opening a special one. The performance of our dancers was a stunning display of their abilities. The Nutcracker is a magical story, but the magic of tonight is not over. Caius?" He turned to Caius.

Caius nodded. His eyes quickly searched the audience until they fell on me. "Celine, would you join me up here, please?"

I swallowed as everyone turned to me. My cheeks burned. Dad gave me a gentle nudge. I looked up at him. He smiled and nodded, his warm brown eyes sparkling. Did he have some part in this?

I made my way through the crowd, slowly climbing the grand staircase to stand beside Caius. He took my hand and smiled down at me. The hall was deathly silent. For just a second, the world froze. Caius removed a little box from his pocket and went down on one knee.

My hand went to my mouth to stifle a gasp. "Celine, you swept into my life at a most unexpected time. You captured my heart when I believed such a thing was impossible. I cannot picture my future without you. I need you. Will you spend eternity with me—will you marry me?"

My breath had already fled my chest. I gazed at him with wide, disbelieving eyes. He wanted me for a wife? For eternity? I tried to answer but my voice just squeaked. My eyes darted down to my family. My mom and dad smiled wide. They must have known!

I returned my gaze to Caius. His silver eyes beseeched me. The truth was, I needed him just as much as he needed me. I was a ballerina—to be a ballerina was to be immortal. Caius wasn't simply asking for a wife, he was asking for an eternity with me, for immortality. In that moment, I made more than one choice. Eagerly, I nodded, smiling and bursting into tears of joy all at once.

The audience cheered and whooped as he stood, gathering me up into his arms. I laughed as he spun me around not once, but twice, before setting me down. Then he took a dazzling emerald engagement ring from its box and placed it on my ring finger.

"It's beautiful," I gasped.

The crowd continued to cheer. Caius led me down the staircase so that our audience could congratulate us properly. As we went, he looked down at me, his face radiating more happiness than I had ever seen. "Am I to understand, Celine, that you have at last made up your mind?" he asked. "Are you ready to become a vampire?"

My stomach fluttered. Truth was, I wouldn't have been a *genuine* ballerina if I did not desire immortality. No more could I give myself to Caius completely without promising him eternity. What was once a seemingly impossible decision, had suddenly become easy. My season of indecisiveness had come to an end. This was my chance to begin *living*. I smiled at Caius and nodded. "I'm ready."

# AUTHOR'S NOTE

When I was younger, I wanted to be a ballerina (and/or a figure skater). My family couldn't afford lessons, so I began teaching myself through YouTube videos. I had friends who danced, and while I did cheerleading and gymnastics during my teenage years, I accepted that ballet was something to be admired from afar. After this, my love of ballet took on new forms. I watched performances, movies, television shows, and read books written by ballerinas. In time, I learned a lot without ever having belonged to the ballet scene.

My first live ballet performance was at the San Francisco Ballet, watching Balanchine's Nutcracker. The experience was a magical one, especially seeing the Christmas tree growing out of the floor. To this day, the Nutcracker remains my favorite piece, though there are so many great works.

When I began writing, I wanted to fuse my secret love of vampires with something fresh. Thus, the story of Blood and Ballet was born. I renewed my passion for ballet by doing more research into the world of ballet. I learned that ballet is a dying art. It reached its height during the Balanchine era, but when Balanchine died in the eighties, its popularity decreased. This saddens me, and I wish there were more ways to make it as popular as it once was. Writing this little novel is my own contribution to the effort, to spur interest in the younger generations.

As I began writing, I stumbled onto the gladiators, and the *Third Servile War*. I conducted research into the history of Rome, and the way the slave rebellions shaped the changes the republic experienced. I enjoyed fusing these different concepts together into a single story of fiction that was meant to be a romance, first and foremost.

After spending six weeks writing Blood and Ballet, I let it sit for almost a year before molding it into something publish-worthy. While it has been a tedious road, I am happy to close this door. Ballet will always hold a treasured place in my heart, and I hope after reading this story, it will in yours, too.

## ACKNOWLEDGMENTS

I wouldn't be a writer were it not for the constant support of my husband. The life of a physics Ph.D. at the largest United States lighting company does not afford a lot of free time, nor did completing my doctorate. My husband's constant willingness to keep up the house and the yard, take care of our dogs, cook my meals, and shower me with love, are the only reasons I was able to take time away from "life" to write. I couldn't have done this without him.

There are others in my life I wish to acknowledge, who also support my writing. My bardic sister, Jeanine, has been pursuing writing alongside me. Our mutual growth has been instrumental in my success. I am so lucky to have her extra set of eyes when my work needs edits, and also her mind, when my plot needs discussing. She was a huge help during the Blood and Ballet writing process.

I must also thank my Wattpad followers. Their feedback throughout this writing process was heartening. I was blessed to have so much great feedback. Those words made the tough days easier to bear. You guys are the best sounding board, and I love the support you have offered. Thank you.

# ABOUT THE AUTHOR

Melissa Mitchell is a physics Ph.D. by day, and fantasy writer by night. She is a California transplant, who moved to Georgia with her husband and three dogs to chase her engineering career in illumination design. Aside from her love of tea, wine, desserts, and writing, she loves reading, playing piano, baking, and bullet journaling (in no particular order). Visit her online at: authormelissamitchell.com

facebook.com/MelissaMitchellAuthor

twitter.com/ladydragonwall

instagram.com/melissa.nicole.mitchell

Made in the USA
Columbia, SC
23 November 2018